INHERITANCE OF THE BLOOD

IMOGENE NIX

Print ISBN: 978-0-9954182-3-3

DEDICATION

I feel like this book has been a labour of a million years. I began writing it 4 years ago, but time, accidents and family issues kept pulling me away.

It was only in the last 6 months that I understood I wasn't ready to go back to it (even though my oldest daughter kept begging for this story.) I'd needed time to work out how the story would actually end.

So here I am, finally writing the dedication in 2017 and there are so many to thank. So, while I will try and include everyone, please understand if I've forgotten you, it's not because I don't care, it's just that my mind is a mush after all this time.

In no particular order (and so I can't get in trouble) to Jan, Eva, JL. Thank you for your insight and plodding your way through this tome!

To Sassie for your magnificent editing. To Victoria Cooper for the amazing cover art!

To Charlotte for nagging, Suzi for kicking my backside into gear. To Beth and the inestimable Mr Nix for understanding this book had to be finished and in it's own time.

To Tracey who is my great friend, Beta Reader and Champion *Par Excellence*!

To my readers, who've waited patiently (and because 4 years is a long time to wait) a very humble thank you.

Without your support, care, attention and encouragement, I wouldn't now be writing this page without all of you.

Imogene

2017

CHAPTER 1

The burning at the back of her neck warned she was being watched. A quick glance didn't clarify it. Instead, she turned around in time to see her mother's face, pale. "Mama?"

She took a step forward, but her grandfather snatched her wrist. The grip was painful, and Kira stilled. "Let your parents talk."

She didn't know what the topic of conversation was, but it couldn't be good.

The dappled sunlight seemed cooler than before.

Her father crooked his forefinger at her grandfather while they stood there. For a moment she wished Vasya had come with them, but he had to work. Just the thought of her new husband warmed Kira.

She only had a few minutes to contemplate her newly defined status as a married woman, when her grandfather pulled at her hand. "Come with me." He tugged and, confused, Kira allowed herself to be towed away.

A glance at her parents' faces stole any feeling of well-being.

"*Grandfather?*"

"*Shh, my love. You must go.*" His grip was implacable and his face stern, but he shivered.

"*What are you doing? Where are you taking me, Grandfather?*"

They moved rapidly through the village they'd visited to sell their wares just that morning, and for the first time since they'd arrived in the market place she felt fear. What was wrong? Was it something to do with Vasya?

"*You are in danger. We must send you away.*" The words confused her further. Send her away? Danger?

"*Where is Vasya?*" She stumbled over a stone, but he kept tugging her onwards.

With a quick glance around, he hauled her into a dirty laneway between the buildings. Kira gasped, trying to drag air into her starving lungs. "*There's no time. We must get you away.*"

A nondescript shopfront lay ahead, and he pushed on the door. It rattled and opened with a loud groan. "*Andre? Andre, are you here?*"

An older man shuffled into the room, bent nearly double from the weight of the load on his back. "*Marat? What do you want?*"

"*My granddaughter. They are coming for her and us. Get her away. Take her now, while you can.*"

The man's face clouded over. "*Are you sure?*"

"*Grandfather, where is Vasya?*" Fright had the blood in her veins pounding.

"*Hush, my precious. Andre will see you well.*" He turned. "*Whatever it takes, Andre. Take her now.*" With surprising speed, her grandfather whirled and was gone.

The man, Andre, eyed her. "*Come this way, child. There is no time to be lost.*"

Eleven years later

The tattoo of her heart and cry of terror woke her, as they usually did. Once again, as she had since that rapid flight from those who sought her, she found herself in a lonely bed. Hundreds of miles away from everything she'd dreamed of, in a house she'd built for them to share. As always, it left her wishing that Vasya had fled with her.

Instead, here she was, exiled without her husband. With a sob, she rolled over and let the tears fall.

****

The sun was shining brightly, but Christina—formally known as Kira—ignored it. "Clothing, food, water. Cash. Papers."

A heavy lump had settled in her chest yesterday, when she'd received the information about her husband, Vasya and her sister, Serina: That they would be the next to come under scrutiny by the special police.

No time to stress now, Christina. Just get the paperwork and move.

If only it were that simple.

Getting into Alvonia would be relatively easy, but getting out? Well, that might require some assistance, the kind that came with favors and lots of money.

The ache in her arm was reminder that time was of the essence now. While Zuor—she tried to ward off the touch of frost that invaded her body just at the thought of him— might be willing to wait a few more days, she couldn't be sure. After the last time... A chill traced its way down her spine at the memory of his last feeding. Memories of the sharp pain, spurting blood and his anger didn't dissipate quickly.

She grimaced as she stretched the muscle in her arm.

Thankfully, the wound site had healed sufficiently and could be hidden with a bandage.

Scooping up the blankets, she ran her eyes over the house one last time. When she returned, she wouldn't be alone. She just hoped her plans and preparation would be matched by their enthusiasm.

Christina slid her fingers into her pockets, curling them around the keys as she dragged the door closed with a thud and a snick of the lock.

At the car, Christina stopped and drew in an unsteady breath. She tugged open the boot and shoved the blankets into the space. One last check showed her that everything was ready. A frisson of excitement and fear zinged through her body as she got into the driver's seat and turned the key.

She didn't look back as she drove down the street and into the gathering darkness.

*T*he sedan hummed along the highway ; a once damaged vehicle she had bought for a song. She'd carefully restored it to an undistinguished grey that would raise no questions. She'd completed the final work to it last summer, and now it looked like any other unmarked car on the highway, though in better condition on the inside. That realization made her shudder. Perhaps she should have been a little less conscientious in the preparations, as she'd yet to pass any other vehicle as well-cared for.

It handled well. Eating up the miles it needed to travel without missing a beat, and the fuel efficiency meant it would go further without requiring constant refueling.

She'd hid her eyes behind dark sunglasses as she drove,

hoping they wouldn't require her, at the checkpoint, to remove them. The contacts she'd worn for that scenario itched, but she daren't change them now. Hiding who she was remained the key to getting in and out safely.

Once more Christina twitched and sighed, hating her current attire. She knew what the officers at the border crossing would see—her toned figure, arrayed for their view. Her clothes had been carefully chosen for this role: Skintight jeans, a low-cut white blouse, and knee-high boots. Her long hair lay in waves across her shoulders, making her seem more approachable. The entire outfit wasn't very official, but it would entice the men to consider her form rather than check her paperwork too closely. She grimaced at the thought of being subjected to their gaze.

She'd even planned the story and delivery she intended to spin during the long hours of driving.

In the pocket of the door was the cheap and easily obtainable phone, though she'd taken the opportunity to slip her existing sim card in the hidden pocket in the handle of the door. She'd pop it into the receiver once she'd regained the safety of her own area. Only one number from her current life was logged into this phone. She may yet need the assistance of her contact.

Customs lay ahead. Her head throbbed, her mouth felt dry, and her stomach churned. While getting through one way should be easy it was never guaranteed. But the hardest part would be getting back over the boarder. Her stomach clenched in acknowledgment to the danger ahead.

As Kira, she'd been a scared seventeen-year-old when she'd been smuggled across the border. She might be older now, and had assumed the life of Christina, a government official, but the coil of anxiety and fear that gripped her belly wasn't any less. Her body felt icy, and cold-sweat trickled down her back and terror thrummed like a fizzing potion in her veins.

This time, she had help waiting for her on the other side of the border. Of a kind, anyway. She held onto that thought; it gave her a momentary sense of relief.

The lights of the border crossing loomed ahead. And for just a second, her ability to breathe abandoned her. Her heart thrummed fast in her chest before once more she settled her reaction by breathing deeply and relaxing her muscles. She released her death grip on the steering wheel. "It's fine. They have no reason to be looking for me."

There was no traffic on the road except her. But at this hour of the night, she'd expected that. Christina would have preferred to cross in the daylight hours, but time was of the essence.

Leaving when she did, she'd become aware that she would arrive at her destination in the dead of night. *It suits your plans*, she reminded herself silently.

Slowing the car, she came to a stop at the boom gate. The guard sauntered in her direction, knowing whoever it was would wait for them. Since the military coup, they'd become full of their own self-importance and were unafraid to make passing into the country far more difficult than it should have been.

She smiled as he ducked his head through the wound-down window. "Papers?"

"Sure." She made a show of looking at him with wide eyes. He was young and, she was sure, he considered himself good looking. Maybe if her interest ran to young men in their early twenties with razor-short blonde hair, he would be attractive, but in her mind rose the memory of a dark-haired man who'd captured her heart years ago.

His gray uniform smelled of stale sweat and other things she didn't wish to question. The stench was almost overpowering, but she ignored it as she smiled, handing over a slim black wallet containing her identification papers. Her real ones had been changed, courtesy of her employer, years before and this set bore even less resemblance to those she used daily. Thank heavens she worked for the government!

"Here they are. Are you having a good night?" Small talk helped the guards relax, she reminded herself.

His gaze dipped down to her breast, then he glanced swiftly at the papers he held in his hands before hungry eyes gazed at her again. Christina fought to contain a shiver of disgust that shimmered through her as his gaze travelled over her body, coming to rest at her ample chest again. She fought to keep the smile on her face, her tinted glasses hiding the disgust.

"All good?" she asked, and it took every ounce of bravado to keep the wobble from her voice. *Remember, you have nothing to hide.*

He dragged his gaze to her face. "Sure. Sure. Yes, everything's in order. Have a good stay." His accent told her he was a northerner, far from where she needed to head.

Christina accepted the wallet back, noting that his hand stayed just a little longer on hers, rubbing his thumb over the tender skin of her wrist. The urge to snatch it away was compelling. She ignored it. "Thanks. I will."

With great care, she stashed the wallet in the pocket on the door. It was important to leave him with the impression that she had all the time in the world.

The boom gate rose, and she gently accelerated. The car rolled through the checkpoint, merged onto the road and kept going, her gaze returning again and again to the rearview mirror.

*V*asya cupped his hand over his brow gazing into the distance as the darkness grew around him. He turned to Gregori, his newly married brother. "We should pack up for the night. It comes quickly."

His brother gave a grunt and wordlessly began gathering the old tools they shared. Times in Alvonia were tough, yet it was family that would get him, Gregori and Serina through...that and hope for the future. He ran his hand absently over the cradle he'd planed. "We'd best get inside, soon, otherwise Serina will come looking for us."

Now Gregori worked in earnest while Vasya contented himself, lifting, and hiding, the unfinished cradle at the back of the barn and behind the hay they'd managed to collect.

"It should be safe there." His brother loomed at his shoulder, the gloom invading the dark interior. "Serina will have prepared a meal." Gregori turned and led the way out into the darkness, toward the house where he'd grown up, together with... He cut off the thought before it could form fully. Going *there* only lead to misery, and the last few years had held more than enough of that. At the door, they slipped off their threadbare boots and padded down the hall.

He was a step or three behind Gregori as they reached the kitchen, but he paused, knowing his brother would want a moment, or several, of privacy with his wife.

Vasya eyed the hall. He'd need to get Gregori to assist him soon. Winter would close in. His family would require the house to be more air tight if every member were to survive the harsh conditions. On that thought, he pushed away from the wall and entered the kitchen. "What's for dinner?"

Serina grimaced and indicated he should sit. "Don't ask and you won't be upset."

CHAPTER 2

The miles sped away, and Christina felt dismay as she passed numerous farmlets. Many of the buildings were falling down. They were a stark testament to the dark economic times in Alvonia. Here and there, dotted along the side of the pot-holed roads, she could see the outlines of rusted vehicles, abandoned to their fate. In her mind, it spoke volumes about the economic situation of Alvonia.

Wisps of smoke trailed up from chimneys as the clouds hung low in the air, the grey ash covering the car as she drove through the old towns. "At least it won't be so clean, now." She gave a tiny chuckle before it melted away under the weight of her concerns.

Redoubling her concentration, she scrutinized the status of the country, and judged that it had seen much better days. In some fields she noted farm animals, and cars and trucks that had been jury-rigged so they could be pulled by the oxen and horses. On the outskirts of towns her eyes skimmed what had once been called temporary shelters.

The illumination of the headlights highlighted their degradation. They were little more than tents made from animal skins. The tools and clothes hanging off them told her these hovels had become somehow long-term abodes.

Hours ticked by as she forged on, and night became day.

Her heart broke as she noted the blank stares of the children trudging along without shoes or coats, carrying baskets of goods for sale.

Christina kept driving, hunger and fear settling like a crater in her belly.

*A*round midday she stopped; exhaustion dragged at her mind. Pulling into an abandoned farm she parked behind an outbuilding to catch a few hours sleep. Until now, she'd only risked stopping for a toilet break and to refuel. She'd reach the largest town between the border and her old home before the need to fuel the car become urgent.

The shade of the outbuilding lulled her into a false sense of security and she let sleep claim her.

She woke at night. Her eyes itched and felt gritty. "Damn it." She'd slept longer than planned. She wasn't fully refreshed, but time was of the essence, and she needed to get *them* out of Alvonia.

Her head and back ached from hours in the car, but all she could do was swallow a pain pill with a sip from the bottle of water. She wouldn't stop again until she reached her destination. At least she'd thought to remove her contacts before her nap. Now Christina popped them back in, aware of the stinging sensation.

The food box on the front seat rattled as the car jittered over the rough road surface and she saw the first signs of her home-town.

Livohka had always been a small town and hosted the royal hunting season, but since the royal family's removal, that source of income had dwindled away. She dimly remembered the profusion of deer and wild game, before the military had stepped in and cut a swathe through the carefully preserved wildlife. It had also been known for the smelting of steel to make the guns and tanks that Alvonia used to suppress its citizens with. Long before that, prosperity had hinged on the production of farming tools and equipment. The political climate of Alvonia, once so stable, had taken a turn for the worse after the coup.

The headlights lit the way, and to her gaze, the township looked small and dirty, the houses in disrepair—all those except the dwellings allocated to the government officials. The sagging corners, splintered fences, and broken windows told their own stories. She'd expected things to be bad, but she couldn't control her moan at seeing how much worse it looked in the glow of the car lights. Dogs barked and yapped fitfully as she drove into the town, her windows wound half-way down.

The thin and angry creatures chased the car.

Christina turned off the lights, driving in the gloomy glow from the few working street lamps that remained. No need to advertise she was here, yet. The hum of the vehicle would keep people inside for the moment, she knew from bitter memory. Her own fear of dark cars without lights sent a shiver through her body.

As she turned onto her old street, she noted the refuse lying on the side of the road. Serina, her only sibling, had been left behind in this squalor, and her heart still ached at that knowledge. It had eaten away at her over the years she'd been absent. But she wasn't the only one left behind.

Hot tears stung her eyes, and she blinked them away.

Allowing the car to glide to a stop alongside the front of the house. She knew the instant it was noted, as a small light clicked on inside in preparation for what was to come.

She opened the car door, placing a booted foot down into something wet and squishy. She didn't want to know what it was; she simply pushed away from the seat.

Carefully and quietly she shut the car door and engaged the locks.

Christina made her way up the rickety wooden steps to knock. Her stomach quivered with fear and nerves as she waited, the sound of steps echoing within. "Open up!"

The door cracked open, and there was Serina; older and finely drawn, but nonetheless, her.

She was half-hiding behind the dilapidated wood door, a fearful expression on her face. "Who are you? What do you want?" The words were quiet, but the eyes peering at her were frightened. Shadows played over the younger woman's pale face.

"It's me, Serina. Kira. Let me in." She said the words quickly, looking over her shoulder for signs of anyone watching.

"Kira is dead. They took her away." The voice was dull, as if stripped of every bit of personality and Serina pushed to close the door.

The words sliced her to the soul. "It's not true. It's really *me!*" Desperation colored her words, and Christina pushed on the door, shoving her foot into the opening to keep it from closing in her face. It took effort, and as she wrestled with her sister, Christina felt another chink in her heart, cracking it further open.

She leaned in, hoping Serina would see that it was her. "I got away and now I'm here to get you out, too."

"No. You lie." Serina's voice was thin and reedy, and it tore at Christina's emotions. "She's dead."

"Serina, remember the scar on your left foot? You got that playing at the water pumps. You were five, and I had to carry you all the way home." Christina was desperate to get her to listen and accept her words. Time was short for her to prove she wasn't lying or tricking her.

She chanced a glance over her shoulder; there was so little time before the PES arrived on this very doorstep.

"It wasn't long before I left, and you cried all the way because you got blood on your dress. Mama had to stitch the cut because we couldn't let anyone know Papa was gone. Plus there was no way we could afford a doctor."

Serina's eyes widened, and she released her grip on the door. "No." Disbelief curled through her voice and Christina took the opportunity to push the door open wide enough to slide through and close it with a thud.

The act of stepping within shocked her. She was finally here, back in the home where she'd passed her childhood.

Serina looked at her, frightened but hopeful. What could she say? Were there enough words to explain the fear and anguish she'd existed in for so long?

"Serina, I'm sorry I had to leave you behind. They came for me and G…" Christina stopped herself, taking a deep breath. She'd promised never to reveal who had helped her. She wasn't going to fail now.

"All you need to know right now, is that someone I knew was able to get me out of here before the PES came for me."

She waited, watching those before her in silence before continuing.

"I kept tabs on you through the years. But I got a note three days ago, saying that the men were coming for you. You and Vasya. I couldn't let that happen." She stretched out her hands, beseeching her sister, but Serina stepped back and away.

"What? Who is coming for me?" She trembled and Christina desperately wished she could enfold her sister in a hug. Her instincts screamed to be patient, and the distance in Serina's eyes warned her any touch would be unwelcome right now.

She breathed deeply. "The Secret Police."

Her gaze took in the state of the building. Shabby didn't even begin to describe it. Never in good repair, the walls now slumped sullenly, bulging in the middle with holes at the top where the joins had given. The gaps left the framework in full view. The mess illuminated by a single, naked bulb hanging from the ceiling on a frayed electrical cord.

Serina had been left here in this hovel, while she'd had the opportunity to experience freedom and comfort. She'd gone to school and found a worthwhile occupation, in the office of Foreign Affairs, helping others to rebuild their lives after escaping Alvonia. Her mind whispered it hadn't been all perfection, but she shied away from the other, colder truths. She'd had it better than her sister and there were many years to make up for.

"I can't go." Serina's words were cool. Remote, even.

"What do you mean, you can't go? Didn't you hear me? They're coming for you next." Christina wanted to reach out, grip her shoulder and shake her.

Serina backed away slightly, touching her belly, and a feeling of fear and knowing ricocheted through Christina.

"No. I'm married and have a baby on the way. Kira, you left all those years ago, and now you want to come back and *save* me? Why didn't you come years ago? When I needed it?" There was a painful thread in her voice, hidden under a steely cold exterior. Serina's words thudded into her brain, driven like steel spikes. Christina hadn't envisioned this situation.

The damning statement reverberated through Christina, leaving her gritting her teeth and clenching her fists. Even knowing the truth couldn't stop the slam of pain that exploded within her.

"I couldn't. Initially I was on the list of people the government was looking for. I couldn't come then." She stopped, gulped, and plowed on. "Since then I've been setting plans in place, organizing things so that I could get you out of here safely.

"But what do you mean, married? To who?" Here lay a piece of information her informant had overlooked, a very important fact that she'd never really considered. Her sister was barely seventeen. How could this be? A brief surge of anger speared her before the fear returned.

"Gregori and I have been married for six months, now. It's his baby I am growing." Serina placed a light hand on her belly.

"Gregori? Vasya's brother?" Shock ricocheted throughout her brain.

Confusion nearly overcame her, but she stopped for a second, allowing her body to calm. *If only I'd known beforehand.*

Sure, she had left eleven years ago, but that would only make Gregori twenty, or at best twenty-one. Wouldn't it?

"Yes, Serina—*my wife*—carries my child." A tall, dark-haired man stepped under the light. Broad shouldered with a curious streak of white in his hair and a brooding look in his eyes, he moved menacingly towards her.

She held her ground and inclined her head. "Gregori, you've grown." She'd been through too much to back down before any man these days. "Let me think."

Christina held up a hand, halting the tone of the conversation and heading off any confrontation, while her brain spun with ideas and improvised plans. Knowing instinctively that they had very little time, she had to convince them before the authorities worked out someone was there who shouldn't be. An idea began to formulate in her brain.

There was no reason she couldn't expand it to include him, but how? She bit her lip as she weighed up the pros and cons of her thoughts. "Well, this certainly makes things harder, but not impossible."

She reached up to rub the knot resting between two tired eyes. "Right, then. Grab your things. We need to get out of here tonight." She closed her eyes. "And where will I find Vasya?"

"Kira? That is you?"

Her eyes flashed open and she looked further into the gloom of the passage.

Vasya.

The man she had dreamed of.

Burned for.

Her husband.

Her Vasya.

Their one brief night of passion had only made her yearn more deeply. She'd loved him for years before they married. Their wedding had been a hasty affair in a time of upheaval.

"Yes." She spoke uncertainly, while her hungry gaze took in all the changes that had taken place on his face and the parts of his body that she could see. He'd become broader in the chest and his face had lost the traces of youth. His hair was still as dark as she remembered, but there were lines bracketing his mouth and eyes.

Inside her chest, the cold knot that had been with her for over a decade warmed, just a little, and its icy casing fractured. She moved towards him, but Gregori stepped in front of him, creating an effective barrier between her and his family.

A greasy pit opened in her belly, but she had to make him understand. "Vasya! You haven't answered my messages in so long."

His eyes betrayed anger and a deeper emotion—stilling Christina in her tracks. The wall of bravado she'd encased herself in cracked, and she swallowed. The lump lodged in her throat, choking her.

"You will not go near him again." Gregori's voice boomed in the silence and she stopped, her gaze flicking to the looming hulk of her brother-in-law.

"What? Vasya, you're my husband." Christina could barely control the pain, and her voice echoed it.

"Messages? You never sent me anything." Vasya snarled; she recoiled as if burnt.

"I... I wrote. I did!" She leaned in, hoping he would read the truth in her eyes. The replies she'd received in the early months and years of their separation had been the only things that kept her going. "You wrote back..."

But he shook his head. "I never wrote, and neither did you."

Gregori squared his shoulders menacingly, and for a moment she was sure everything was lost.

"If you didn't get them or reply..." The words died away

as knowledge bloomed. Her heart thudded harder and faster than before.

"Gregori, step aside. It's fine." Vasya moved forward, sliding past Gregori with the same smooth movements she remembered.

"Kira, getting out of here is not simple..." His eyes slid past her glance, though, as if disbelieving that she was here to help them.

That alone cut deeper. She pushed the pain aside, knowing she only had one chance to get this right.

"I know, but I've put a lot of work into this. I have contacts that will help us. Contacts you couldn't possibly imagine." She shivered inwardly at the thought of some of her contacts.

There was one in particular...she shied away from thinking about what he would ask for in payment as the ache in her arm flared briefly.

"You need to get Serina and Gregori out of here..." Vasya spoke, half turning away. "I will remain."

Christina laid a hand on his meaty arm, feeling the muscles tense below her grip. She stilled, as did he, and drew a breath.

"No. It has to be the three...and a half... of you. I can't leave any of you behind, because there'll be no coming back." She released her grip on Vasya and watched as he stepped back.

Their eyes met in a silent battle of wills. "Why?"

"Why am I doing this now? Because I can, Vasya. Please. I can get you all safely out of Alvonia, but we don't have a lot of time for questions." Icy tendrils curled down her back, but she blinked once, the only action she allowed to betray her fears that they'd refuse her assistance.

The pregnant silence stretched. She wanted to scream at

him to hurry, but it was clear he was weighing her words. The shrug he gave was slow and measured. "Fine!"

He nodded to the others, and she released the pent-up oxygen in her lungs, just as tiny black spots appeared in her vision. "Grab only your essentials. Papers, photos and the like."

She shoved a set of folding bags she'd withdrawn from her pockets in their direction. "Bring only what fits in here. You'll have to leave everything else behind, so it looks like you have only gone for a day or two at most, just in case they stop us at the checkpoint. I have special hidey holes set up in the vehicle for these, but can't fit anymore."

She pushed forward in the direction of Vasya again, but Gregori barred the way. His brown eyes remained cold and flat. "No."

"No?" She trembled.

"We will not leave."

She scrunched her eyes up, thinking about how best to discourage any further arguments: How to get them out of there, when he blankly refused her assistance. The truth, that the PES were coming, was about the only thing that came to mind.

"Damn it, Gregori, if you won't do it for me, then do it for Serina and the child. I have assets and holdings that will help you to make the transition, and I can get you out of here. Safely." *My contacts can make just about anything happen, for a price.*

"If we don't leave now, there'll be no future child. I can ensure you have the best attention, medical help for the baby and Serina. Please. You have to let me help you." Her words broke as she pleaded with him, watching as his eyes narrowed.

"I can get us out of here, but you have to help me help

you. We have to go now." Christina turned her head, and her gaze met Vasya's. "Vasya? Please?"

A tic at the corner of his mouth jerked.

A wild, hysterical bubble rose in her chest, but she stopped and closed her eyes, searching for the calmness deep inside her soul. *Hysterics won't help anyone.*

"Gregori. Stop." Vasya's voice broke the silence.

She knew then, how much she had lost. Her eyes settled on the man in front of her. Her husband of just over eleven years didn't know or trust her. That hurt most of all. The years spent apart had torn the tiny flicker of connection that had existed between them.

In that moment, she wished she'd never been forced to go. She's been homeless and friendless for so long. At least he'd had family, friends.

She'd live for and dreamed of him, of the connection that could be forged again, and she'd expected, erroneously it seemed, that he'd feel the same thing. That knowledge now burned her.

He'd moved on, and she'd remained stubbornly loyal to him alone. She took a step back, swallowing the cry of pain that bubbled up from her chest.

Serina's breath caught, and for an instant, Christina was sure her sister wavered, in the way she twisted her hands. It was just as she'd always acted as a child when thinking something important over.

"How do we know you aren't fooling us? Lying about what you can do?" Distrust was clear in her words, and another nail was driven into Christina's battered heart.

"Realistically, you don't. But to be honest, whether or not you trust me makes very little difference now.

"They could be here as early as tomorrow. Maybe even

tonight if anyone has tipped them off that I'm here. You know that."

She watched as Serina blanched. They all knew who *they* were. The secret police, known as the PES or Paranormal Enforcement Squad. These men and women were the ones who took people away, and very few ever returned after being taken in. Those that did were never the same again, either physically or emotionally. The stories they told were nightmarish tales of torture, death, and things that were better left unknown.

Everyone in Alvonia lived in fear of someone informing on them or their families. At any time, anyone could point a finger at their neighbors. In these dangerous times, it was akin to signing their death warrant.

"By the time they get here, I could have you over the border and traveling towards a new life. Can you afford to not take the chance? Can you risk your *child* for that possibility?" Christina played the trump card, seeing the fear in her sister's face and the way her hand slid over her flat stomach. It made Christina feel unclean, to use it.

Christina waited as Serina thought it over, and saw the cogs in her mind turning as she measured the words and truth within them. With a nod to Gregori, she turned.

He huffed and followed close behind her sister as she disappeared into the small room Christina had shared with Vasya for one short night.

The door closed behind them and she heard the murmurings and thuds from within. A sound drew her attention and she turned back to her husband.

"Vasya? What did you mean about the messages?" Her chest hurt, but she needed to know.

"I don't know anything about any messages. I never

heard from you again." His lip curled, and a cold band wove around Christina's heart.

If he didn't, then who had responded? And why would they have duped me?

"But you did. I have them. Every one." She couldn't help the desperation in her voice, as hard as she tried. The lump that lodged back in her throat was surely bigger than before.

"They're at home in my bedside drawer. You told me about Serina being sick during the winter. The market raid, and even when the Grozhani's disappeared." She let the words trail off as his eyes narrowed.

"I didn't tell you those things."

Her heart stopped then began again, thudding erratically in her chest at his words.

"Oh God. Someone intercepted the letters." *They know*. "We need to get out of here, and now!"

Something in her agitation must have indicated her honest terror, because he turned in silence toward the room at the back of the house, the one that had always been Serina's. Without waiting for an invitation, she followed him.

Even as he grabbed a bag from under the sagging bed, she was overwhelmed at how graceful his movements were. Within minutes, he'd pulled clothing from the drawers her sister had used as a child. An item, small and white, grabbed her attention, but he quickly stuffed it into the bag before zipping it with a quick motion.

On the wall was a photo of his parents; she grabbed it up and looked at him, handing it over slowly. He accepted it, stuffing it into the shirt that nearly covered his broad chest. He grabbed a jacket and the small bag before turning to look at her.

"Come on then, if we need to be quick. We should get

the others and get out of here." His words were hurried as he moved back into the hallway.

She nodded at his back as she followed him down the hall. Gregori carried two bags and a pitted motorbike helmet. "I'll follow you." The words were cold and forbidding, but she shook her head in dismay.

"No, that will alert them that something is up. Depending on the size of your bike, we can put it in the back of the car, otherwise..." She shrugged. They couldn't risk them catching on that something was happening, no matter that it could be the most valuable thing he owned.

"They rarely check the boot of cars at the moment. And we have...." Vasya looked questioningly at her; she broke off and shook her head.

She'd nearly blurted out the truth of what she was. To do that would be the end of any hope, right now, that they'd accompany her. Her mind looked for a suitable alternative explanation.

"They don't check too closely if there are officials in the body of the vehicle."

"Officials?" Vasya leaned forward menacingly.

Christina flinched. "Not like that. I'll explain in the car, but right now we don't have time to linger. Please. We have to hurry."

Christina grabbed the bag from Serina's hand, slipping the door open a crack to peer around the corner, searching for signs of people watching. Satisfied that she could detect nothing, she motioned them forward. "Looks clear. Come on."

They flowed down the steps, and she saw Gregori move around the corner of the house. While he was gone, she quickly unlocked the car, glad she'd muted the beep while restoring the vehicle.

He returned only a moment or two later, with a small motorbike in his hands. It was grimy and dirty, but she understood what it represented. In a place where people didn't have much, every possession was meaningful.

Christina unlocked the boot, motioning him to swiftly place it within, and sent a soundless word of thanks to the designers for the ample boot space. She scanned here and there for signs of movement, heart thudding wildly as she hurried them along.

Next she laid down the old blanket she'd thrown in for this kind of eventuality; she tugged the document bags from his hands and shoved them into the carefully made hiding spots. She'd retrieve them once they'd got through the checkpoint. She refused to consider they'd be located beforehand and give away the whole ruse she was relying on.

Next, Christina had Vasya place the bags on top of the bike, hiding it below and glad the wheel well was deep. She made an urgent motion. They climbed into the car, shoving the empty bottles and wrappers of food to the floor.

No one said anything, although Vasya raised an eyebrow. She turned the key in the ignition, strapping in, ignoring him again as she checked the rearview mirror. Biting her lip, a mixture of frigid terror and hot flashes of a deeper, hungrier emotion rippled through her body.

Gregori settled Serina in as Vasya made himself comfortable in the front. She inched the car away in the dark, creeping through the streets, not wanting to turn on the lights. They would give her away, and the improvements she'd made during the restoration allowed her to key off all the lights in the vehicle from the steering column.

At the edge of the township, she accelerated into the dark even as she spied a flash of light in the distance behind her. Twin bursts of light, which told her it was a vehicle. It turned down the road they'd just left, and she breathed deeply, hoping to quell the unsteadiness that racked her.

They had only just made it in time, she was sure. After all, who else would be driving in the gloom in Livohka? No one except the PES.

It felt like hours, though it was barely ten minutes before Christina judged it safe to turn on the lights, but by then they were well out of town, hidden by the sparse woodland that lay at the edge of Livohka.

CHAPTER 3

Weariness dragged at Christina as she drove through the dim moonlight, the headlights cutting through the fog, as Serina dozed in Gregori's arms. She longed for privacy so she could talk to Vasya, but discussing their situation would have to wait, at least until they were safely out of Alvonia. Each time she glanced in his direction, her soul froze a little more. Instead of the man she'd dreamed of, the reality was standoffish. Forbidding.

She wished she knew what he thought, although it was a given that he was still angry that she'd left without so much as a word. Even so, she wasn't sure he'd accept that she hadn't had a hand in that.

Did he think that in the intervening years she'd somehow ignored him? There were so many layers of secrecy that she'd have to work through and yet she'd truly tried, sending letters regularly though her contacts. At least until he'd stopped answering, and hard on the heels of that thought, her stomach clenched hard. Who had received them and replied if not him? And why?

In her mind, she tossed over the list of concerns that seesawed inside her. Would he turn away from her? Would the truth, if he knew it, put the ultimate distance between them?

It was true, she'd experienced more freedom in leaving her family behind, but it was never her choice.

Not every secret was hers to share.

Lost in her rumination, she hit a pothole, and the car swerved.

"Kira? You are sure you can drive this vehicle?" Vasya spoke for the first time in hours, and she blushed deeply.

"Yes. And you mustn't call me that. Please. My name now is Christina. It's vitally important that you remember that."

He answered her with a grunt, cutting like a knife to her heart.

Instead, she focused on the task of driving, avoiding the ruts and rusted abandoned vehicles that dotted the roads as she redoubled her concentration. "What happened here, Vasya? When did it get this bad?"

He shrugged. "It didn't happen in one hit. It's been gradual."

Things had certainly become worse and she'd not been able to help them before. *I'll make their lives better now, whatever it takes.*

That brought her to the next issue. She'd spent many hours planning how to get out of Alvonia without being caught, but that had been dependent on the three of them—she'd not factored in Gregori's presence. She had an idea of a plan, but it would need more assistance, and she wasn't sure if any of them would be receptive to her plans.

She extended a hand, and reached for the bag on the floor. "Vasya, I have papers for you in the bag. The red envelope contains identification for you and Serina. You are Vasya Alzona, an itinerant worker I was sent to retrieve on behalf of my government."

Vasya started at her words, but she kept her voice steady and continued. "You need to understand this, so you can play your part. This was the only way I could arrange to get you out of here. So, before you say anything, just listen.

"You are a resident of Misrand Province, particularly Lelucani village. You and your accomplice absconded with a large sum of cash." He grunted angrily and she shushed him, understanding why this information angered. The way he scowled at her and his fingers turned white on the packet had her breathing fast.

"Let me tell you the plan first, okay? Gregori? I don't have papers for you, but as they aren't searching for you just yet. You should be able to just use your identification and, I'll arrange an Authorization to Travel."

"How? What have you done?" The dripping anger in his tones slammed into her like a ton of bricks.

"I'm working with people who get those in danger from the PES out. So work with me, okay?" She checked for movement in the rearview mirror and nearly sighed when he nodded.

"Serina is Saraya Alzona, sister to Vasya. Also an itinerant worker. Both are wanted by my government for related crimes." Her eyes burned as she felt the waves of hostility washing over her. It was clear neither liked the tag of thief. Vasya moved in his seat, ready to argue.

She held up a hand once more and relaxed her grip on the steering wheel as he subsided.

"White collar crime is usually the best bet in these instances. It will allow me to arrange for easy retrieval and transportation through customs, particularly if they think you are from Lelucani, where we have some contracts. There wasn't really any other option to arrange your retrieval as there are no reciprocal legal arrangements accepted by the Alvonians."

She glanced to the seat beside her and saw that Vasya glared at her. "I have warrant papers, in the packet, and both of you are coming peacefully." She hurried on, hoping they would accept what she said at face value. "They aren't real warrants, though, just official-looking enough to get you through customs without too many questions.

"If there is any talking, let me do it. You need to act worried, be quiet, and don't interrupt me. Once we get out of here, I'll deal with the papers through the Foreign Affairs office. It's just—"

How the hell did she explain that none of this was real? The Alvonian's weren't as unsuspecting as they made out, but they allowed the ruse to continue in return for favors and cash. Unless it was a person of particular interest to the PES, and she knew Vasya and Serina were now tagged.

Peering through the rearview mirror, she glanced at Gregori still cradling her sister, before turning back to the road, her heart twisting. "Gregori, as her partner you have chosen to come along also to support her. Now, I'm about to ring someone who can prepare the paperwork to cover your transit."

She chanced a look and let loose a frustrated sigh at the dark expression on his face and his turbulent eyes. "If every-thing goes to plan, it should be waiting for us at the check-point when we get there in an hour or two. At least, I hope so."

The words were harried as she suddenly noted the vehicle behind them. A small blue sedan had been following them for the past fifteen minutes, but she felt an uncomfortable itch burning at the back of her neck. She thanked every deity she knew of for the foresight to take a wide and circuitous route away from Livohka.

She picked up the phone and dialed, speaking as soon as it answered. "Phil, I need a favor. I have a Gregori Illyvich with me. I am about to leave Alvonia through the southern checkpoint and need an Authorization to Travel ready for when I arrive in about an hour."

She listened as she drove, the tinny sound filling the vehicle and she thanked the stars for hands free, all the while keeping an eye on the car following.

"Have you got a cover story in place?" His tone was surprised and she dug deep, hunting for the tone that wouldn't tip off her concern.

"Yes. It's all in order as per the current paperwork."

"Fine, then. The papers will be drawn up and waiting at the checkpoint on your arrival."

"Great, I'll call you just as I hit the checkpoint, to make sure they're waiting there for me."

"You know I'd do anything for you." His words echoed, and she gave an unsteady laugh while refusing to look at her husband, sure the banter wouldn't help their current situation.

"Phil, I honestly don't know what I would do without you." In the past he'd always cut her off before she thanked him, now it was just second nature to show her gratitude without saying thanks. This time though, she couldn't stop herself and the whisper of his sigh floated down the line.

"Don't mention it."

Even as she disconnected, Christina thanked her lucky stars that he'd chosen to help her. After all, she rarely went into the field these days, and that too had caused him to raise eyebrows.

Vasya grunted, "Who was that and what did you just do?"

"I am a Displaced Persons Officer for the Department of Foreign Affairs, so I was able to call in a favor of one of the men in my unit." She let the words drop as she produced her ID from the door of the car, showing him her papers. What she didn't tell him was that she headed up the department.

"When I got out of Alvonia, I had a lot of help. The Department was new and dealing with the few fugitives like me who were smuggled out ahead of the squads." Of course, there was little she could tell him, so she hurried on with her explanation. "Since then I attended university and have a degree in Social Services."

The grip of her teeth on her lip left her wincing but she waited as the silence stretched. When she was game to scan his face, she noted it hadn't changed from the cool expression he'd worn since getting into the car, except for the few brief flashes of anger.

"My name was changed, because those in the government felt it was important to ensure my safety, just as they do for all fugitives smuggled through our channels. So instead of Kira, I am Christina." She shrugged and yawned. "Pass me the water please, Vasya. I need to stay awake, just a little longer."

As he reached down to snag a bottle from the floor, she cranked up the air conditioning in the vehicle. "There are blankets on the floor in the back if you want them, but the cold air helps keep me awake." It was a lesson she had learned with the years of covert work she'd done, getting people out of the country.

She yawned again. *I must be out of practice.* She hadn't run an operation on the ground in over two years and she conceded that perhaps in the future she should leave it to their operatives. Yet, this time was different. She had a personal stake in ensuring everything went to plan.

Have I bitten off more than I can chew? She hoped not, but just the thought of what could go wrong… She shied away from even considering it. Negative thoughts had a way of attracting him. The ache welled again, and she glanced down to the strapped bracelet she wore, hiding the truth from those who looked for such things.

"You are too tired to drive safely. Let me drive for a while." Vasya's voice cut through the frosty silence. She sipped at the water, the moisture trickling down the back of her throat, wetting the dry membranes in her mouth.

"I can't. If we get stopped, they'll wonder why you're driving, and that puts the whole plan in jeopardy. No, I need to keep driving. It's only another little while." She suppressed a yawn and rubbed her eyes. "Talk to me, and we should be fine."

"Why didn't you come for Serina beforehand?" Gregori's words from the back hit her like a body blow. She expected it, just not now and not here.

"Ahh, that's a long story and better for another time." She shrugged. His anger flowed over her in a rage-filled wave at her non-answer, but right now she didn't have a choice. "I'll tell you everything when I can and where it's safe. Just not now, and not here. Suffice it to say, until now, it either hasn't been possible for me to get in safely or get Vasya and Serina out."

He didn't believe her. That much was clear from his snort and the hard set to his mouth.

"If I had known about you, I would have made provision, Gregori." He grunted again, and she wondered if she would have believed those words either, if she'd been in his position. "Once we're safely out of Alvonia, I can share most of the story, I promise. It's better for you if you don't know much at this point." The atmosphere in the vehicle was fraught with tension, and for the first time it occurred to her that this would help with the ruse she had to carry out.

Now that the conversation had stopped, she drove in silence. The enervation that dogged her made driving difficult, and the lines wavered before her tired eyes. She wanted to pull over, but they were less than ten minutes from the checkpoint, and she needed to get them across that damned border. Once that was accomplished she could let her guard down.

The road finally gave a twisting turn, and she followed it as she drew a ragged breath as the car that had been following them curved off in the other direction. *They weren't following us. Either that or—* Those thoughts wouldn't help, she reminded herself. *No use in borrowing any more trouble.*

Christina dialed Phil again, grateful for the opportunity to talk to someone who wouldn't judge her. "Phil, I'm just about there, have the docs been sent?"

"Yeah, now there's a couple of things you need to know."

She listened intently. "You have the receipt number? Hang on and I'll get it written down. Vasya? Grab a pen and notebook from the glove compartment." She indicated and watched as he grabbed it and a notepad.

The bronze of his skin, stark against the white paper, reminded her of the man she'd known before her life had irrevocably changed. "Write down A77-4GH52-9YTZ. Yep, they're down. Okay, I'll make contact on the other side. Thanks again Phil."

She silently disconnected the phone and slipped it into the pocket of the car door. In the distance, the bright halogen lights of the checkpoint loomed. In her mind they became scary beacons of death. What would the guards see when they scanned the vehicle and paperwork?

She dismissed the paranoid thoughts and straightened in her seat. "Gregori? Wake Serina, quickly tell her what I told you then stay quiet. Let me do the talking. If we're going to get out of here in one piece, you're going to have to be silent."

His nod told her effectively that he would follow her lead, but she didn't have any illusions. He'd also blame her if it all went wrong.

She listened as Gregori carefully shook her sister to wakefulness and shared the information.

Dawn was creeping across the sky, extending fingers of light through the gloom of the receding dark. The line of cars at the border crossing was filling quickly.

With care, she aimed the car into the line of vehicles, and inched forward. A different officer was on duty, and she sighed. She maneuvered the vehicle to the indicated zone and dropped the window. She ignored Vasya, breathing deeply, and brushed her hair away from her shirt. Her actions accentuated her assets for the guard to view while she smiled broadly.

Inside though, she quaked, wondering what scathing thought was going through Vasya's mind. No doubt he thought she was loose now.

"Your papers." The guard in the threadbare uniform thrust his hand through the window, accidentally brushing against her skin. She wanted to flinch but didn't, as she reached for her ID wallet. The whole time she focused her gaze on the guard, she could feel Vasya glaring at her.

She grabbed the envelope and the sheet of paper Vasya had written on and thrust it at the guard. "Here they are. I am CDPO Christina Alward. I'm delivering Vasya and Saraya Alzona and Gregori Illyvich Vizara, partner to Saraya Alzona, to Madona for questioning in a legal matter as per the standing agreement between the countries. You'll have received an Authorization to Travel from my office via email. Here is the receipt number."

Her stomach soured as nerves assailed her. If they questioned her paperwork now, she had sentenced them all to death, and a long, painful one at that. She held onto the tendril of hope that they'd all survive and their ruse would go undetected.

What if they refuse to let me take them through? The thought hammered at her mind, even as she worked to contain them. Rarely did anyone in her position attend to the transportation of those in custody. If they refused and checked the vehicle and their identities... The thought rode her hard, and her head thudded with pain from the headache she'd been attempting to ignore.

Christina wanted to drum her fingers on the door of the car, but stilled them. Her nerves jumped and jerked beneath her skin. She needed to hold onto her calm persona for just a few minutes longer.

The guard took her bundle of papers over to the building, where he talked with his colleague. He gesticulated, arms flying over the paperwork then the other guards nodded, accepting something back before stalking over. "You are free to go through."

He handed the wallet and papers through the window, and the boom gate rose.

She smiled her thanks, not quite game to say the word,

and moved the car forward into the no man's land between the two checkpoints.

This was the most dangerous time, she knew.

Either side could decide not to let them through. Her fingers tensed on the wheel as she kept the vehicle moving slowly across the rutted asphalt on her way to freedom.

Fifteen kilometers was the speed limit. No faster. No slower. Each time she looked at the speedometer, she felt a prickle of sweat trace down her back. It could still go so wrong.

Here and there tufts of grass broke though the road surface, testament to the lack of will to work together from either side of the border.

Each and every jostle woke her a little more, as the rising sun heated her skin.

Serina started, and she was sure was about to speak. "Not now," Christina muttered, shaking her head, and thankfully her sister subsided in the back once more.

The second checkpoint loomed, better tended buildings rose through in the distance, and heavily armed men in fresh blue and red uniforms stood ready as she rolled forward and dropped the window once more. "CPDO Christina Alward. I have Vasya and Saraya Alzona and Gregori Vizara with me. Here are our authorized documents. PDO Phil Garcia has also sent through an Authorization to Travel that you will have received via email." The man snapped to attention as he intently surveyed her documentation.

"Ms. Alward? If you could please proceed through the checkpoint and come into the office, there is a matter to be addressed before you leave."

She nodded. *Payment was due.*

"Of course." She addressed the man at the gate, and he gave an infinitesimal smile.

As the gate lifted and she drove the car forward, she turned her head to address the others within the vehicle. "Stay in the car, do not leave it for anything." She knew there was a rattled quality to her voice, but she couldn't help it. Fear and loathing welled up inside her. "I'll be back as soon as I can."

She crept the car forward, and turned the corner. In front of the building sat the parking area the officer had indicated. She drew a ragged breath, realizing they might need to relieve themselves after the long hours of travel. "If you need bathrooms, they are straight ahead in that building." She pointed to a low squat block in front of the parking zone.

Turning to the backseat, she spied her old lightweight blouse and caught it up. She'd need the sleeves to hide the ravages of his feeding, and it would save a lot of questions when they left.

She turned off the engine. "I won't be long." *At least, I hope not.*

The door clanged open, and Christina winced as she tugged on the blouse she'd just donned. In the bag she dropped on the counter was the bracelet and white shirt she'd replaced. *Zuor would be inside and require his payment immediately.* Of that she was sure. And he didn't like waiting.

For her there was no escape.

The young man behind the desk waited. His face was pallid under the lights and he shook and sweated. Most people usually reacted like that when they were confronted with Zuor.

"Ms. Alward?" His face betrayed his concern for her as his eyes widened, and he started to shake his head.

She laid a quiet hand on his and smiled. "I can take it from here, just show me where and then stay out here. No matter what you hear, do not enter. Do you understand?"

Pity surged. It was probably the first time he'd been confronted with a nightmare demon. Sadly, in the last eleven years, she'd had a lot of experience dealing with them, and in particular, Zuor.

He nodded, head bobbing up and down in agreement. These demons weren't the type of creatures anyone really wanted to meet, and his quick agreement fortified that belief.

"Christina. Come in." The booming voice flowed over her, and she closed her eyes before entering.

"Zuor ElAmaray, I greet you." Her voice was calm.

Her stomach might be a seething mass of knotted snakes but she'd be damned if she'd let him see it.

His black skin glowed slightly, and his coal-colored eyes glittered in the half-light. Soul Stealer, she'd silently dubbed him—didn't like light, and would extinguish it on every possible occasion. They tolerated only as much as their donor required for the completion of their feeding. They preferred the deep night, where they could hide in the darkness and bring terror to their prey.

He motioned her to the chair. "I have come for my payment. Vasya and Serina are through. Now you owe me. Once again."

She shivered and nodded, taking her place in the seat as she pulled the arm of her shirt up for him to access his favored feeding spot. She knew most people considered the mythical vampires to be the ones who stole blood, but that couldn't be further from the truth.

No, it was the demons that fed off human blood. Those, like Zuor, were angry spirits and relied on sustenance in the form of blood and emotions. He'd been her companion since her flight so many years before, the day she had escaped from Alvonia.

Even those in her department were unaware that she'd been classified a donor—just as her mother had been before her. It was a secret you took to your grave. As one passed, another from the next generation was chosen, groomed and used until they too passed their expiration date.

She'd never understood why she'd been chosen instead of Serina, but right now, having heard of her sister's pregnancy, she was pleased it was herself that was linked to Zuor.

The very association between Christina and the demon was the reason for the danger, and she was responsible for dragging Serina, Vasya and now Gregori into this dangerous mess.

She remembered that fateful day. They'd been in the market place, the day after she'd wed Vasya.

"Grandfather, come see. Mother says..." Her words broke off as she witnessed the intense emotion he clearly struggled with. "Grandfather, is all well?"

His face, pasty in the daylight, had drooped. "I must take her. It's time."

He'd dragged her along, fingers digging into the flesh of her wrist. People had watched. Fingers had pointed and he tugged mercilessly as she tried to pull away. "Grandfather, you're hurting me." Fear bloomed as he had tugged her into a small building. "Where's Vasya?" He hadn't answered, simply pulled harder, made her move faster as icy dread seeped into every pore.

He'd entered a small shop. "Andre?" The man had come out and seemed to slump.

"It's time?"

"Yes. Take her. Save her, Andre." Then he'd gone, leaving her alone. So alone...

She shook away the memories.

Everything had changed the day she'd been spirited away.

The true government of Alvonia had fallen, and a new and far more dangerous threat to the supernaturally-connected had risen. The coup had been powered by a radical faction of the military that had promised to wipe out anyone with links to these creatures.

Zuor ElAmaray had been the Soul Stealer her mother and grandmother had served, as had earlier members of her family. It was he that endangered them, but he was uncaring, so long as his needs were met. All she knew was someone, somewhere had alerted the authorities, shared their fears and concerns and ensuring Christina's parents and grandfather had been taken away for questioning.

Over the years, Christina had learned it was Zuor who'd alerted her grandfather to the danger. It was the only way they'd managed to smuggle her out of the country. It wasn't much to be thankful for, though.

Thankfully Serina had never shown any signs of this curse, but the government didn't care about those niceties. And they hadn't known about Vasya. She was grateful for that, too.

She dropped into a small chair, knowing he preferred her to be lower than him, even during this hated ritual.

Her mind wandered unchecked, only dimly noting that

Zuor grabbed her hand. Then she felt the slide of his incisors straight into her vein as he clamped down.

Her small gasp of pain pleased him momentarily until his anger rose. Now the pain she felt was acute as he fed from her. Positive and bright memories dimmed slowly as he fed, sucking and thinning her soul and gorging on her emotions.

As always, sadness and fear descended on her. Tears dripped down her face, like a hot river on her frozen skin. The lights of her soul dimmed, as they always did, and the well of hunger and need swelled.

The snort of anger told her seconds before he detached that he was once more unhappy with her. A quick spurt of blood jetted as she swiped her fingertip through the saliva, knowing it would seal the bleeding vein almost instantaneously.

His jerky movements away from her highlighted his anger. "You are thin. It was not a good feed. Fail me again and...."

Christina wrapped her hands around her shaking body. "I'm sorry Zuor. I'll try harder."

He snarled, his fist balling. "I will be back to take payment-in-full soon." Right now, though, there wasn't much she could do to ameliorate his anger.

The last few years, his patience with her had worn away, and lately he hadn't bothered to be careful as he finished feeding. Instead, more often these days, she'd had to wear long-sleeved shirts to hide the welts and ragged tears he left on her arm. The gushing of blood stilled, but the wounds remained as ragged gashes in her skin, the scars ropey and hard.

With a final roar, he disappeared from her sight, but the memory of his touch and feeding remained, leeching the last vestiges of heat from her body. She looked around for tissues or a cloth; anything to clear and cleanse her skin.

The tissue box lay just out of reach, and as she stood, a wave of dizziness descended. She slid off her shirt, taking care not to stain it with the blood that had started to congeal on her wrist, then slumped back down into the seat.

The darkness pulled at the edges of her vision, and her body swayed. She fell forwards, her undamaged arm reaching for the floor and breaking her fall. It was cold and hard, and she must have called out.

The young officer raced in, his eyes darting around the room as if expecting to find Zuor awaiting him. "Ms. Alward? You need rest and assistance?"

"No. I'll be fine soon, just pass me some tissues and help me into the chair. I'll be fine in a minute."

But it wasn't true. After feeding she always felt terrible. She needed to rest, to eat and drink. But she had Vasya, Serina and Gregori in the car. A fuzzy recollection of warning the officer not to enter rose.

"I told you not to come in here."

"I heard you cry out. I just…"

"If you are ever in this position again, do not enter. They don't appreciate disturbance during their feeding." She watched as he paled. "The punishment is extreme."

She wiped at the ragged flesh, each touch like a knife in her arm—the blood swiped away. Wordlessly, the officer passed her a package of adhesive bandages, and she applied them with great care, then carefully slid the shirt back over herself and rolled down her sleeve, hiding the evidence.

She pinned the young man with a stare and he blanched. "Say nothing. No one is to be told. This never happened." She stood gingerly and moved towards the door.

"If you say nothing, then you have a good chance they won't find you an acceptable donor."

The young man nodded at her words, but she paid him no attention as she carefully opened the door and moved down the stairs to the car.

❄

"What's wrong?" Vasya's words cut through the air.

"Nothing. We need to find a motel so we can stop and rest." She brushed off his words, but knew her hands shook even as she started the car. Her arm throbbed and the wound site screamed as she used it. She could only hope it wouldn't resume bleeding as she drove.

"You are unwell." His brow furrowed as if he were sifting through his thoughts. "Something happened in the office." His dark eyes stared at her.

God, I wish I could tell him everything. But the reality was far too dangerous. And she didn't want him to turn away from her just yet.

Instead, Christina shook her head, hoping he wouldn't ask any further questions. "Nothing happened. Just some work things I had to clear up." She was as evasive as always when someone enquired. The reaction was so deeply ingrained in her now that it was second nature.

Christina pulled out of the parking lot and maneuvered the car onto the road, heading toward Madona, the city she now called home. The sun was high in the sky so she knew it would be quiet. Just what she needed right now.

They still had at least a full day of driving ahead of them. She also needed to make contact with groups that would help them rebuild their lives, change their identities, and find employment, before she could leave them to their own devices.

"Pull over and I will drive." Vasya's voice filled the cabin of the vehicle.

"No. I know where we're going and there's a motel in a couple of miles."

He grunted, and while she wanted to chance a look at him, knew her resolve was far too thin right now. "It's not that far."

CHAPTER 4

A light shone ahead. The motel had a seedy air, but the vacancy sign flashed red and green. She needed to rest, wash the demon's smell from her skin, apply the salve and bandages she kept on hand for these times, and she desperately needed food. Serina also looked strained and tired. Pregnant women needed sleep and comfort, she told herself.

Flicking the indicator, she turned into the drive. "I'll get us some rooms, and then we can order food and rest." She climbed slowly out of the vehicle, and she noticed Vasya did, too. "You can wait here, while I arrange everything."

His eyes narrowed. "No. I think I will come with you."

Too tired and utterly defeated to argue, she turned and headed to the small office. Entering, she found an assistant at the small desk.

"I need three rooms for today. One double and two singles would be perfect."

"Nope we only got two doubles left. You can have them though for the night rate."

Her eyes closed. "Surely you have one single left as well?"

"Nope, that was booked about ten minutes ago." *Damn. Zuor ElAmaray was no doubt making her pay.* If the situation had been different, she wouldn't have thought it was him, but experience was bitter and she knew the way he reacted when stymied.

"Fine, I'll take it. How much?"

The clerk named a price, and she pulled the cash from her wallet, handed it over and filled out the room card before she handed them over too. Her arm ached and her eyes burned. She swayed as she stood waiting for the keys.

"I will drive the car. Which rooms?" Vasya grabbed the key to the car before she could argue, and she accepted the room keys. Thankfully both rooms were side by side, just behind the office.

She trudged out the door and around the corner. She fitted the key into the first lock, opening it up and glancing inside. At least it was clean, and there was a rudimentary bathroom with tea and coffee facilities.

Serina and Gregori met her at the door. "Here's your key. If you need me, I'm next door."

Christina could hear the rumble of the car as she moved to leave the room and Serina reached out, brushing soft fingers over the bite site. She couldn't hold back the yelp of pain as Serina's eyebrows rose. Grabbing her hand, she pushed back the sleeve, to reveal the bloodied bandages below. She tugged them off, and Christina couldn't control her yelp of pain.

Serina stared at the two large tears in Christina's flesh. "Oh my God. You're a donor!" The words breathed out as Christina's head flew up.

"What do you know?" She could barely fill her lungs; fear overwhelmed her in a billowing, greasy cloud.

"I'm not an idiot, Christina. There were others in the village. And kids, well, you know how they talk." Serina glanced at her. "Is this why—"

"Don't, Serina." She backed away, refusing to see the loathing in her sister's eyes.

"It is, isn't it? When did this happen? It's fresh." Serina's eyes took in the wound, and she lightly touched the ragged skin as Christina's knees almost buckled. "The one you feed isn't kind, either. From what I heard, they usually feed and go but don't inflict this kind of injury. It's rare that they leave those sorts of marks, so I've been told."

Christina refused to consider Serina's words. In Alvonia such information was almost as dangerous as being connected to the underground supernatural community. The PES would hunt anyone with such a connection, and they would disappear. Forever.

"Please don't, Serina. I can't talk about it right now." She needed to get out before Vasya heard.

She pulled free of Serina's grip, wrenching the sleeve roughly down her arm. She didn't want him to know what she had done. She couldn't let him know the price she had paid for their freedom.

He didn't even seem to like her anymore, and she'd rather die before he understood what she had done, she thought hysterically.

"But Vasya..." Serina's voice was tense, but Christina felt like she was tugging what little dignity she had around herself like a brittle cloak.

"Don't. Please, Serina, you can't tell him."

She looked to Vasya's brother, who'd walked in and now stood like a statue, staring at her. She didn't want to consider if there was hate and distaste in his gaze. It was too much. Her emotions were too raw to examine deeply right now. Maybe when she was more settled and time had passed.

"Gregori? Promise me you won't tell. It was the only way I could be assured of getting you out of there safely."

She spun back to her sister, silently pleading with her to understand and accept what had happened. "He's been watching you for me since I left Madona and— He promised to keep you safe, but something changed and I..." She closed her eyes as the sound of footsteps intruded, knowing that tears burned behind the heavy lids of her eyes.

"Is there a problem?" *Vasya.*

"No. None. I'm just making sure Serina and Gregori have everything." Her voice sounded strangled, but she squared her shoulders and turned back to her sister. "I'll order a pizza to be delivered. If you need anything else, I'm just next door." She backed away as Vasya stepped into the room.

With a quick movement, she hurried to the other door, fingers trembling a little on the key as she pushed it open. A large bed sat in the center of the room, and she stepped inside, ready to drop.

She denied her exhaustion just long enough to regain her equilibrium. Sitting down gingerly on the end of the bed, Christina palmed her cell phone and hurriedly ordered two pizzas delivered to the rooms. She had pulled out her credit card to make the payment as the door snicked open. The call was quickly finished, and she looked up to see Vasya watching her.

Her stomach churned wildly. Whether it was hunger or fear she couldn't tell. Not that she really wanted to examine that right now, anyway.

"So now, what?" He watched her, hard eyes flicking over her in the dim light. Probably totting up the many ways in which she was a failure. He would do so much better without her.

"I'll shower and change, you grab the pizzas when they arrive, and we get some sleep. We have at least another day on the road before we get home." She rose jerkily.

The end of her energy loomed, but there was one more thing to do. "You can have the bed, and I'll take the sofa." She stood, grabbing the bag he had pushed into the room with her good arm, hefting it towards the bathroom.

He reached for her, but she dodged. "What happened back there? You are favoring your arm since you left that office."

"I pulled something. I hurt it last week, and it's still healing." The lie came easily to her lips. Just like they always did.

His eyes narrowed, but he didn't say a word and she steeled herself for an outburst of something. Anything.

He nodded. "Fine. Shower and then we eat and sleep."

She turned to the bathroom and shut the door.

CHAPTER 5

She was hiding something. She had favored her left arm since the office at the checkpoint, and any color she had had was gone. She was also extremely jumpy.

It was clear that some momentous event had taken place.

Then when he had entered Gregori and Serina's room, they, too, were involved in the secret—and he dearly wished he knew what it was.

After eleven years, he didn't know the woman he would share a room with. At seventeen she had been open and soft, with sparkling eyes and perfect for him. At a mere twenty, he'd felt like a king when she had become his bride.

Within a day, though, she was gone. Disappeared after leaving for the market with her parents. Later that day, the PES had come for her family, and they'd taken her parents and grandparents, leaving young Serina, for all intents and purposes, an orphan.

They'd never returned, although he'd searched. At first, he was sure they—the PES—had taken her at the markets, but gradually he'd pieced together the truth from those in the market place that day: Her parents talking animatedly, and her grandfather dragging her away.

He'd prayed at first that she'd return, but the years piled on and that hope withered. Died. Until now.

In his mind, he recalled the day the soldiers had broken in and taken her mother.

The door shivered under the onslaught as men, the PES, bellowed for them to open up.

Serina's mother had gripped her hard. "Whatever happens, stay with Vasya. He'll look after you." She'd stared at him. "I'm sorry, Vasya. So sorry."

His mind spun. "What's happening?"

"The PES are here. They'll take us away. Look after Serina. No matter what happens, protect her for us, please."

The man in charge thrust a hand inside as the door splintered, then shoved the wood out of his way. "We're here to take you and your daughter into custody."

"She's gone." Kira's father filled the doorway, blocking the men from Serina and his family. Vasya tensed, knowing exactly what this meant. The PES had powers that extended like tendrils of evil. When they came, people disappeared and never returned.

They swarmed, the men in long grey coats, and when Vasya would have fought, Kira's mother shoved Serina into his grasp. "No. This has to happen." Her sad eyes beseeched him, and he had dragged the screaming girl close to him as the PES rounded up her family, shoved them out of the house and down the steps in near silence, while his body felt encased in ice.

"Where is the girl, Kira?" He towered over Vasya as the little girl cowered beneath his arm.

"She's not here." It broke his heart to say that, but he was sure she'd reappear when it was safe. He'd lie to protect her, his Kira.

The sour breath of the man wafted over his face. "We'll be watching, and when she returns, we'll take her, too." His eyes glowed —the merest hint of red flaring in the blue then was extinguished.

Eleven years later, his wife was a stranger. Cool and distant. He'd seen a flash of pain at the house when she came for them. The sadness that she wore like a cloak surrounded her, and it pulled at him on a deeply emotional level. It also confused him. She'd been so full of life and laughter years ago.

He didn't know her, though. She might be his wife, but she didn't sound, look, or even act the same. This was a cardboard woman.

He turned around at a knock on the door. Through the peephole Vasya saw a massive, dark-skinned man, with a set of boxes in his hand. Pizza.

He'd tried the delicacy once. It reminded him of a pie with cheese and assorted foods on top. Mouthwatering and tasty came to mind.

He opened the door, only to have the boxes and a bag shoved at him.

The delivery-man grinned.

"You need to be paid?"

"Already paid. Tell the lady, Zuor says hi." With that, the man turned and was gone, the door slamming in Vasya's face.

Confused more than ever, he retreated to await Kira— no, Christina he reminded himself—she didn't take long. She wore a long sleeved, peach-colored top with light pants; strange clothing choices, for the warm weather. "Do you want me to take one to Gregori and Serina?" He asked, glancing toward the pizza boxes.

She nodded absently as she reached into the package.

"Take them one of these too. Garlic Bread." She smiled sadly as she turned away.

"Right." He picked up the small foil packet and box and made through the doorway, before turning the corner and knocking quietly. It opened quickly, and he shoved the food into his brother's hand. Gregori grunted his thanks before shutting the door on him.

Vasya shook his head with a smile as he made his way back to the room. For a moment, memories of him and Kira seeking privacy stirred, but he shut them off, the way he had many times before. Whatever they'd had was now gone.

Once back in the room, the wafting smell of pizza hit him. Food had been something jealously guarded, and yet here it was delivered to his hands, in a box, ready to eat. His mouth watered at the thought of the tasty food he had to look forward to.

Christina took a sip from the bottle she held, and for a moment he watched a drop of water balance on her lip. The urge to brush it away rose. Sexual hunger flashed, hot and wild, as she swiped it away with her tongue. Sighing, he willed his body to relax.

The man's words came back to him. "The delivery man said to say Zuor says hi."

She blanched suddenly, the tracery of blue veins standing out in stark relief on her visage. She had been pale before, now the word colorless came to mind as she clutched her arm.

He moved swiftly towards her, she turned away, but not before he could see the panic and fear in her eyes. *My wife has secrets. But what could have made her so afraid?* "Kira—?"

"No. Please." Her words tore at his emotions. He felt the burning emptiness of loss. His wife should have been able to confide in him. Was there someone else?

Anger curled in his gut, hot and burning, like the fire in winter. But just as quickly as it bloomed, it seeped away. She wouldn't have done that, not his Kira. The woman he'd known would never consider turning to another man for solace.

"Kira? Are you okay?" He kept his words low, not wanting to scare her.

"Yeah, I'm fine." She whipped her head around to look at him, but she didn't appear "fine". She looked hunted. Somewhere lost in her damaged psyche was a woman who hated something, or at the very least had a vast fear of something. He couldn't guess what it was, but deduced it was terror that spurred her on.

"Come on, we should eat before it goes cold." She moved towards the table, flipping the box open and the scent assaulted his nostrils, his stomach growled with hunger. Food had been scarce in the last while, so he and Gregori had hunted, finding anything alive to eat by stunning it with rocks in a slingshot easily hidden in a hollow tree behind the house. There had been many a day where he hadn't asked what he ate. When that occurred he was just happy his belly was full.

He picked up a piece, inhaling the smell before taking a bite, chewing deliberately and slowly as he savored the explosion of flavors on his tongue.

Closing his eyes, Vasya let his mind make the most of the tastes. The textures of the pizza fulfilled a need long denied, and as he pushed the last bite into his mouth, he opened his eyes.

Christina still hadn't bitten her slice. Her eyes downcast, like the droop of her mouth. She placed the pizza back into the box. "I'm not very hungry right now." Her words were soft, and her skin ashen with a green tint. "I might just retire." She turned away, grabbing a single pillow from the bed and reaching into the cupboard to pull out a blanket and headed for the couch.

"No, you get the bed, I will take the chair."

"No Vasya, you have longer legs and you need the bed. This will suit me perfectly. Good night."

She lay down, rolling towards the back of the chair as she pulled the blanket over herself. She might as well have pulled the blanket over her head, as she retreated physically and emotionally from him.

He reached for another slice. The Kira he remembered would have stayed up and shared the pizza to the end.

He frowned. She'd changed a lot.

CHAPTER 6

*V*asya finally retired, his soft snores filling the air. Fatigue dragged at her; her senses pulled tight, her eyes stung and her headache intensified. From experience she knew there'd be no relief anytime soon.

If they were going to make it safely home, she needed to sleep, but that remained elusive, even with the blinds and curtains tightly closed.

Her thoughts turned to the home she'd lovingly made for all of them. Perhaps she shouldn't stay with them, but leave it so the three could make a home without her? It seemed more likely that was what they wanted. What would be best for everyone?

Her chest ached with the tears she'd ruthlessly held onto. Watching the joy on his face as he ate the pizza had forcefully reminded her of what he had missed, and what Serina had missed.

The combined thought increased her quotient of misery. *It wasn't right.* No one should starve like an animal while the ruling elite gorged on resources. In a fair world, no one would be terminated just because of his or her associations.

There'd be no need to smuggle people out. But Alvonia wasn't fair, or even just for that matter.

She'd been reminded of that time and time again with her work. So many she'd offered a new life to, but for every one they'd saved, hundreds more had perished.

Now in the semi-darkness, her thoughts turned to Vasya's comment about Zuor. Her chest had nearly exploded with fear. Zuor was toying with her, showing her he could come and tell them, tell Vasya what she was: A slave to his need for her blood.

Her stomach congealed as waves of nausea swelled.

"Oh God!" The words erupted and she slapped her hand over her mouth even as she cast a quick glance in the direction of the bed. Vasya muttered in his sleep and turned before sinking back down. Her outburst had nearly woken him, and that would lead to questions of the kind she feared most.

It was bad enough that he might learn she was no better than the pizza in the box to Zuor. And as with everything she'd achieved on her own, Zuor would spoil it, smash her happiness like an angry child.

The churning of her stomach started subsiding as she slumped back, closed her eyes and flung her hand over her face.

She knew Zuor considered her disposable. But if he decided she was no longer a usable commodity, he might settle on Serina as an acceptable replacement. The thought set her belly churning wildly again. She'd just have to make sure he didn't feel the compulsion to replace her, which meant giving in to everything he demanded.

He wasn't going to do to Serina what he'd done to her. Even if it killed her, she would protect the three— four, she mentally corrected herself, allowing for the child that Serina carried—with whatever she had left in her to give.

She tossed and turned on the lounge, trying to find a comfortable place to lay her body. But with an unsettled stomach, a throbbing head, and the sting in her arm, sleep was further away than ever. "I wonder if this is a new tactic of his?" In the silence there was no answer.

She could envision it, though, as his latest favored method of discipline. He'd only started this hurtful feeding method in the last several months, but it didn't work, because although he needed her blood, which she produced on demand, he wanted her emotions, too. Positive and happy memories and experiences, but she couldn't give him what she didn't have.

Christina closed her eyes, trying to envision the good times, but they swam through a hazy cloud too far from her grasp. The act of taking on another identity had stripped away the fragile connections that had kept her afloat, and over the years all that remained was the fear and uncertainty.

All that came to mind were the negative experiences, and the knowledge that any chance of a future with Vasya had slipped away. It shredded her heart and soul.

As the sun dipped in the sky, she finally dozed.

Christina woke, groggy and sore, the gnaw of hunger her companion. Memory came slowly, finding Vasya and Serina after all the years of separation. Vasya, so cold and unwelcoming: her sister un-trusting and so damn grown up. Not to mention married with a child on the way. And Gregori. The young boy who'd held her hands as he'd learned to walk was now distrustful of her. She couldn't blame any of them, though. She'd been gone for so long.

The emptiness of her life weighed on her. Christina wanted to cry for the lost years and dreams. Now they were little more than ashes scattered on the floor. She sighed. *Feeling sorry for yourself won't get us safely out of here, Christina.*

One more moment passed, she squeezed her eyes shut and a single tear escaped between the aching lids.

Her back ached as she turned on the unfamiliar and lumpy bed—no, couch. She'd slept the day away and the night too. No wonder she felt starved! Christina stared at the box sitting on the table. Cold pizza. The scent, muted though it was, teased her and she ate, ravenous bites until what remained had been consumed.

Her gaze settled on Vasya still asleep, which was probably for the best. Grabbing her clean clothes, Christina slipped into the bathroom, resting her toiletries on the small shelf.

Looking in the mirror showed a wreck of a woman with long, dark hair standing up at the ends and eyes ringed with black shadows. "Good thing I'm not here to impress anyone. All I have to do is get us home."

Shrugging out of her clothes took some effort, as she slipped her sore arm slowly out of the sleeve and turned on the shower. The wetness sluiced over her body, and she welcomed the awareness that came with it.

Feeling refreshed, Christina turned off the taps and reached for a towel before drying herself with an economy of motion. The towel was a little scratchy, but dry and clean. She sat on the toilet, taking a good look at the wound site. The bandage she'd applied late yesterday left a gluey residue on her skin.

A quick inspection of her arm revealed the bluish-purple bruising around the damaged flesh. She reached for the toiletries kit and inside spied the small first aid stash and applied the adhesive strip to the site after cleansing the wound.

"At least it's healing, though." Maybe not as fast as in the past, but Christina was thankful it didn't ooze and was only stiff and sore.

She stood and reached for her pants and light shirt, brushed her hair and cleaned her teeth, then opened the door.

He waited just beyond the door, hearing her move around. He remembered the morning after their wedding. She'd been too shy to dress in front of him. It had only made his need for her more urgent.

In his memory, he still saw her, high breasts and trim flanks. Miles of skin he'd touched and caressed the night before. His body tightened as it always did.

The door opened softly and Kira's eyes turned wide with surprise. She stepped back into a pool of water and slipped. He caught her just as she would have connected with the hard tiles, grabbing her by the arm.

Her yelp of pain surprising him, and he let her go without a sound.

She dropped, landing in the puddle of water.

His gaze drawn to her white face and he leaned down, inhaling the scent of her sweet perfume.

"What did you do that for?"

"You were obviously pained by my grip. I let you go."

"But now I'm wet and need to change. Again."

He spied a scarlet ribbon, blood seeping through the

white cotton of her sleeve and his stomach tightened. "Wait, you've hurt yourself."

"It's nothing." She made to hide the injury behind herself, but he reached out and grabbed her wrist.

"It is not nothing. You're bleeding. Let me see."

"No!" Christina stood up clumsily, but he crowded in.

He reached for her shirt and she batted his hand away. "It's fine. Truly."

"No, Kira, it isn't. I hurt you, and I will now minister to you."

He spoke softly as if she were a startled deer. He frowned considering that thought. She acted as if someone were about to hurt her. This wasn't the girl he'd known all those years ago.

"You don't have to—"

"I do. I would never hurt you, Kira. Even after all these years, I wish you no harm." His words cut her off.

He pushed at her shirt, and when she tried to push him away, he grabbed her hands lightly and restrained her gently. "I need to look, Kira." He tugged the sleeve up, but it wouldn't give enough, so he started reaching for her buttons, carefully slipping them out of the loops that held them.

His body reacted, every muscle yearning and his cock stirring. Breathing deeply didn't clear the sudden hunger that singed him from the inside out. If anything, her scent aroused him further.

A flare of heat shot through his veins then he saw at the bandage. *Scarlet blood staining the stark whiteness.*

Kira closed her eyes as he touched the side of the bandage, carefully peeling it back until it was removed. He stopped. His gut churned.

Horror, freezing blind terror replaced the heat, leaving

him giddy as his mind worked to process the view before him. "What happened? What caused this?" The words were hoarse, as if he was strangling on them.

"Zuor, the demon did it." The words were whispered as she looked away.

Christina yearned for him to show softness or a hint of something else. Her need wasn't rational and her touch was unlikely to be welcomed, she berated herself, now he'd learn the truth and that knowledge seared her to her soul. She wished they meant he loved her, but she had to be sensible. The fantasies of eleven years were just that. Fantasy.

How could she handle the disgust on his face?

"How?" His gaze collided with hers, and so many questions were present.

"You know what this means. I'm a donor, Vasya."

"A donor? How long?" The words stung liked barbed arrows through her heart.

"It's hereditary. Some call it the Inheritance of the Blood. It's a curse, though. It was discovered years ago."

Now his eyes widened and he opened his mouth.

Christina shook her head. "Eleven years ago, yes. The day they came for me. The day after our wedding. Zuor... the one the delivery-man mentioned? That is Zuor ElAmaray. He hungers, and I feed him." She whispered in shame.

"When? When did he do this." She accepted the fury in his tone, felt the burn and firmed her chin.

"Yesterday." She wasn't going to tell him anything he didn't ask for. Not unless he asked.

"When, yesterday?" He growled the words and she shrank back from him.

"At the checkpoint. Or just after."

He pushed away from her as if he couldn't bear to touch her. She stayed where she stood while her heart shriveled.

He won't ever want me now.

She heard his angry footsteps on the floor as he marched back and forth, muttering under his breath.

"How long? How long have you known about this Zuor? When did you find out?" He stopped pacing. "Before our wedding?"

"No. The day after. It was only as they smuggled me out that they told me."

"You ran from me because of this?" The words were anguished, so she raised her head.

"I didn't run. Grandfather knew the authorities had been told, and they were coming for me. For all of us. He had me out of the country so fast, I couldn't even say goodbye.

"I wanted you to come with me. You and Serina, but he said there was no time left. They said... they said they would try to get you out, but it never happened. I don't know how they found out or who told them. All I knew is that my family, everyone except you and Serina, died because of what they found out." The words erupted on sobs that caused her chest to heave.

"Why didn't someone tell me?" He didn't move, but so much pain filled his voice. She wanted to go to him, but the anger and vitriol, which had passed since their reunion stood between them like a stone barrier.

"Because it wasn't safe to know these things. Not in Alvonia. I didn't even know until the day we went to the markets.

"That's why my parents and grandparents disappeared. Someone told my grandfather, who informed my parents. He took me to a shop, to someone who smuggled people like me out of the country."

The ball of misery inside her chest grew. "If I had

known, I wouldn't have married you, because it placed you in danger, too." The tears coursed down her face, scalding rivers of anguish.

He moved swiftly to her, grabbing her in his arms. "I should have known. You should have told me!" His fingers and words were angry.

"But *I* didn't know. Not until then. It was kept a secret from me, too. And then my grandfather didn't even allow me to go home. Before I knew it, one of his friends had me hidden in a crate. They took me through the checkpoint."

He let go, and she closed her eyes.

"It's okay though. I have a plan. When we get to the city of Madona, I am going to leave the three of you at the house. There's a unit in town I can use while I get things sorted. You won't even have to see me."

Vasya didn't look at her. He remained still with his head bowed and his hands covering his eyes. His broad shoulders acted like a wall protecting him from her.

She balled her fists, her voice low and hard as she fought back the tears. "You'll have freedom and help. I'll arrange for you to be met by other agents, helped to transition to a new way of life and I'll stay out of your way. You just need to put up with me for the next day or so until we get to Madona and sort out some of the basics."

With a jerk, she scooted back her eyes on Vasya as he spun around, dropping his hands and she felt the heat of his gaze as she headed to the suitcase.

She flicked the bag open and grabbed fresh jeans, slinging them over her shoulder along with a light shirt. "You won't ever have to see me again, if you don't want to. I'll make sure you have your freedom."

She glanced over her shoulder at him, but he hadn't moved. His body was stiff in the tight position he'd assumed, his gaze averted from her. She swiftly made her way to the bathroom, shutting the door.

Her heart was shattered and the ache in her chest threatened to crush her. The injustices of her life left her wishing she could scream. But she wouldn't. It wouldn't help anyone, least of all her.

Christina moved to the sink, ran cool water, and shoved the white face-washer from beside the sink, under the faucet before applying the cold-water compress to her face.

"I'll save face now. Because that's all I've got." The words echoed in the tiny bathroom as she stared at her red eyes. He knew the worst now, but she'd wear her dignity like a flimsy cape.

Once satisfied she'd repaired the worst of the damage, she stripped the wet pants and shirt off and in disgust threw them into the garbage. She wanted no reminders of this exchange as she tugged the clean ones on.

With that thought, she pulled open the door and looked around. Vasya was nowhere to be seen.

Sighing in relief, she grabbed the suitcase, heaving it down off the metal bench it sat on, and headed to the door. She swung it open and moved to the back of the car. Once the key was inserted in the lock, Christina raised the boot, throwing her suitcase inside on top of the motorbike under the blanket.

She sighed. Yet one more issue to deal with, she thought, another problem in the litany of errors and mistakes that made up her miserable existence.

The door to the room Gregori and Serina shared opened, and Vasya, her sister and Gregori moved out. "I will get my things from the room."

Vasya hardly looked at her as Serina watched. Christina felt the curiosity in her gaze before she jerked away. "We need to get moving, it must be close on ten, and we still have a long way to go."

Gregori nodded, making his way back into the room and emerging with the bags he had carried in just that morning.

Vasya exited their room with his small bag in hand, and she nodded. "Right, I'll return the keys, then we can go." She turned and walked toward the office.

*V*asya watched her walk away. There was no slump in her shoulders. This woman would show no fear or pain now, not to him, but he could sense the tense fragility that hung around her. He didn't know what to say to her, so he kept his counsel.

When she returned she unlocked the vehicle, and they all got into it. Gregori and Serina sat in the back seat as they had before, and Gregori commenced clucking over his wife like a mother hen. That small slice of sanity brought a smile to his face, but it quickly melted away.

It should have been me though. Us. With Kira, excitedly expecting my child. The thought had occurred to him before, and for a moment he allowed his eyes to close, imagining Kira, her stomach rounded, lying beside him, laughing. The same girl he had married, so happy and carefree.

None of that girl seemed to exist in the Christina who was pulling out of the parking bays.

Now, the only emotions she exuded were loneliness and frailty. How hard it must have been for her! Dragged from her home to a new land, no family, no friends?

"What do you do, in your work?" The words surprised him as they escaped from his mouth.

"I help displaced people and those who have been

rescued from the Secret Police in Alvonia when they arrive in Madona. I help them to find work. Offer assistance in changing their identity if necessary, and assist them in tracking down other family members who have escaped."

"You enjoy this? Helping people?"

"I find it rewarding." Her curt answer told him she'd rather not continue any discussion with him, so he settled back, considering her answers. For all she indicated there was pleasure in her tasks, there was no sense that any form of enjoyment filled her life.

He glanced at her, as she focused on the road ahead. There still remained some puffiness around her eyes, and the pinkness he associated with the end of a crying jag.

It had never been his intention to hurt her, physically or emotionally, yet he'd achieved it.

Vasya derided himself. He should have understood. He'd let his festered hurt and anger lash out, never realizing she carried such a heavy burden.

He looked out the window of the car as they sped away from the border town. "What can you do for me?" He needed to talk to her, but couldn't think of anything else that made sense right now.

"Pardon?" He winced at her frosty tone.

"What can you do to ease me into my new life? If you help all these other people, what can you help me with?"

"Well. Umm, let's see. Are you still working with wood?" She flicked a quick glance over at him.

"Yeah, I'm a master wood crafter. How can you help me?"

"Well, I can introduce you to the head of Madona's Guild of Wood Crafters. He'll want to see a sample of your work, I'd imagine. Then my people can help you to decide if you wish to work with someone or by yourself. Assistance is available by way of low interest loans to purchase any equipment and find premises for work, if that's what you wish."

He watched, amazed, as she rattled off the numerous ways she could help him rebuild his life. "If required, we can replace your papers. We will even help you apply for Zoyonan citizenship. That's just the tip of the iceberg, of course."

The information wove itself into a web that intrigued him. In Alvonia, he'd had to do the bidding of the political masters. For him, it had been about building monuments to their government and masters. To their *achievements*. For a moment he did wonder what they'd make of his vision of their achievements.

He smiled, considering the possibility of a home of his own. He could even become a master in his own right. Perhaps his fortunes were changing?

He looked at Christina. *How will she fit into my new life?* Would she be the old or part of the new? He didn't know, but he wanted to look for a way to make it fit, especially if the girl he'd love still existed in Christina.

"I want to teach." Serina's voice filtered from the back.

"Okay, we can help you with that, too, Serina. But your first priority is to find a doctor and get you settled. Then we can look into the options that are available. You finished school..."

"How do you know that?" Serina's voice was sharp.

"I...umm..." Vasya could see she was flustered, taken by surprise at her sister's query. "It was part of the deal I made with Zuor. He kept an eye on you, made sure you remained safe, until I could get you out."

He closed his eyes. *She had bargained for their safety? For eleven years?* His gut churned at the thought, but he needed to be sure. All those years in Alvonia meant that he was slow to trust. Even Kira.

Especially this new, cold Kira.

"So you bargained since when? Kira?"

"My name is Christina now." He heard the ragged tone in her voice. "And you don't really want to know the answer to that."

His ire rose. "I wouldn't ask if I didn't wish an honest answer." He winced, realizing what he had just demanded.

"Fine. Ever since I escaped Alvonia. Is that what you wanted to know?" Her voice was fierce and angry. She swerved the car to the side of the road and pulled to a stop, the tires screeching their displeasure while the smell of burning rubber assaulted his senses.

"Go on, then Vasya. Tell me what else you want to know. I would be *so happy* to tell you about my time and experiences. Let's start with loneliness, shall we?"

She wasn't quite yelling, but her face reddened and her eyes swam with unshed tears. He sat ramrod straight in his seat. He'd asked the question, and now he would hear it all.

The knife in his chest twisted as she gripped the steering wheel, the knuckles of her fingers white with the ferocity of her hold. "How about not having a decent education so I had to go to school at night while I worked during the day? Every day was a struggle because I was exhausted?"

The hiccup sounded in the air as she dragged in a ragged breath. "How about trying to remember a new name, because the government needs you to change who you are. I had to make sure the Alvonian Government didn't realize *I* was the girl they'd been searching for. They hid me in the Displaced Office of Madona—an office the Alvonians refused to work with. Then there were the constant threats from their people."

Each comment pounded into him. Hammer hard blows that left his senses reeling. "I had to learn to use equipment, to drive a car, but I had no one to share that with. But the worst? That was the holidays everyone else takes with their family, while I was always alone." Her words died away, and he swallowed the lump of pain that lodged in his throat.

Her face glowed with hurt and sorrow long bottled inside. The tears started again, flowing freely. She put her head on the steering wheel.

"Kira?" He put a hand out to touch her shoulder, but she flinched away.

"Please, don't touch me." She looked out the window, fumbling in her bag for a handkerchief and quietly wiping her eyes. "We need to keep going. There looks to be a storm brewing on the horizon."

Her voice was hoarse, but when she looked back, her face was composed, even though her eyes were watery and red.

"I apologize for my outburst. It was unwarranted." She smiled, a cold, distant movement of her lips, and it chilled him to the core. The hurt he had caused unthinkingly had brought forward this cold, soul-less woman.

"Christina—" He reached out toward her, but she shook her head, warding him off.

"Don't worry about it. It's done." She flicked the indicator and pulled back onto the road.

*D*amn! She shouldn't have lost control of her emotions like that. Christina pulled the vehicle back onto the road, heading northbound towards a cold, empty life that lay there. But she hadn't said anything that wasn't true.

I shouldn't have tried to wound him with my words. It wasn't the way to cope with the anger and frustration she'd lived with for so long. He, too, had struggled in the long years that had passed.

Vasya had been left behind, not knowing if she'd return. He'd taken on caring for her sister after her parents had been taken. She knew from working with other survivors times were hard, with little food and even less freedom.

During the years, she'd woven impossible fantasies of reuniting with Vasya; of maybe making a family with him. Instead, she'd gone home to find an angry and distrustful man. It was clear he blamed her for choosing to leave. If only that choice had truly been hers, she wouldn't have taken it.

She pushed harder on the accelerator. The sooner they were home, the sooner she could unravel the mess she'd made of her life. Petition for divorce, so he would be free to live his life the way he wanted to.

Her eyes blurred with tears again, and she blinked them away as she thought about the choices that had led to this point in her life.

She never saw the other vehicle, just heard the screech. She slammed back to reality, her hands fighting to control the vehicle. Vasya's hand reached for the wheel, to wrench it back, but it was too late.

"Oh God!" The only answer to her outburst were yells and screams.

She pulled hard on the wheel, yanking it to the right. The road sheered away, dropping down toward the boiling sea below. The tires lost traction on the road and slipped over the edge.

Christina screamed, "Hang on!"

The car moved in slow motion. Another scream tore from her as the vehicle pitched over the edge. Through the windscreen she spied the jagged rocks below a line of bushes.

The car careered wildly into the scraggly shrubbery. The engine screamed even as the car came to a stop.

She closed her eyes, shaking as the momentum pulled her forward into the wheel, her head making contact with the glass. Without thought, she reached out and turned off the engine, then gave a tiny laugh of surprise.

Her stomach hurt.

Not just the gut churning that had been going on since she'd realized they were still alive, but a deep, tearing pain.

"Vasya! Serina!" A grunt and groan from beside her brought her back to her senses, but she couldn't move. Something held her against the steering wheel.

"Vasya?" she wheezed.

"I am here, Kira. Are you okay?" His voice was panicked.

"I think so." One more little white lie won't hurt now. She knew she'd sustained an injury, but how severe...

She wanted to shrug but was afraid to move more than needed. "What about Serina and Gregori? Are they okay?" She turned her head a little to the side to see him. A thin trickle of blood slipped down his face, but he moved easily enough, and he didn't seem to be in any real pain.

"I'm fine. Gregori?" Serina's voice was thin but sure.

"I'll be okay in the morning, Serina. We just need to get out of here."

Vasya was pulling on his door; she could see he was favoring his arm a little, but he managed to get it open and slipped out of the vehicle. Heading to the back, he opened the door for Gregori and Serina.

"Come on, Kira, you need to get out. Now, before the bushes give way." His voice was harsh.

"I can't, Vasya. I'm stuck. Take my cell." She fumbled in the small pocket in the arm of the door and handed it over, "Get the others to the road, then dial six-five-five and ask for Phil."

His eyes narrowed but Vasya took the small device realising as he saw the dribble of blood at her lips, that she'd been badly injured. "Explain what happened, and that I need help. He'll know what to do."

Her chest hurt, as if something was pushing the breath out and she couldn't seem to drag in a full replacement. "The bushes won't hold too much longer." She kept her tone neutral and watched as he looked at the spindly green growths that stopped the car from sliding further.

She closed her eyes, coughing slightly, feeling a wetness seeping out of her mouth. She had a sinking feeling Zuor wouldn't let her go this easily, though. He would come for her before it was too late. After all, he still needed to collect on their deal.

When she opened her eyes, she could see horror on Serina and Gregori's faces. She refused to look at Vasya. "Go. Until you call for help, I can't do anything." She looked forward and closed her eyes.

CHAPTER 7

*V*asya ushered the others up the side of the ravine, looking for reception then dialed. He had only used one of these devices a few times in the past and kept watching for the bars everyone said were so important.

People stopped to look at the vehicle lying partway down, held in place by some spindly bushes. He ignored them. She'd given him instructions and he'd follow them through.

"Phil here. What's up, Christina?"

"This is not Christina. There has been an accident and she told me to ring you."

"Who is this?" the voice demanded, and he winced a little as the ache in his head bloomed.

"I am... I am a friend." Vasya didn't know why, but he wasn't yet prepared to give voice to the tangled relationship he shared with his wife. "She is hurt. Badly I think."

"Okay, do you know where you are?" The man's voice became deep and intense through the speaker.

"I don't know. We've been driving for some time. She's in

the car, trapped in a ravine. There are some bushes holding the car in place, but her situation is precarious." He needed to make that clear, because heavens knew how else he could save her. "She's bleeding from her mouth, too."

He'd seen the dribble of blood at the corner of her lips. Heaven help him, he wasn't going to let her die now, not now that he knew the truth. She'd risked everything to give him and her sister their freedom.

"Right. Hang on the line and we can use the GPS to find your position. Don't hang up, no matter what you hear." He waited and listened. It took time and thuds and clanks filled his hearing.

"I'm back. We found you and a rescue team is on the way. If you can get down to her safely tell her, she'll be calmer knowing help is coming." This Phil guy sounded very concerned, and a seed of jealousy raised its head.

"I can go. I will be safe."

"Right then. From what I can tell, the ravine will have no coverage. I've been told they should arrive there in the next five to ten minutes. Just tell her to hold tight."

The phone clicked off, so he slipped it into the narrow pocket at the back of his jeans before he prepared to carefully lever himself back down the steep embankment.

"Vasya? What about—" Serina sagged in his brother's arms, and he took a moment to swipe the tip of his finger over her cheek.

"Help is on the way, Serina. Stay here and be safe."

Down he headed. The soles of his sturdy boots slid on the loose rocks and dirt. Some slipped free, hitting the vehicle with pinging and crunching sounds.

He felt Gregori's gaze and heard Serina's sobs as he made his way slowly back down, much more slowly than he had gone up.

The car rocked and creaked quietly. "Kira? Can you hear me?" He wanted to grab her, but was concerned that to do so might destabilize the vehicle enough to move it off the shrubs. Not to mention the further damage it could do to her.

"I can hear you." Her eyes remained closed, her words faintly slurred.

"Phil says to hang on. He has crews on the way and they will be here shortly."

"Yeah, I'm hanging in here. You know though, Zuor won't let me go. Help would have turned up anyway, don't you know? I'm his meal ticket." She said it dispassionately. Her words concerned him as much as the way she said it.

"Go up now. I'll be fine." Then she slowly turned her head towards the front again.

As if a spell was broken, he backed away. He didn't like it, not one bit—his heart screamed to stay with her.

As he reached the top, vehicles screeched to a halt, and skidding rocks flew. Vasya flung up his hands to shield his face.

Traffic had stopped on both sides, and groups of people huddled, watching Serina and Gregori. They gaped at the emergency vehicles and they whispered, while some were brazen enough to take photos.

"Voyeurs." He bit the word off grimly while making his way towards the men striding in his direction.

"What happened, here?" A big burly man in his mid-thirties demanded. Vasya sized him up for an instant before his brain told him he was here to save Kira.

"We swerved to get out of the way of the traffic and the car rolled over the edge. My...*wife*...is stuck in it and can't get out. It is resting on the bushes. She's injured."

Another man climbed out of the vehicle slowly, his eyes

moving restlessly as if summing up the situation. Vasya got the impression this was the man in charge.

He, along with a couple of others, fastened a rope to their waists and made their way carefully down to the car.

When the men reached the bottom, Vasya noticed how gingerly they touched the car—each working quickly to save Kira.

One watched and gave instructions, another talked to her, and he could see him making notes and carefully reaching inside. He couldn't hear what was being said, and the sense of helplessness left him clenching his fists. The last man fastened a heavy chain to the precariously balanced car.

A cry went up, and one of the men scrambled back up. His face streaked with dirt and sweat as he moved to the back of the vehicle. Vasya noted the heavy gloves and the way the muscles on the man's arms strained.

The chief materialized beside him. "We can't get your wife out safely down there, so we're unsure of the extent of her injuries. Getting her back up here is the safest bet, but even that isn't without risks to her.

"However, once we get the vehicle back on solid ground, we'll be able to make further decisions." The chief patted his arm in what he probably thought was a consoling manner. Vasya felt no comfort from the action.

The car groaned as the back end came even with the ground, stopping for a moment while one of the men, who Vasya was sure was some kind of medic, checked on Kira.

Like an ailing crab, the car finally crunched over the edge, and the watchers sent up a ragged cheer. He moved as if to go to Kira, but another man grabbed him around the waist.

"You need to let them do their jobs. They'll do whatever

they can for your wife. You just need to be patient a little longer."

Patience was something he usually did quite well, but after eleven years and almost two days of spewing hurt, his chance to make everything right with Kira hung in the balance. As did her health. He wasn't going to let her go easily.

So he waited on the sidelines; finally able to see how she was wedged between the car seat and steering column, and his mouth grew dry.

Her shirt had blood on it. It was a huge, spreading stain of scarlet, and his heart nearly stopped. "Kira." A spike of metal protruded from the steering column and had clearly punched into her shirt and the flesh beneath.

In horror he watched her eyes close. For just one moment he thought the worst—his heart stopped beating in his chest, and he must have made a sound of distress.

The Officer came over and clamped a hand on his shoulder. "Just hang tight. If it was that bad, they'd have her out of there by now." It was only when she re-opened her eyes that the world righted once more.

"Vasya? She'll be alright, won't she?" Serina burrowed her tiny hand into his pocket, like she'd done as a child.

"Yes, I'm sure she will." The honest truth was he wasn't so damned sure. Men crawled over the vehicle, emptying the trunk, and Gregori stepped forward to grab his bike. Their bags and blankets were piled up a little away from the wreck, topped with the special satchels she'd insisted they place all their documents and photos into, but Vasya couldn't bring himself to be thankful. Even though it was now all they had in the world, he was more worried about Kira, and all he could do was watch others care for her.

"Vasya, they can't be too much longer, can they? She

needs to be attended by a healer." There was fear in Serina's voice.

"I don't know. I don't know what they're doing, not really. But I think that man is a medic; he seems to know what he's doing." He hunkered down beside Serina, and rested his tired head in his hands. All he knew right now was fear.

If he were honest, he'd accept that his anger and demands had caused the accident, and that knowledge ate at him. That she might leave him for good—die without giving him a chance to see if something of their marriage and love could be salvaged—burned him. It wasn't an outcome he wanted to contemplate.

CHAPTER 8

Christina woke in darkness; nothing more than a pinprick of light relieved the inky cold blackness. "Where am I?"

"You are here, in my realm. Where you will be my servant for as long as I wish it." Zuor. He was here, wherever 'here' was.

"I want to go back." Her voice trembled, and he laughed. A cold, frighteningly dark laugh that sent adrenaline coursing throughout her body—where it throbbed from the pain of her injuries a trickle of warm liquid oozed. Instinctively she knew it was blood, well before the coppery tang confirmed her thought.

"You don't make demands. Only I do." His voice filled the dark, soft yet hiding an inner bite that stole her thoughts.

Her stomach quivered at his words. "Please." She couldn't contain the small pleading word, and he laughed again.

A chilled touch drifted down her naked back. She gasped, leaning away.

Cold metal touched her neck, clasping around it, closing with a snick. She tried to raise her hands but couldn't. They too were secured.

Something scratched at her skin and she shivered once more, realizing she was naked. She glanced down as best she could, but all she could see was the faint outline of her skin, pale in the gloom.

As if someone had illuminated a spark, light grew, until she could see more clearly. Zuor stood beside her, and she faced an old-fashioned mirror. Its burnished face glittered slightly, and she shook, shocked at the sight reflected there: Her arms fastened to the wall with cold manacles. A black metal collar encircled her neck. A gaping tear in her side, oozing dark blood. He skin dotted with bruises and scratches.

In the mirror she spied Zuor watching her, grinning. His coal black eyes glinted as he assessed her, his gaze running over her body, while his tongue swiped his lips. The dark hunger twisted her stomach further.

"My nightmare realm is so... appropriate don't you think?" He waved a hand, and the mirror melted away, leaving her instead overlooking a field. Or what may once have been one at some time; instead, it was littered with a seething mass of black and bloodied bodies, and only the bare limbs of trees rose above the ground, with rocky rubble springing up beside the bones.

Revolted by the sight in front of her, her stomach heaved. The dry retching pulled at her innards, wrenching at muscles and flesh already compromised.

"None of that, my dear. This will soon be your home. And one day, you will be my consort." He turned to look at her, his eyes roaming over her naked body again as he dragged a single, elongated fingertip over her shoulder.

Christina shook with revulsion.

Dizziness assailed her, and she closed her eyes at his touch. His cold slimy hands slid over her bare stomach. The muscles clenched involuntarily, even as she strained against the bonds holding her in place.

"Not yet, but soon." He crooned the words, and she opened her *eyes, watching as he leered. "Soon you will be my consort. Then... Then you will plead for my touch." His face tightened. She watched him raise an arm, then he snapped the fingers on one hand and melted away.*

Silent, hot tears dribbled down her face. "Vasya!" She screamed his name, knowing it was pointless. He couldn't hear her here, not in this dark prison.

She slumped, feeling the bite of the metal into the soft flesh at her wrists. She let the fiery hot sobs escape, and the pressure in her chest grew as her body heaved with the ferocity of her emotions.

How could this happen? She knew the answer already: Zuor was determined to make her pay his price, the one he had demanded for the safe release of Serina and Vasya. Her torment was the price she had unknowingly agreed to.

The only bargaining power that she'd had with Zuor had been exhausted.

She gulped down the bubble of misery lodged in her throat.

The steady drip-drip-drip of water was her only companion, and she welcomed the sound. It was a hint of normality in a world she could neither comprehend nor escape.

She wouldn't give in yet. She couldn't. That's what he wants, her mind told her. She already knew that he fed on happy feelings, sucking them into himself leaving her nothing but fear and terror. Loneliness and heartbreak.

But he would release her soon. His need to feed soon and to relieve her of the happy thoughts would consume him. At least she hoped so. The thought comforted her.

The air cooled; a touch of frostiness now nipped at her as the light dimmed. She shivered in the gloom. If only she could wrap her arms around herself, to clutch the last traces of warmth to her body. But even that small freedom was forbidden.

Her eyelids fluttered down as she shivered once more.

"Vasya..." The moan filled the air as the tears flowed freely once more.

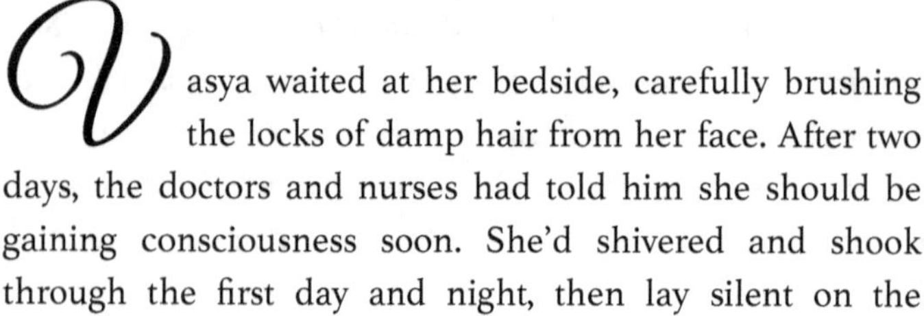

*V*asya waited at her bedside, carefully brushing the locks of damp hair from her face. After two days, the doctors and nurses had told him she should be gaining consciousness soon. She'd shivered and shook through the first day and night, then lay silent on the second.

The horror he'd felt watching as they'd got her out of the wreck never left. It remained, replaying in his mind like a movie causing him to reconsider his feelings. The emotions that had churned since she'd turned up—loss, anger, fear, uncertainty—melted away at the very real truth that he could lose her, after she had only just reappeared in his life. In one single minute, his feelings had become crystal clear: He still loved his wife and would take any chance to rebuild the connection that had snapped between them.

He ran a shaking hand through his hair. Why hadn't she woken yet? *If only...*

"I need to check her, and you need a break. Go have a nap or grab something to eat." The nurse interrupted his stray thoughts. Her words were kindly enough but firm.

He trudged down to the waiting room—the white walls and black seating offered nothing soothing to the eyes—but while Christina lay deathlike in the hospital bed, she remained the focus of his thoughts.

A commotion in the hallway caught his attention. "I'm Phil Hausbauger. I've come to check on Christina." A tall man stood at the nurse's desk.

"She's just being attended to, then you can enter." The woman smiled.

Before Vasya could interrupt, the younger nurse, the one who'd ejected him from her room, spoke to the man who'd just arrived, then ushered him into Christina's small hospital cell. The door closed, and silence fell again.

Jealousy pushed its way inside him.

"He shouldn't be in there." He huffed, scrubbing his fingers through his hair. Minutes ticked by before the man left the room and took up residence in a seat opposite him.

Vasya noted the dark-grey eyes hidden behind slim, gold-rimmed glasses. And a lean but muscular and toned body lay hidden below the severe black suit he wore. Vasya felt grubby and threadbare in comparison. His clothes betrayed what he was, a poor artisan with nothing except the small bag of items he'd come away with.

The tall man nodded once, leaving no doubt that he was well aware of Vasya's identity. And the beaded sweat across this Phil's top lip told him just how deeply he cared for Kira.

His mouth tightened with anger and a primitive emotion kicked in. *She's mine.* He couldn't deny the primal urge to hold her close to him. To keep this man away. To protect what was his. *I will never let her go again.* The knowledge of the years of terror and loneliness that she had survived continued to cut at him as surely as the sharpest knife he had ever wielded.

"You're Vasya, right? Her husband? I'm Phil, Christina and I work together... You know, she never mentioned any of you." Phil's voice broke the silence in the soulless waiting room. "You'd think after all those years, working together, she would have mentioned you." He shrugged. "But then, she's always been so self-contained, so private that I never pushed it. I guess I thought I had time."

The knot inside Vasya's chest released—just a little bit—at Phil's words. So they'd never been together. If she were still the woman he thought, she'd never permit a relationship on any level without being brutally honest. She wasn't the kind to engage in a romantic entanglement while still married to him.

But is she still the same woman? After all these years, she might not be, his mind offered; he closed his eyes against the thought. After all, he really didn't know his wife anymore. "You... You work with her?" He heard the uncertainty in his voice, wincing.

"Sort of. We mainly work separately, but she oversees the section we are all associated with." Phil was frowning at him. "What she does... it's dangerous."

"What do you mean? Dangerous, how?"

Phil shook his head. "She needs to tell you. It's not for me to disclose." He leaned back in the chair, leaving Vasya struggling to contain his anger again.

The negative emotion floated close to the surface; vengeance and jealousy were unfamiliar emotions to him. He was a contained man. The urge to create something new called, a pale imitation of the emotions that had swirled within him since Kira had returned to his life.

"Will you be remaining here until she is released?" He watched the man, waiting for his response.

Phil shrugged. "It depends on how soon she comes around and what the doctors say. For now, I have arranged to stay in the same hotel as yourself and the rest of your family."

Damn. He didn't want the man around. On some level, it would probably make things easier, but it also slammed home how little he knew of Kira's new life. It should be him making the arrangements, caring for Kira, yet he didn't know how to do that here. He bitterly hated the feeling of helplessness. "Ki..."

Before he could finish her name, Phil sat forward raising one arm. "Christina. Her name is Christina now. You go calling her that, and no matter that we're on this side of the border, she'll be in more danger than you could possibly understand."

What. The. Hell?

Just what was Kira involved in that would cause her so much danger? He made a mental note to find out once she had recovered enough. For now, he nodded his acceptance to the man.

Soft footsteps echoed down the corridor and he raised his head. The nurse walked up and eyed both men. He could see the confusion in her eyes. "Umm. Ms. Alward has recovered consciousness." She smiled at him as he rose.

"I can see her?"

She nodded. "But only for a few minutes."

When Phil made to rise she shook her head. "I'm sorry, only her husband will be admitted right now."

Phil flushed, and Vasya couldn't contain the feeling of elation, laced with a sliver of pity from rising. He would see her, not this Phil.

CHAPTER 9

Her ears detected the soft beep-beep of machines, and wherever her gaze touched, she saw tubes. Her side ached viciously.

Zuor must have allowed her to live, just as she'd expected. He wouldn't be one to let his donor pass away that easily. The last recollection she had was of him whispering in her ear.

His intentions when he toyed with her like that were always cruel. He taunted her, while she made every effort to ignore him, but the more she ignored him the worse it became. He would make her pay—next time.

Christina learned over the years to be prepared and to accept the punishment he mete out, because there was no other choice. When alone she could answer him, but in public... She never wanted to deal with the looks of scorn if she didn't control her reactions.

A whisper played at the edges of her memory. A fleeting emotion that made her breath catch and chilled her to the marrow. She tugged at the white sheet, unsure and worried at what he planned next.

The door cracked open, and she looked up. Vasya stood there, his eyes deeply shadowed and with at least a three-day growth shadowing his strong jaw. Instinct had her reaching for him, feeling foolish for giving in to the urge she stopped her hand, and held herself rigid.

"Hello, Vasya." She looked at him, waiting for a tirade, but none ensued. She frowned.

"Kirai... Christina, I owe you an apology." He shut the door behind him and pulled up the plastic visitors chair beside the high bed. "I shouldn't have..."

"No. It's my fault entirely. I should have paid more attention." If she had, they wouldn't be in this position. "How is..." She stopped, ignoring the shaft of pain and forced air into her lungs, then tried again. "How is Serina?"

"The doctors checked her. They say she and the babe are well."

She nodded, thankful that her thoughtless actions had not wrought the worst of outcomes.

"Good. I'm pleased." She glanced away, to the wall, hoping to soothe the ragged feelings within her heart. "Gregori and yourself? You are both well?"

She looked back to see he nodded. Then she waited, wondering what else he wanted. Christina lifted her chin a little. *Let him say his piece and leave.* The silence drew out, broken only by their breathing and the beeping of the electronic equipment. Her nerves pulled tight; at any instant they could twang, and she would break down. She couldn't let that happen.

His eyes roamed over her face.

"Ki... Christina, please. I never..." He swallowed, and her eyes followed the movement of his Adam's apple, the convulsive gesture betrayed his emotions. "I shouldn't have reacted the way I did."

"It's okay. Honestly, Vasya. I understand." Her heart ached, but even if it killed her, she would make sure he didn't feel bad. She reached out a hand, touching his for the first time since the altercation in the bathroom.

Her body reacted to the contact with a frisson of electricity dancing up her arm, stronger than she'd ever experienced before, and a bubble of pain rose up, nearly choking her.

Memories of the shy lovemaking they'd shared on their wedding flashed through her mind. And then by the lake... She thrust them, away with an effort.

"Christina... You didn't do anything wrong." He laid his other hand over hers. "But I... I want a chance to start again."

Oh, God! No doubt her outburst had made him feel he ought to give their relationship another chance.

"Vasya, it's okay. It's been eleven years. Way too long for whatever is between us to work." Her heart ached but the words had to be said. "I understand that, now. It's okay though. I will let you go, once I'm back on my feet." She kept her voice as soothing as possible even while her heart cracked wide open.

He shook his head. "No. That's not what I want."

She smiled, holding onto her sanity with the tiniest grip while withdrawing her hand. "When you're first placed in a new environment, you want the familiar. I understand that. Really, I do." His eyes widened but she plowed on. "It's something we all experience. But you've got Serina and Gregori."

"That's not..."

"Shh. It's okay." She breathed deeply, letting her mind clear. "I'll do everything I can to make this as pain free for you as I can. I'll even hand your case over to Phil, if you prefer."

"No!" He nearly shouted the word, and she jerked back watching the thatch of black hair moving wildly as he shook his head forcefully. "I don't want you to do that. I want to be with you."

His hand recaptured hers, and he placed a gentle kiss on her palm. She shivered at the subtly erotic movement, but a ripple of pain ran through her body at the motion and she moaned.

She'd longed to hear those words for years, but reality was intruding. She couldn't be what he needed. He'd be in danger, and with Zuor prowling... well, she wasn't going to allow that.

Christina tugged on her hand, but he wouldn't release it.

"I want us to find a future together. Christina?" Uncertainty colored his tone.

Her eyes stung, and she had to turn away, dashing at them with her free hand. "If only you knew." She whispered the words.

"If only I knew what? Christina...."

A knock on the door interrupted the moment.

When he released her hand she should have felt relief, but it felt more like loss.

CHAPTER 10

His fingers tapped out a ragged beat while he waited for Christina—he still struggled with calling her by that name. During the last fifteen minutes he'd been waiting, he fought to stave off the worry that was his constant companion: Was she all right? Was she being discharged too early? The invariable questions gnawed at his mind.

Phil had offered to stay and help, but she'd refused, instead, sending Vasya and Gregori to find and purchase a car before collecting her from the hospital. She'd told him, that with his paperwork and the cash she handed him, that would be the easiest option. He'd followed her instructions to the letter, purchasing a SUV, large enough to carry his brother's motorbike and their meager collection of items.

Phil left yesterday, promising to be *only a phone call away*, leaving Vasya to stew over the friendly relationship the man and Christina shared. "Damn Phil!" The words slipped out, and he looked around, hoping no one noticed. He wasn't a man given to sharing his emotions publicly.

Vasya had feared that she might take the chance of

ending their tenuous relationship by leaving with Phil. "I won't let her go." He took strength from the confidence in his voice.

He'd have to engineer a way to keep her by his side while he proved the connection between them burned hotter than ever before. He needed to prove to her they had a future—together.

Sitting in the tiny parking area just beyond the entrance of the hospital and looking over the view before him, he mentally prepared for the days and weeks ahead. He welcomed this opportunity to be alone, when he could gather his strength like a cloak in preparation for what loomed like a battle ahead of him.

After less than a week, the doctors had informed her that if she were cautious, she could travel home. She still had little stamina, and walking around the ward exhausted the small measure of energy she'd built up.

Kir—Christina, he forcefully reminded himself, again— had been adamant. "I'm going home, Vasya. I've had enough of hospitals. And besides, I need to get on with my life, and so do you."

Those words had speared him. He planned to ensure she got what she needed, but deep in his heart, he knew that meant she needed him too. If only he could make her see that truth.

Gregori and Serina had insisted that they would help her to the doorway. Anxiety weighed him down. So much could go wrong—she could slip and fall, or be too tired to reach the portico. It was the only permitted place to collect patient from, and he chafed at the restriction.

The doors slid open, and he sat up, watching her ginger footsteps, her face still carried a pinched, white look to it, which he found alarming. She leaned heavily on Gregori and used the cane the hospital supplied. The wound at her side would take time to heal, and the doctors had cautioned her to not place any pressure on that area, or to exert herself.

He'd tried once to remonstrate with her as she prepared to leave, but she'd merely pinned him with one of her cool and remote glances before she spoke. *"You really shouldn't concern yourself, Vasya."* After that, he'd tried to keep his counsel.

Jerking back to the here and now, he watched Gregori act like a human barrier, preventing anyone getting too close to her. Serina offered silent support and smiles. Inside his belly the cold knot that had formed started to melt away.

His family rallied around her, and he was glad they could finally support her. Gregori must have seen Vasya moved the car up to the pickup zone and made to get out. Gregori shook his head, so he stayed in his seat and waited while Gregori opened the door for her, hovering like an anxious father.

"I'm fine." She pushed away from his brother and slowly moved herself into the car, swiveling until her legs were directly in front of her. He saw the nerves in her fingers jumping and the tight way she held herself before she visibly relaxed.

Curling his fingers, he stopped himself from reaching out to touch her.

"So, how do we get home?" he asked when Gregori and Serina where in the car.

She gave careful and concise directions to the city of Madona.

Gratitude filled him once they were on the other side of the accident scene. He worried that passing it would be too much for Christina—after all, it was still too raw in his mind. He followed the highway heading in the direction of Madona, the capital city of Zyonan. Instead of old buildings and smatterings of abandoned cars, tanks and carts that littered Alvonia, the roads were well maintained, the houses reasonably well kept, and not an abandoned car was in sight.

The further they drove, the more he wondered at the differences between the two countries, even though they were side by side. Passing through a tiny seaside town, he heard the exclamation of surprise from Serina. "Look at the beach." Her tone were almost reverential.

People had flocked to the sandy expanse, umbrellas dotted the shoreline while children played. On their faces he spied grins of delight. It was so alien after their drab existence in Alvonia. Tears burned his eyes.

"Our child will play like that." Gregori spoke from the back, and pleasure suffused him. Gregori and Serina deserved to be happy. However hard he tried to ignore it, though, an empty space filled a tiny portion of his heart.

"Are people generally so happy?" He turned to Christina, unable to contain the surprise in his question.

"Yeah. Most people here live a good life. Education is free and so are medical services." She shrugged. "It will be good for Serina and the child." She turned away from his gaze to stare through the window.

She'd been remote with him since waking after the accident, as if she had locked her emotions behind a wall of ice, one he was struggling to chip away at.

"What about learning to be a teacher?" Serina's voice came from the back seat.

"I spoke to Phil before he left. He's going to make some enquiries and get back to me once we get home. And

Gregori? He's making arrangements for you to finish your apprenticeship with a master craftsman."

Vasya smiled to himself. She had unknowingly betrayed the depths of her emotional ties. Her attention to their needs, healthcare, education, training and housing filled him with warmth and gave him hope.

If only she would see how much she needed them, he might have a chance to woo her and to win her back. He held onto that thought as he drove on.

The two days on the road had been trying, with an overnight stop in a small motel. He'd been adamant. "You need to rest."

"I am. I'm not driving." But the truth was the minute they stopped and she'd lain down, the relief had been overwhelming.

By the time they had reached the outskirts of Madona, it was clear that Vasya wouldn't do for anything other than treat her as an invalid.

She was pleased to see the little house ahead. She told herself, it had nothing to do with the need to be alone with or without Vasya.

The house might be small, with only two bedrooms, but it was hers. She would have to ensure that Serina and Gregori took the larger bed in the master bedroom, now that she knew about Serina's pregnancy. Her needs would take precedence.

Besides, the large bed was too lonely for her on her own. Her heart lurched at the thought.

Thankfully she had another, smaller bed in the second bedroom. She hoped Vasya would find it comfortable enough, while Christina would take the couch. Her mind ran through the linens she had on hand, pleased to remember there was an older white set she could use on the sofa. She'd have to grab clothes from the closets so she wouldn't need to intrude on anyone's privacy, but it was certainly easy enough to arrange.

She pushed the door open on the car and winced as her body protested, her muscles ached as her stitches twanged.

"Christina, let me help you." In a flash Vasya was there, reaching into the car. It was an action she was slowly becoming accustomed to. *For now*, her mind supplied.

"I'm fine." She tried to shake him off, but he held on.

When her step faltered, he scooped her up in his arms.

Not wanting to argue, Christina rattled around in her bag for the keys. They jangled and she sighed, realizing she still carried the ones for the wrecked car as well as the house.

Once he inserted them in the lock of the door it swung open. The scent of stale air escaped from the tiny wooden house.

Christina breathed in deeply though. It was home. Hers for now or at least until she was able to move into the small unit in Madona, kept in readiness for emergencies.

Vasya stopped, and she looked up, watching his face. Saw his smile as he took in the restful room. "This is good, Christina."

She startled, realizing he'd called her Christina. Until now, it had been a stop-start version of her name.

She shied away from thoughts of how he was trying to adjust his thinking, and instead concentrated on what Vasya might see, upon entering the room.

A three-seater sofa sat in the middle of the room facing a small white coffee table. There were also two single recliners in the same blue material as the sofa. The plain white walls were unadorned but the floor teamed with pretty white and blue floral tiles. The room was compact, but she'd decorated it carefully, pouring her hopes and dreams into every decision.

The tiny dining room, hidden behind a curved wall, featured a heavy wood table and matching chairs. She'd rescued them from the side of the road and lovingly stripped and re-polished them during the first festive season she had passed in Zyonan. *Alone.*

A bubble of pride filled her, and she smiled in spite of herself. "Let me down and I'll show you around." She wiggled in his arms, and he reluctantly placed her on her feet. She slid down his tall frame and heaven help her, her body reacted to his proximity, warming through to her core.

She gulped and hoped he hadn't noticed the flare of heat on her face.

Gripping the head of the walking stick, Christina led him through to the galley-kitchen. Previously she'd always thought it felt friendly and welcoming, but now it felt crowded and intimately small. She grimaced, knowing this would be an area of difficulty until she left.

"The kitchen." Christina cleared her throat.

She turned with a swift motion, but instead of edging by him, Vasya moved close. With an *oomph,* she crashed into his chest.

His hands gripped her shoulders, steadying her, and she gasped as her body reacted to his proximity again.

Her face flamed. "Sorry. I didn't mean..." Christina looked up into his eyes and was lost all over again.

"It's fine Christina. Besides, we need to talk." His face softened losing the harsh edges that she had seen for the last two days.

I don't want to talk. Her traitorous body wanted him and her mind screamed that it was a continuation of the eleven-year fantasy she had indulged herself with.

She stepped back. "How about you..." She had to clear her throat, before continuing, "go grab the stuff out of the car. The garage is just up the side. Tell Gregori to put the bike there, it'll be safe." She turned away, stumbling slightly.

He must have read her determination accurately as he half bowed. "If you want." His words weren't a statement though, as much as a query.

"Yeah. That would be great."

He stayed still a moment longer before turning. At the small doorway he glanced back. "We will talk. Soon." Then he turned, leaving her in turmoil in the middle of the kitchen.

*V*asya stalked out to Gregori who was pulling his bike from the back of the small station wagon.

"Still ignoring you, I see." Gregori smiled as he spoke.

"She has some misbegotten idea that I feel indebted to her." He ran his hands through his hair, wishing desperately for something physical to do; to work off the anger that coursed through his veins.

Gregori's smile faded away. "Eleven years is a long time."

"Eleven years, four months and two days." He frowned, knowing exactly how that made him sound. "You need to bring that around to the garage at the side." They walked together while he thought over Gregori's words. It was a long time. They didn't know each other anymore. And to make things infinitely worse, she was injured so it wasn't like he could drag her off to the bedroom, love her and make her see and feel what he did. He needed to think carefully before he acted, in case he scared her away.

"She's going to need a bed. I saw a large one and a smaller one as she showed me around the house. If I read her right, she'll try and claim the chair."

"I remember how she was always mothering Serina and the younger children from our town. Including me."

Vasya grunted at Gregori's words. They pushed the bike into the small, dark garage; shelves ran the wall, with everything laid out neatly. "She won't be able to help herself. She should have the big bed. Serina and I can take the smaller, that's what we're used to anyway."

Vasya shrugged, knowing that his brother and wife would be more comfortable in the larger one, but right now, he wasn't going to argue. "With the child on the way, you should be comfortable, or at least Serina should be."

"You'll want to stay with her, given what we now know about her feeding." Gregori scratched his head, pushing the bike against the walls. "I doubt this demon, Zuor, will leave her alone easily. I know..." His brother broke off the statement as a frown creased his forehead.

"They must feed regularly. Yes, I'm aware of that." While Gregori was correct, he doubted Christina would be happy to let him share her bed, let alone hold her through the night.

They'd have to think of another way to keep Zuor at bay. "Maybe we should let Serina choose?" Neither of the sleeping outcomes suited him, but this way, maybe he had a chance of Christina accepting the situation.

They walked back to the vehicle, both lost in their own thoughts. "What is your plan of attack?" Serina waited by the car. The pile at her feet told him she'd been pulling the blankets and rubbish out. Her blunt words stopped them both.

Vasya didn't pretend to not understand her demand. "I don't know, Serina. She won't even stay in the same room as me, without making a comment about how she thinks I'm only doing this because I feel lost, or it's gratitude. That is, when she will actually let me talk to her." He shook his head. "She's been damaged during our time apart and I don't know how to reach her."

Serina reached up a small hand and patted his face. "We all treated her badly and have to do a lot of work to make up for it. She gave up a lot to get us out. But your situation is different. The only thing you can do is keep trying. We've, all four of us, got adjustments to make and I'm finding it hard not knowing what to do or how to help. I know Gregori wants to do something too."

Serina smiled as she glanced at her husband, the fierce light in her eyes fading away and the droop of her lips returned. "Give it time. She's been on her own for a long time with only this Zuor character to keep her company and I personally don't know how she's survived under those conditions."

"About the beds..." Gregori spread his hands and Vasya shook his head, his brother was determined to change the subject to something infinitely less emotional.

Serina smothered a frustrated groan. "She is insistent that we take the larger one. I accepted for tonight, but she said that she'll organize another for Vasya tomorrow. When I mentioned that she should take the other bed she just shook her head and said it wasn't *negotiable*." Serina made a frustrated face. "I told her you wouldn't be happy." Serina shrugged. "She just laughed it off. But at least I tried."

Serina looked so downcast that Vasya briefly folded her

in his arms. A prickle of unease made him raise his head and he looked around. At the door stood Christina, watching them. She'd obviously witnessed the scene unfolding, and for a moment stark need and hunger flashed over her face. The constant ache in his heart settled deeper as the emotion on her face disappeared. Now she replaced it with the blank expression she wore like a mask.

When Christina turned without a word and retreated within the house, he wanted to follow her.

The need to remind her that she too, belonged here with them, a part of this family rose. He shrugged. He knew that right now she wouldn't accept it. As if he'd seen their brief non-verbal interaction, Gregori laid his hand on Vasya's shoulder. "Go after her, Vasya."

Instead he let his shoulders slump. Right now what did he have to offer her? The knowledge that she kept locking him out cut deeply, but he knew she was protecting herself as much as she thought she protected him and all he had to offer her was empty hands and a bruised heart. It wasn't enough.

"I don't think she would welcome me right now." He felt like he was merely shadow boxing with his demons and hers.

"Vasya... Maybe if you shared...?" Serina bit her lip.

"No." He turned away from Gregori's concerned gaze. "She isn't ready to hear it yet."

"Leave it for now, Serina. There is nothing you or I can do. Vasya and Christina must sort this out for themselves."

Vasya heard his brother's words. Not knowing how to fix this mess was stealing his ability to think, so instead, he acted by picking up the bags lying on the ground with a grunt. Gregori and Serina followed him as they headed for the door.

The house settled as she tossed and turned on the small bed. She'd managed to talk Serina into accepting the larger one, mainly because she was pregnant. But when she'd tried to talk Vasya into accepting this bed, he refused. *Point blank.*

She could almost see the look of frustration that had painted his features before her. "*If you would prefer it, I could sleep on the floor, but don't expect me to use this bed. You're healing from injuries.*"

In the end, it had been simpler to accept defeat and take the single narrow bed for herself. So she'd scurried into the bedroom, changing and carefully climbing in before he could push the argument further—the one where he'd stake his claim on her and the larger bed. The stark hunger that, from time to time, coated his face disconcerted her and she questioned her choices and decisions endlessly.

Now she lay awake, scanning the white ceiling. Even though she was exhausted and her body screamed for rest she kept the sensations at bay, kept her mind occupied. The painkillers soothed the fire at her side, lulling her slightly and she fought off the clutches of worry that crept around the edges of her mind.

The last few nights had been horrific.

Zuor had somehow managed to find his way into her nightmares. Each and every night, she tumbled back into the dark. The rank odor, the terror chilling her marrow and he was always there. Watching her as she fought the bonds. Stripped naked, both emotionally and physically she had no way to fight. Except to stay awake.

She'd kept this a secret though, insisting on three rooms wherever they stopped. Tonight though, Vasya was in the room opposite and she knew he'd hear if she called out. The fear drove her to struggle against the rest her body craved, because that realm was where she'd end up inevitably if she fell asleep.

She turned, searching for a comfortable position, her hip discovering another lump in the mattress and Christina wondered if she should have grabbed a book. But it was a little late now.

A shaft of light illuminated the room slightly, from the crack between the curtains. Christina levered up carefully, brushing one curtain open to peer out at the stars. Then she lay down, looking out onto the quiet garden and hoped the light would keep her awake. Instead, her eyes grew heavy and the call of sleep captured her.

The manacles bit into her wrists once more and she opened her eyes. Back here, in the cold dark room where she had been kept night after night, she feared for her sanity. Sobbing, she wondered if she would ever break free of Zuor's hold on her.

Each night she sank lower into the morass of fear and loss... Just as each day reinforced it. Today she'd seen Vasya with his arms around Serina, comforting her, while Gregori had supported him.

In the window before the wall where she was chained, the images rolled before her over and over again.

Her mind whirred, considering the day and the night. The duality of her very existence... A new thought took root. Maybe that was the key to beating it? A small interrupt caught her attention, making her force back the hysteria that had taken root.

The door slammed open and Zuor stalked in. "What are you doing?" He roared the words and she cowered. The action instinctive in this cold hell he'd created.

"Nothing, Zuor. I'm still here." She rattled the iron at her wrists and gulped.

He moved toward her. She shrank back but the waft of decay about him still caught in her nostrils. She flinched and he leered, bending closer to her near frozen and naked form.

"You are mine. You were always meant to be mine." He ran a possessive hand from collar to breast and she heaved, unable to contain her reaction to his caress. He laughed softly, running the nail of his thumb over the tip of her breast. For a second the touch stilled, then he gave an excruciating flick and she cried out as pain radiated.

Another sound intruded... Zuor lifted his head, baring his long incisors and roared...

"Wake up, Christina. It's a dream." Warm hands touched her body and she flinched, feeling the burn.

"No! Don't touch me..." She writhed against the touch, still lost in the netherworld.

"Christina? It's okay. It's me. Vasya." Warm arms circled her as the shaking took control. Shudders racked her entire body, leaving her teeth rattling in her head. She opened her eyes to see the fear and concern on Vasya's face.

A sluggish finger of warmth penetrated through the iciness and she shivered again. The warmth was winning, stealing its way into frozen bones.

"What is it, Christina? What haunts you?" The little trickle of warmth slowed then stilled as she tried to pull away, but his arms held her close against his body.

"Please Vasya, I don't..." A tear dribbled down her cheek and she turned away, dashing at it with a shaking hand.

"You can't bottle it up Christina. Otherwise, it will crush you. It'll steal your life."

She pushed at him. "No Vasya. You can't understand." Her voice sounded husky and she swallowed.

A hand moved up and down her back, the action as sensual as it was comforting and she couldn't help herself.

Christina arched into the caress. Her thought processes became molasses-like. Her body craved his touch after being denied it for so long.

"Christina..." He whispered the words and she turned in his direction. The heat of his breath upon her lips battering her mind.

"Vasya..." Her limbs refused to move, even though she knew she *should* push him away.

"It's been so long." His mouth touched hers and her body exploded as delight and wonder filled her.

The thought fled as his lips roamed gently over hers, as if learning, for the first time, their contours and softness.

She moaned, wanting more. Her lips opened just a bit and he must have felt it, as he deepened the kiss. His tongue pushed and parted her lips so that it surged into her mouth.

The taste of him, so warm and musky called to her on a level she had forgotten existed. Sensations coursed through her body...

Sounds intruded. Voices...

She pushed away. "Oh. My. God." She stared at him. "I'm sorry, Vasya."

The door to the bedroom stood opened a crack and as she looked up, Serina peered around the corner, taking in the tableau.

"Is everything alright? Vasya? Ki... Christina?" Serina's gaze no doubt noted the disarray of Christina's hair, and the closeness of their bodies as she lay entwined in Vasya's arms. Serina pinked a little. "I... I'm sorry." As she backed away Christina felt the burn of heat on her cheeks.

"You should go too, Vasya." She turned away with an uncomfortable moan, hoping he would leave.

"No." His firm voice startled her.

"What?" She turned back. "What do you mean no?"

"I'm not leaving you alone." He looked deeply into her eyes. "Whatever these nightmares are, you need someone to keep you safe. You need me to chase them away."

Christina shook her head, but knew it was a vain effort. "Alright then. But you need pillows..." She made to rise and his hand was there, stopping her.

"You stay. I'll go get them." She watched as he left the room, the casual movements of his body, radiating strength and safety. She closed her eyes, disgusted at her lack of fortitude.

CHAPTER 11

*H*er stomach fluttered as she stood in the kitchen trying to sort out what the hell she should do next. The roiling mad jumble of nerves each time he came near made concentration difficult. *How can I face him after last night?*

Her mobile rang, the jangling sounds making her jump. She reached out, grateful for the interruption. "Christina Alward." She waited.

"Phil here. You're home now? Safe and sound, I guess. Look, we have a small problem. The unit is going to be needed from today, so it's not available. We have an emergency extraction underway."

Christina closed her eyes clutching the bridge of her nose between finger and thumb. The unit she planned to move into. Damn. "Will it... Will it be used for long?" But even as she spoke she knew the answer. There was never any way to tell.

"You know the answer to that." Phil spoke quietly and she nodded to herself, feeling foolish.

"Yeah, I do." She picked up the coffee and sipped. It was

cold and bitter. Much like her life, she mused. "Fine. I'll be back at work day after tomorrow. I have some things to sort out here first."

"No you won't." Phil's voice was firm over the line. "The doctor said you're to take it easy. I've given everyone instructions that you aren't to be bothered for at least another two weeks."

"Phil...!"

"No. Two weeks. I mean that, Christina. I've already updated the section director and he agrees."

"But—"

"Christina, something big is happening. I have all the teams available for call out attending today. The unit is going to be needed and we're under the pump here and I can't spend time thinking about whether you're overdoing it."

"But you'll need me." Christina gripped the receiver wanting to do something that took her away from her introspection.

"No. If anything, having you around as an invalid will make things harder. Take the time. Get better, then we'll re-evaluate the situation. Besides, I'm thinking it's time for some of the junior officers to find out just what all the perks they complain about really are."

Damn! Two weeks here, locked up in the house with the others, facing them and the whole damn bunch of regrets.

"Look, I gotta go. I'll ring you tomorrow and tell you if we've learned any more. See how you're getting on. Okay?"

"Yeah. Thanks Phil." She hung up and waited for her mind to rebel at her enforced break.

Since they were all going to have to make the best of it, for now they needed to sort out the sleeping arrangements. It might pass at least half a day. Then there were other things, clothing and necessities to be bought. That would fill several more hours.

There was a tiny furniture store not far from here; she'd seen it advertising a sale before she'd left. Maybe they stocked a single rollaway. Vasya would need a proper bed and she would take the mobile one. It couldn't have been comfortable for him on the cushions.

With that in mind she hurried, as quickly as possible when hobbling with a walking stick, toward the bedroom, and dug out her purse.

"Ki... Umm Christina?" *Serina! Thank heavens it wasn't Vasya.*

Christina turned to face her sister. "Yes, Serina?"

Her sister blushed beet red and she watched her fighting for composure. "You need your room back and we feel bad that you can't sleep in your bed. So, is there some way we could make arrangements...?"

"I don't mind..." She truly didn't. Did they think that she'd ever filled that big bed by herself? It had been bought purely with herself and Vasya in mind. A silly foolish pipedream that she'd hopefully put to rest!

"But Gregori and I do. And after last night..." She stopped and Christina felt a twin heat burn her face.

Christina took a step toward her sister, needing to rein-force nothing would have happened. It was a mistake of the moment type of thing. "It wasn't what you thought. Serina..."

Her sister lifted a hand. "No. You're still married, even if you have been apart for so many years. It's not my business." She smiled. "But you need your privacy to talk. Gregori and I would feel more comfortable in this room, if it can be managed."

Without meaning to, Christina rolled her eyes, feeling as if their thoughts were a conspiracy. She sighed, before nodding. "Okay then. We can sort it out later, but right now, you might like to come with me and do some shopping."

"But we don't need..."

She stopped Serina. "We need to order a bed and have it delivered and the three of you are going to need new clothes."

Serina looked down and grimaced. "Are they...?"

"No, they aren't that bad. But you're going to need some other things because you'll have doctor's visits, lawyer's visits and have to come into the department offices as well."

Serina's eyes almost bulged and a small smile bloomed. "Well, if that's the case..."

So easy. Christina had to suppress a grin. Her sister was still a girl, with all the normal hankerings and weaknesses. Help her on the first shopping experience and from there it would be easier. It was heartening to see the smile on her sister's face. She glowed and Christina basked in it for a moment.

"Come on, I need to get my keys and someone to drive me. Unless... Can you drive?" She glanced at her sister.

Serina shook her head. "No. Gregori wanted me to learn, but I always expected to stay home, so..."

"You'll need to learn that too. Okay, since it looks like neither of the men are available..."

"I'll take you." Vasya's voice nearly made her jump, but she kept a calm expression on her face and turned.

"Excellent. We should get moving then." She moved with purpose grabbing her keys and phone before ushering the three, since Gregori now made an appearance as well, out the front door. "Come on. The sooner we get there, the sooner we can be organized."

Once more Vasya took control of the vehicle, while Christina gave directions to the small furniture store nearby.

Large *Sale* and *Closing Down* flags hung in the window and Christina sighed. "I don't know what they have left. I hope they have a trundle bed."

Vasya looked at her. "Trundle?"

"A bed that folds up and slides under a full-size bed. That way, they're easily stored." He frowned at her words but she ignored him. As they entered the shop her stomach dropped. There was so little left and she worried that she wouldn't get what she needed.

Christina headed directly to the beds and was shocked to find only three left. All large, probably queen sized at that. Not a single to be seen.

The salesman sailed over to her, with a smile plastered on his face. His immaculate hair and matching ensemble were better suited to an office, she thought. He held out a hand, but she dodged it. "How can I help you?" He looked at Vasya and Christina cleared her throat.

"A bed. We're looking for a bed." Her eyes scanned the offerings, wincing at the posted prices.

"Then you're in luck. We have a beautiful maple sleigh bed left. Perfect for a couple who like their comfort." He steered them over to an ornately carved bed. Vasya frowned, running his hands along the surface. He would have made a sturdier and more beautiful bed, she knew. But their need was urgent.

"It's not real maple. The joints are also weak." Vasya inspected it carefully and a roll of warming emotion filled her. His eyes narrowed as he inspected the wood.

The man shook his head. "No. No. It's a lovely bed." He frowned slightly, as if trying to remember his spiel and then smiled. "Look, we're clearing stock you can have it for half the ticketed price."

"But I really wanted a trundle."

"A trundle? Nasty and uncomfortable things. No. You, dear lady need a quality bed." He patted the mattress with his hands. "It's a pillow-top mattress, and I'll even throw that in to sweeten the deal." He grinned. "Besides which, we don't have any trundles left and we really need to clear the stock."

Another full-size bed would make her yearn for something she couldn't have. Another reminder. But she couldn't magic something out of what wasn't there and the bed was nice looking, she guessed. There wasn't much choice if she wanted it today.

She tried to pull away but he pushed her toward the bed. Tripping she ended up sitting on it with a gasp.

"You try it. Hop on."

Vasya grinned and lay down. "It's a very comfortable mattress." Then he patted the side next to him and winked. Her breath caught, as her body reacted to his offer, falling back before rolling closer. The next thing she knew, she lay next to Vasya and his eyes searched hers.

"This is better than the one we shared." His whispered words filled her with heat, as she remembered their single night of wedded passion. Her mouth dried and she couldn't say a word, only stare at him, mute.

After that, she couldn't get out of the shop fast enough. The quick transaction completed, she arranged a same day delivery and refused to look back, more than aware of the salesman's conclusions about them. Her face burned.

"That was embarrassing."

He smiled, the corner of his mouth crinkling. "Why?"

"Because he thought..."

"He thought we were married, Christina. Which we are." His careful tone stopped any more comments for now.

They left the store, meeting with Gregori and Serina

outside. As they climbed into the car, Christina wasn't sure that something hadn't changed.

In him...

In her...

In them!

CHAPTER 12

A little flare of heat filled Vasya, warming him all the way through his body. He knew she wanted him and fought against it. The knowledge had come when he'd seen the flush of pink over her cheekbones in response to his comment.

The way she'd scurried away from his side as soon as she could, gave him the confidence to continue pushing the barrier between them. The little gasp she gave as he helped her up from the bed had been breathless and for an instant, he'd nearly leaned in to taste her.

"It's not enough, damn it!" The mutter was louder than he planned, but he couldn't hide his fascination for his wife.

She glanced in his direction. "Did you say something?"

"No." He turned away quickly, but knew she'd heard him, even if she hadn't caught the words.

It wasn't enough. Once he'd tasted her sweet lips again, and felt the lush curves tight against him, the desire flared hotter than ever before.

His blood thickened in his veins and other parts of his body firmed in ways he'd almost forgotten.

Desires long dormant awakened in a rush, and he wanted to vent his frustration and scream his anger to the world. Or to push his wife down on the bed and kiss her until she was moaning and quivering with the same need that haunted him.

He curled his hands into a fist, knuckles burning as he fought to contain it.

The worst part was, he had no compass. He couldn't... He wouldn't confide in Gregori.

The fact that I can't get my wife to accept my advances isn't something I want to broadcast. Even though he already knows. It unmanned him, realizing his younger brother and bride understood the driving hunger that gnawed at him.

He pulled into the small shopping center that Christina had directed him to and she hustled them out of the car and into a large store in the center of the complex. "We should be able to find everything you need." Christina indicated to the rows. He gaped, amazed by the sight of so many clothes, books and electrical goods. While he drank in the sight, she grabbed a trolley.

"I've never..." It was like a wonderland of commerce. Something he'd heard of, but never before seen.

Christina laughed. "We've only just begun." For a moment he basked in the warmth her pleasure gave him, before her smile died away.

"We should..." She waved a hand and he nodded as Christina pushed them to the clothing section.

Christina picked up items and dropped them into the cart, and he watched as Serina's eyes grew wide. "We need to get you a wardrobe together." Serina started to protest about the costs but Christina shook her head. "I've been preparing for this for a long time. I have a decent nest egg and the government will pitch in too. So don't worry about the cost."

Serina looked uncomfortable and Gregori frowned unhappily as well. It was clear neither of them liked the idea that Christina was going to pay for everything.

It pricked his pride too, he admitted, watching her steer them through the throngs of happy shoppers and into the men's clothing section.

He was a man. It should be him caring for her, not the other way around. At that moment, he determined that as soon as he was able, he would pay back everything she had outlaid. Even if she had no interest in working once their situation stabilized, then he would move heaven and earth for her to do as she pleased.

Slowly she steered them around the store, filling the trolley with collections of items. Shoes, toiletries and even underwear found its way into the metal basket until finally she was satisfied.

"Just one more thing. Vasya, we need to get sheets for your new bed. Is there any color in particular that you prefer?"

He stopped himself from saying brown, the color of her gentle eyes. Instead he shook his head and she shrugged at his silence. She ended up choosing a heavy cream-colored set, together with pillows and even a comforter and let them drop in with the other goods she'd deemed necessary.

They headed through the checkout, and he growled as the total appeared on the computer screen in front of him.

Once everything was paid for, he stilled her hand as she reached for the bags. "Let us do this."

For a moment he was sure she would argue. Her lips flattened and her hand curled tightly around the handle of the heavily laden trolley. Then she stepped back, clutching the cane in one hand, and Serina and Gregori settled the last bags on top.

"I'll repay you."

She glanced at him with a grin. "You don't need to. It's fine. Honestly, my finances are strong." She pulled away, signaling the end of the conversation. But he'd barely begun. They would discuss this. *Later...*

Instead of leaving the complex though, she headed toward the back, further away from their vehicle. At the food store, she took hold of a new trolly and relentlessly continued on, scooping up fresh fruits and vegetables, meats and milks, the whole time keeping up a commentary about what she'd do with them.

After another hour, it was clear Christina had overdone the activities of the day. She moved slower, her gait less graceful than before the furniture store, and she leaned more heavily on the cane. "Wound hurting?"

She looked at him, the small lines around her lips white. "A little. Nothing I can't handle though."

He reached out to her, steadying her as the cane caught on an uneven patch of asphalt. "You should rest."

"I'm fine." The dismissal of assistance frustrated him and his mouth settled into a hard line as she made her way slowly to the vehicle.

At the car, she went to help unload the goods but Vasya moved her to one side before he and Gregori accounted for everything. Serina grabbed the trolley before Christina could do so much as grope for it and he watched her gaze narrow.

She'd been stubborn eleven years ago, now she refused to give up any control willingly, he mused. That extended to driving the car, even though they all knew she shouldn't.

"I'll return it." Serina moved quickly and Christina's gaze followed her sister.

With a small huff, she made to the front and carefully

lowered herself to the seat as he watched. The hiss that escaped tore at him, and Vasya determined that once home she would settle into a seat and rest.

Gregori caught his gaze and he shook his head, looking away, before he made a comment that wouldn't help the situation.

The drive home was silent and Vasya was grateful.

Perhaps if she was introspective, it meant she was thinking over the ways he'd showed her that he wanted her still? Quick on the heels of that thought came another— she'd probably already decided on her actions.

If she set them in motion, then time was of the essence. If that was the case he needed to find a way to stop her before she could move out of the house.

The driveway appeared in front of the windscreen as his temper flared. He gritted his teeth hating the necessity of relying on her for every scrap of information.

The clues she would have given off in the past, when he used to know her, no longer existed. This new Christina seemed to live more inside herself. She was so... he hunted for the right term. She was so *contained*. The word Phil had used previously frustrated him further, but no other term seemed to fit quite so well.

The vehicle rolled to a stop and he was moving as soon as the handbrake engaged. Serina and Gregori had also climbed out and headed for the back of the car. "Open the boot Christina. We'll get everything inside." With a clunk the rear door opened upwards.

Meanwhile Vasya headed to the side where Christina sat. He noted the beads of sweat on her upper lip and the way she breathed raggedly.

"Christina?" She closed her eyes, the pallor of her skin

frightened him. He reached out to her and she shook. "Dammit, why didn't you say something?"

"I just…" One deep breath, then another passed. "I just need a minute." As she moved, Christina gave an audible whimper and he knew he wouldn't be satisfied until he had her inside, resting. With great care he slowly retracted the seat, reaching to unfasten her seatbelt.

"Please Vasya, I just ahh…" The stark sound of pain married with the tight closing of her eyes as she held herself still punched the wind from his solar plexus.

He slid his arms beneath her before carefully lifting her against his chest. "Give me the keys *dushka*." She reached for the keys, still in the ignition, while he held her close. Any other time he would have enjoyed the way she rested her head against his shoulder, and the way she curled in to him. But not today and definitely not now.

She groaned.

Vasya looked down, horrified to see the red seeping through her shirt. "You've opened the wound, Christina. Why didn't you say?" He stopped his words as anger clawed his gut.

Vasya hurried for the door, fumbling to unlock the house and then headed to the bedroom, carefully laying her down. She groaned and he damned himself a million kinds of fool.

*T*oo caught up in the pain that pulsed at her side, she missed the expression on his face, only realizing his anger had grown when she heard his outburst.

"If you weren't so damned stubborn this wouldn't have happened. Why didn't you tell me you'd hurt yourself?"

Right now, she ached too much to deal with him. If he wanted to rage or argue, she'd just live through it until he was done. Right now, she just wanted the pain to go away.

In and out.

Careful breathing.

Soft movements caught her attention, pulling her from the miasma of pain she was buried in as he carefully undid her buttons. "Hey! What do you..." She started but he carefully pushed her back to the bed.

"Shh, Christina. I just need to see where you've hurt yourself and fix it. You're bleeding but not heavily." He spoke so tenderly that tears burned in her eyes. She furiously blinked them away.

"Darn. I didn't realize. Look, I can..."

He stopped her words with a small shake of his head. "No. I need to do this for you. Please? Let me."

Christina winced at the pleading tone. After so many years of dealing with everything herself, it was disconcerting to have someone help her. Especially since it was Vasya.

She lay still and looked at the ceiling. "Okay. Just..." Christina inhaled deeply." Just let me deal with the top." She made to move but he stopped her again. "No. I'll do that."

His fingers shook a little and the red crest of heavy emotion captured her attention. Vasya was careful, almost lover like and tears welled as her breath hitched.

Could it be her imagination or was there more? Each pop of a button was loud to her hypersensitive hearing. Each move fanned the desire that consumed her thoughts.

When he reached her bra their gazes collided. The hungry question in his eyes burning her. "I, uh..." Her voice sounded choked and she cleared her throat, breaking the fragile connection.

He gaze drew back down and he frowned as he reached to the blood stained cotton he'd uncovered.

His hand brushed over her skin and the soft touch hurt. Christina hissed in reaction.

"Stay there. I'll find something to clean this blood away. Where will I find bandages?" He spoke gruffly and she breathed deeply trying to gather her scattered wits but it was difficult when the scent of him still dragged at her mind.

"You'll find... Look in the bathroom cabinet."

He left. The door thudded shut as he walked out the room. The prickle of tears burned brighter but she controlled them once more. "I am not going to feel sorry for myself. I will control my emotions." Fortified by her stern words she objectively considered the coming days. They would be difficult, but once the unit was free she could move out and on. "It's time to come to terms with the truth. To let go of my delusions." The words filled the room and left her gut churning.

She was banned from work for two weeks and, according to Phil, something big was going down. Her husband was a stranger and her sister married with a child on the way. So many changes!

"Oww..." She struggled up to a sitting position, her shirt falling to her lap just as the door opened and shut with a shudder. His gaze captured hers.

Then, ever so slowly it ranged over her body, and she felt herself heating up. Her insides liquefying as desire rose.

He moved. Advancing toward her and as his amazing eyes narrowed to pinpricks, she gulped.

It felt like forever, before he sank down onto the bed beside her.

Heaven help her, she stopped breathing altogether.

He reached out to her, his fingers tracing over her flesh as he pushed her back against the pillows, his eyes glancing over the mounds of her breasts.

Her nipples puckered beneath the bra and she felt them stretch and distend, hungry for his touch.

Where he touched her skin, it burned—the connection between them sweeping away the empty ache deep inside her belly.

The emptiness of her loins called out... pulsing, as if in preparation for him.

"I need to clean..." He cleared his throat, and the tips of his ears turned red. "I should cleanse the wound site." With his simple words, the spell broke and horror crashed down on her. He wasn't planning on seducing her, simply attending her wound.

His heart thudded in his chest, crashing wildly as he tried to shift away from the arousal that curled within him. The minute he'd said he was going to clean the wound site she'd shifted, lifting her luscious breasts higher. The peaked nipples captured his attention, along with the expanse of white flesh. Flesh that right now was dotted with blood. Reminding him that she was injured and needing care and attention.

He glanced at her again and his mind was captured by the silky texture of her skin, the purity of it. The slight coppery tang in the air called him back to reality.

He placed the bowl by the bed and crouched. "This is going to hurt a little."

Christina waved her hand to tell him she was ready, but

didn't speak. He dipped the cloth in the water then gently began bathing the area.

He concentrated hard on being cautious while he wiped away the drying and crusting blood. Still, he knew she must be in pain. But she didn't move or speak, she didn't even whimper.

It wouldn't be any better if she'd been screaming or pulling away, but her none-reaction left him frowning in concern. "Christina?"

"Keep going, please."

Vasya sighed then gave his full concentration to the task so he wouldn't hurt her any further. He slathered on a thick white antibiotic salve, before he reached for the dressing.

She lurched upwards. "I can do that." Her voice sounded husky and she pulled on the packet in his hands.

"No. I will do this."

A silent battle of wills followed until Christina slumped back down. He peeled away the wrapper before applying it with care.

Satisfied that he'd done all he could, he rocked back on his heels, catching sight of marks on her shoulders and back, little more than well healed white scars, but he leaned in.

"Christina..."

His words must have sparked something deep within her, for she rose, quickly.

For the first time he spied the white lines on her back, old crisscross marks and his stomach bottomed out. She moved to the side of the bed, and tugged on a robe hanging on a hook at the door. Christina shrugged it on, holding it close against her body before she spun back to him.

"Thank you for your help, but I need you to give me a few minutes alone." Her cold response caught him unaware and he stood there, hands full of bowl, cloths and littered packets.

"I..."

She grabbed him by the arm, the robe gaping slightly.

"Christina?"

She shook her head and one careful thrust had him through the door she'd wrenched open, then slammed.

CHAPTER 13

$\mathcal{C}$hristina stood still, looking at the door. Her chest heaving. "What am I going to do?" Misery didn't even come close to describing how she felt. Realizing she had just thrown her husband out of the bedroom he'd been using.

She wanted to yell, to scream. To melt on the floor in a miserable puddle, but she knew she couldn't. Instead she opened the wardrobe with a vicious yank and groped for the suitcase, searching desperately for a way to stave off the negative emotions swirling inside her mind.

Piece by piece, she hauled out her collection of clothing, folding each item and placing it into the bag. It filled quickly and she reached for the second bag. She hauled on the drawers, dumping underwear and casual clothes in with whatever shoes and accessories she owned. "I can't stay here."

She stopped for a moment, the darkness outside, the sunset she'd missed impinging. She wouldn't be going anywhere tonight, but she could prepare. Christina turned back to the bag, ready to close it when the door rattled and she chanced a look in its direction before returning to emptying her wardrobe.

"Christina... I can hear you in there. Let me in!" Vasya's demands and the ache of her wound slowed her but she knew what she needed to do. "Dammit Christina! I need to talk to you."

A cool breeze swept through the room and the glow of the bulb above the bed dimmed. She gulped knowing exactly what this meant. She shivered and quaked. This... This would be why she'd reacted so violently and negatively. He was here. *Zuor.*

"Turn around Christina. I've come for my payment." The sulfurous growl chilled her.

Her stomach curdled in the middle of the upheaval and memories of the last feeds had her nauseated beyond belief.

From the other side of the door she heard a thud, the wood shuddering beneath the onslaught. Another thud erupted and she tried valiantly to ignore it, to give into the seed of hope that grew and seeped into her chest, even as she began rolling up her sleeve. Aware that for her there would be no reprieve. There never was.

The heated touch of a claw at her shoulder had her turning even as a final thud sounded. The door splintered and Vasya pulled the remains of the wood out of his way.

His shocked gaze landed on the demon of despair and for an instant Christina was filled with the fear that Zuor would attack Vasya. Instead he bared his teeth, swinging towards her. "What is the meaning of this?" He indicated to Vasya with a roar before he disintegrated, trails of black vapor wrapping around her. The remains of the door hung drunkenly on the single hinge.

She stared at the ruined wood, her thoughts splintered while the rapid beating of her heart left her gasping. "I..." She turned her head to stare at Vasya stupidly, while her hand clutched her once more aching side.

"What was that?" Vasya extended his arm at the receding cloud, while anger and something even deeper inhabited his eyes, leaving them sparking like arcing fires.

It was so primal and wild that she couldn't even begin to guess its source. All she knew was that it chilled her to the bone. His eyes glittered with a silvery tone and his skin darkened while her vision wobbled and greyed at the edges. Then, for only the second time in her life, she fainted.

*W*hen she came to, she was lying on the bed, her head throbbing as nausea assailed her.

Watching her with an intent look on his face was Vasya. He must have noticed her eyes open because the tense look on his face lightened slowly and he reached out a shaking hand. "You gave me a fright."

"Yeah, I guess it would. Don't worry. He doesn't usually turn up like that." She knew she misinterpreted his words, but it was easier to do that, than face his concern and anger.

"No Christina. I was worried for you. Who was that? Was it...?"

She gulped. Not really wanting to name him. She made to turn away but Vasya stilled her actions.

"Who was it?"

"That was Zuor. The demon. He came for his payment, or at least an installment." She spoke softly, but each word drove a spike of pain into her chest.

After seeing the coal black demon who owned her blood, Vasya would surely turn away from her. She felt so dirty—unclean. Unworthy of the man she'd loved for so long.

Instead of pulling away, Vasya reached out and cautiously moved a lock of hair away from her face. "He won't come back again. I won't allow it."

Christina wanted to sigh at the expression on his face and his hard eyes. She would have laughed, if she hadn't known his words were serious. "He will come back. He's entitled to. He owns me. And I owe him."

Vasya stood abruptly, pushing away the chair as he spun away, his hands burrowing deep into his midnight black hair, tearing in frustration and anger. "He doesn't own you. You belong with me. *You are my wife!*"

When he turned back with a jerk she sucked in a deep breath. "I have no intentions of letting you go. *Not now. Not ever.*"

With an angry move, he swept the suitcases from the bed. Clothing flew through the air and the bags clattered to the floor.

Christina stilled, stunned by the force of his outburst. This Vasya was vastly different from the one she'd known before.

Gone was the innocent boy she'd married. Now before her stood a man, one who made her shiver as she considered his sensually-full lips and his arrogance. For the first time since the house she'd grown up in, Christina let herself scan his body. His arms had filled into a musculature way that she knew from experience many women would want. His face, so beautiful before, was a man's face, with harsh planes and the shadow of growth edging his jaw.

Over the eleven years of her absence it had become chiseled, the hard edges sharper than before in the throes of his angry outburst. But the thing that amazed her most, was even after learning her deepest and dirtiest secret, he still wanted her. He enfolded her in his arms, but Christina turned away, tugging out of his embrace.

"You say that now. But when he comes back and feeds... When he tears my skin and leaves bruises on my body you'll think differently. When he demands me at a time that suits him... You won't want me then." Turbulent emotions roiled in her chest.

His lips thinned. "You are no longer his to command. You are mine. My. Wife!" With that pronouncement he stepped forward and took her hand, pulled her to him.

His lips crashed down upon hers, urgent and hungry. His tongue demanding entrance to her mouth and with a moan she gave in. Needing this as much as he did.

Even in the midst of passion, he was gentle and careful, avoiding her injury. His hands roamed her body, settling on her breasts, covered only by the plain white cotton, and she yearned for him to touch more of her skin.

A cough at the door pulled them apart and she knew her face burned with embarrassment.

She spun away, her heel caught on carpet while vertigo hit and Christina nearly fell, except Vasya folded his meaty arms around her again. She felt his thudding chest against hers.

"What do you want?" He demanded, his voice gravelly.

"I saw the door. I didn't mean..." Gregori was silent for a moment. "I will go find a door."

He must have retreated as she felt Vasya loosening his grip. "I didn't..."

Christina pulled away. "It's okay. Umm I should finish..."

"No." He cut off her comment. "You are not leaving. Not now. Not ever."

"Look Vasya, this has been very emotionally..." She tried to think of a word to describe their situation, but couldn't. Instead she let the thought peter away.

"No. I was wrong when I said there was no us before." She heard the strain in his voice. And, heaven knew, she wanted desperately to believe him. The facts hadn't changed, though, had they?

She pulled away from his embrace. "Nothing has changed Vasya. I'm still me and you're still you. This..." She fought for the words, her mind jumbled. "This thing is still there. No matter that we're both still physically attracted to one another, it doesn't fix the distrust you have of me."

Vasya pinned her with his gaze. "It makes more difference than you know." He stepped forward. "And you aren't the only one with secrets."

❋

*V*asya sighed, realizing he'd have to explain everything to her. He indicated the bed but she shook her head in refusal. His heart ached. She looked so sad and alone as she stood there, pale and shaking. His gut burned, knowing he probably should have told her his secret years ago. Back then, it had all seemed so farfetched. He'd not believed, not really.

"Please? Sit down. I need to tell you something." His tone must have alerted her to the seriousness. Her eyes opened wide and she acquiesced without another word, he followed her, perching uncomfortably beside her, clasping his hands together.

He cleared his throat, knowing this would come as a shock. "Gregori and I are more than humans too."

She pulled away, an angry look on her face and he sighed.

"More than human?" He stilled her words with a soft finger against her mouth.

"The night before we married, my parents recounted the story of the Sky Flyers... Many here would call them angels. They are the ones who protect the weaker. Particularly the feeders."

Her face remained still and pale and he leaned forward, resting his elbows on his knees. It was so important that she accept what he was about to tell her.

"If only I had known... It explains so much, now that I know the truth about you. We're the ones who protect against the worst ravages of the demons like Zuor. That's probably why he reacted as he did, disappearing the way he did. We're natural enemies." He laughed but it was cold.

He could almost see the cogs in her brain turning over. "Hang on... Does that mean...?" An incredulous look crept over her face. "But if you..."

He nodded. "We both carry those genes. But we've never completed the ceremony. After your family disappeared, my parents refused to consider it. Then they too passed and the knowledge was lost, along with who could help us."

She bit her lip and looked away, but not before he saw the crest of red slash her cheeks. "But... That means your genetics affected your drive to protect feeders, like me, from the demons like Zuor. Maybe that's the source of your feelings for me?"

He shook his head, understanding she was looking for an excuse—some way to give them both an out. He moved from the bed, squatted in front of her and with thumb and forefinger he turned her face so she'd see the truth in what he said next.

"No. That's not at all true. According to what I was told, we are drawn to the one we protect and love. When we fall in love, it's forever. Like our souls are bonded together. You and I..." He dropped his gaze to her mouth. Wanting desperately to kiss her, to show her just how much he loved her. "We are two sides of the whole. I can never be whole without you, Christina. Never. It's why I never sought another once I was sure you were gone. The hollowness always remained." Then he fastened his mouth over hers, unable to stop the natural reaction to her closeness.

*H*er heart rate soared and her head spun, but, by God, she wasn't going to pull away. For far too many restless nights and long days, she'd dreamed of this. She'd dreamed of being in his arms and feeling the pull of arousal at her body and the spark of awareness that filled her mind when he touched her. She melted within his embrace.

He pulled away with a savage grunt. "Not now. We need a door and privacy."

Her brain whirled.

"You need to put your clothes away."

She grimaced, before she remembered an important fact. "But this is the room you'll be sleeping in."

A grin crested his lips. "The new bed is due any time now. I'll get Gregori to help me move it into the other room, then Serina and Gregori can move in there."

When he left the room, she stood there, more confused than ever by the strands and tendrils of magic that had brought them together. With efficient movements, Christina followed his instructions.

After shrugging on a clean shirt, she hurried into the other room in time to see Vasya and Gregori tipping pillows and coverings to the floor followed by a quiet Serina who collected the discarded linens. She watched in silence as they heaved the bed through the doorway and out of sight.

Amid grunts and complaints of poor quality, they returned carrying the repaired door, fresh hinges and screws and a set of screwdrivers.

"How did you...?" She shook her head deciding she really didn't want to know. Christina rolled her eyes, watching the men work. The heat from outside filled the tiny house. Gregori had shed his shirt, but it wasn't his form that interested her.

Serina sidled up to her. "He's good looking isn't he?" Christina spared a startled look at her sister's face and realised she was talking about Gregori, not Vasya.

A bark of laughter escaped. "Yeah, I guess." Her sister snickered at her circumspect tones but her eyes remained on Vasya, watching the play of muscles.

The men stopped their work and looked at her and she ducked her head, thoroughly embarrassed to be caught ogling them.

"Well?" Serina demanded.

Against her will, Christina had to nod and respond. "Gregori has definitely grown into his skin."

That drew a snorted, "You're Vasya isn't too bad either." Then her sister laid a gentle hand on her arm. "He's a good man. He grieved when you left. But I have never seen him as pleased as he is now. He loved you and took your disappearance hard."

The lump of guilt that had nearly disappeared during

the day settled back in the bottom of Christina's gut like a large solid rock.

She hadn't had a choice. Though, that wasn't something she could say to Serina, was it?

Instead she watched the men finish their work.

CHAPTER 14

*C*hristina slipped her hand over the fresh linens, wondering what the night would bring. Her stomach quivered as she tossed over the options.

Vasya hadn't asked the question aloud, but her nerves pulled tight at the thought of where he'd sleep.

Would he reclaim the empty spot by her side? Or should she just wait until he was asleep and settle on the lounge? A soft knock came at the door and she turned in time to watch the man in question step inside, his eyes shadowed.

"I wasn't..." He stopped and looked at her uncertainly. *Could it be that he too, was unsure of their next step?* Even though they'd been lovers for one night eleven years ago, it felt like everything was for the first time.

Neither knew the other's thoughts. Both were unsure of each other's feelings and priorities. She knew the dangers of assumption, so she attempted to control her growing nerves.

The heat coiled deep inside her belly. The urge to ask him to claim her was strong and yet she fought it.

"Vasya..." Her body betrayed her, pushing her to step in

his direction. The wanting rising as she yearned to take what she hoped he was offering.

The silence between them drew out. Her nerves wound tight. Her breathing grew shallow and her heart beat rapidly. The membranes in her mouth dried and she licked her now parched lips.

When Vasya stepped forward, there was a question in his eyes that caught her like a ragdoll and shook her with its intensity. This time she refused to avoid the query. In that instant, she understood there was no choice to make. It was their one last chance—and he was surrendering the decision to her.

Slowly Christina extended her fingers and felt his hand surround hers, the emotions that rose clogging her throat.

Heat flared between them, scalding her. "Christina, I've wanted you for so long. Dreamed of you…" The he folded his arms around her, pulling her flush against his firm chest. It seemed like forever before his mouth settled on hers, and then all rational thought fled.

His lips firmed against hers, while his tongue plunged within. She moaned. Encircling his waist with her arms she gloried in the answering rhythm of his pulse against hers.

The thrust of his erection dug into the softness of her belly through the layers of clothing. And she felt the spread of emotions at the same time: Excitement, heady pleasure and hope. She burned and ached, while emptiness grew in the pit of her stomach.

She ached for the thrust of his body deep within hers. And only he could fill it.

He lifted his head. "There is no going back, if we…" His eyes glittered and his watchful gaze told her he needed her to confirm that she understood and agreed.

"I don't want to. Going back means emptiness and being

alone." She gazed deeply into his eyes, confirming the words she was about to share. "I just want you."

With infinite care, she burrowed her hands under the back of his shirt seeking the reassurance of his hot flesh as his lips descended again.

She opened her mouth and welcomed him. Sipping at his lips, before raking his back lightly with her fingernails. He arched at her ministrations, gasping and clutching at her. Then with a swift jerk he pulled her shirt over her head, flinging it aside.

He caught her mouth up—the feeding rapacious while his hands found and released the clasp of her bra. Her breasts sprang free and he caught her gasp of shock. Swallowed it as they shared another deep and sensual kiss.

Firm fingers found the twin globes of her breasts and she was sure her knees would melt at the lightning sensations that rattled her. A moan tore from her throat.

More. She needed to feel more of his flesh.

Christina wanted him to burn with sensation and heat. She tugged at the hem of his shirt. Vasya stilled his movements. Lifted his head and in his eyes she read the twin yearning. "Take it off."

His lips curved at her soft command, the small dimple in his cheek appeared and she stepped back, her nipples budding tightly in the cool night air. His gaze raked over her, its heat scorching. Nervousness nearly had her covering herself, but the hunger in his eyes told her he more than appreciated the view.

He tore at the shirt and buttons flew through the air, landing with a soft ping on the floor. She didn't care that clothes were ruined as inch after inch of broad chest was bared to view. She curled her fingertips against the burning need to caress his tight muscles.

Her palms ached to rub over the skin of his chest. When she gave in to the temptation she sighed in pleasure, while he tensed beneath her careful ministrations. Then she stepped back into his embrace, ready to explore the next layer of sensual exploration with him.

Christina placed her shaking hands against his impressive pectoral muscles savoring the sensations. She hissed in reaction.

"You like?" His words rumbled and she laughed, unable to contain the sheer joy filling her.

"I more than like." She dotted small kisses on his chest, rising on tiptoe to find the curve of his shoulder.

Vasya allowed her sensual exploration though she felt the shudder as passion rose within him. She traced the curve of musculature with soft fingers and he groaned, lost in her web of passion.

With fluttering movements, she inched her fingers toward his leather belt and rested there, unsure of how to proceed. Her experience limited to one man and one day and night.

His large hand covered hers.

Sparks flew where their flesh touched.

"This time let me." He stepped away.

Christina reached for the skirt she wore, slipping it down over her hips while he dispensed with the rest of his clothes. As she slid hers down her gaze settled on him, her body heating at the sight of his nude form.

He wore no underwear and she swallowed as a lump lodged in her throat. *Commando.*

Her body was awash with sensation and her brain was overloaded by the erotic vision before her. All she could think was at least neither of them were wearing shoes. *Thank heavens for that.*

Her gaze ate him up, travelling over his body until she reached his eyes. He grinned and waited, while her heart pumped quick and fast.

The length of his erection jerked slightly, once more capturing her attention and she almost moaned at the sight. She wanted to touch him there, to feel the steely hardness she vaguely remembered.

The recess between her legs grew damp and she squeezed her thighs together hoping to control the sensations that burned her from the inside out. Instead the action increased her arousal, the quickening sensations heightening her level of arousal.

His smile fled. Her husband stepped toward her. His face flushed and his eyes smoky with long denied passion.

When their mouths fused it was cataclysmic.

Vasya was voracious—taking and seizing her, while his hands roamed urgently up and down her flesh. He squeezed and cupped, caressed and firmed with exquisite tenderness.

Christina dug her fingernails into the tightly packed muscles, as he became her anchor in the sensual storm he wrought.

"I have dreamed of you. So many nights, I've remembered sinking into your flesh. Of being one with you." Every word battered at her, increasing the tension that wound tighter than a spring inside her.

With a quick movement he scooped her up and laid her on the bed, following her down into the softness. She cupped the back of his head, tangling her fingers in his dark hair as he kissed her slowly and evocatively once more. The paced slowed, and he drew away, panting slightly.

"Vasya?" His fingers hooked under her panties and she lifted her hips, allowing him to slide them down her legs.

With clever hands, he caressed the flesh of her legs,

sliding upwards, stopping every now and again to knead the flesh he discovered. She whimpered as he drew closer to her burning, empty core. "I've missed you Christina. So much."

Her eyes burned. "I've missed you too—every day and every night. To have you here..." She had to stop, her chest burned.

"Now we are together again, I will never let you go. You are mine." Vasya dipped his head between her legs, his tongue lapping at her. She squirmed and cried out at his ministrations. "Vasya, please!"

She pulled at him and he relented. "Next time, I will have you like that, my Christina." His darkly sensual words drugged her further and his mouth fastened over hers; musky and flavored with her own essence.

Vasya pulled away and his wicked mouth roamed while his hands kneaded. She urged him on, gripping the soft flesh of his buttocks and opened her legs wide before winding them around him. Clasping him tight.

She gloried in the slight abrasion of the hairs on his thighs, greedily drinking in the sensations.

The hot tip of his erection settled against her, nudging at her center. Burning need drove hard. "Please." The word was a breathless entreaty for him to continue the slow inch forward.

"Vasya..." She chanted his name, before, with one hard thrust, he seated himself fully. Her body wanted to splinter. Her chest bellowed as she closed her eyes, wanting to slow the coil of pressure that wound tightly within her chest.

"Forgive me..." His murmur broke while the jerking pulse of his veins thrummed at his throat. He gripped hard the sting of flesh at her pelvis telling her wordlessly just how much this homecoming meant.

Long, fraught seconds passed before they moved. A slow

nudge at first as her flesh adjusted to the unfamiliar sensation of being filled.

Each movement scalded her and she gasped.

His careful actions heated her and drove her harder towards the looming climax. Their rhythm became jerky and uncontrolled as they moved faster.

Together their bodies grew slick and damp.

"Oh God!" He groaned against her lips and she opened, accepting the invasion of his tongue as the muscles deep within her body began to pulse. Christina exploded in a mind-blowing orgasm, which felt like it stretched into forever—her body bowed as it took control and reality splintered around her.

She recognized that Vasya was shaking as he gave one last shuddering thrust then joined her, emptying himself deep within her womb.

Tears leaked from her tightly closed eyes. *Oh God! How I've missed him and this.*

*C*hristina's pulse settled and Vasya disentangled before rolling to one side. Catching her close, he dragged her hard against him.

"I'm so sorry." His quiet whisper filled her with heat and heaven help her, her own eyes burned and scorching tears rolled down her face.

She was scared, but had to ask, "What for?"

"For not understanding. I should have known you would never have left me without cause. And not in the way you did." Her heart began a slow thudding roll as she settled into his embrace. The frustration that had gnawed, melted to be replaced with belonging.

What about when the dreams came? That banished the feeling of well-being. A cold heavy lump settled in her belly. Would he be able to stand by while she accepted the nightly ravages? After last night, she knew they would return and would likely be darker than previous.

Weariness pulled at her, and sleep dragged her into the world of the night.

The manacles were still there, locked around her wrists—she shivered. In this nightmarish realm was there ever going to be a time when she could break free?

With a tiny jerk Christina pulled on the chains, they clinked together, but for the first time, the bonds seemed looser. A wisp of light appeared before her and Christina shivered in reaction, tugging eagerly against her metal bindings.

She gasped. "I'm going to get out of here, even if it's the last thing I do." The words helped. She felt the power they gave her.

Christina tugged harder, feeling the tearing of flesh but uncaring of the pain, determined to escape.

She'd been here in this nightmare-based prison for eleven long years. She'd slept with the terrors of what she would experience in the night realms. With a grunt she tugged once more, a clunking crunch met her actions then with the restraints loose she fell to the floor. The cold gritty surface grazed her hands and knees. She bit her lip, instinctively stopping the cry of pain that rose. "I won't let him beat me now."

Christina stood and looked towards the glowing light. Light meant heat and her body was chilled in its nakedness. The dungeon was always cold.

Clothes would be a priority but she needed to get out of here before He *came back for her. That thought alone propelled her in the direction of the door.*

She grasped the metal latch and pulled, crying out when it refused to budge.

Then she heard the sound she dreaded, the heavy footfalls that meant Zuor was here.

She gulped back the bile rising in her throat. She wasn't a weakling. She wouldn't give in to the fear and loathing.

The door moved and she tensed, ready to rush it and escape... Strong hands grabbed her. The impression she got was slimy and cold. Nails like talons tore at her skin.

"So. You think you can escape? You are mine. You were mine before you were conceived... Mine."

He thrust her back against the cell wall and she screamed, her legs failed and she fell to the floor.

The light that had been guiding her grew in intensity, Zuor stiffened and whirled. "This is not your realm!" He bellowed, but the light grew...

"Christina, wake up! It's just a dream!" She shivered and shook as he pushed at her shoulder, still half caught in the grip of a nightmare, but he pulled her close.

His body warming her chilled skin.

"Wake up, Christina!"

Her wrists screamed with pain, as did her knees, and her head ached. Even with his shared warmth, her bones radiated a frigid chill. Her teeth rattled in her head under the force of the shudders racking her body and she burrowed closer, seeking the warmth of his chest.

"What...?" She squirmed in his embrace.

"You had a nightmare. At least, I think it's a nightmare."

She raised her hand, noting how they hurt. "Owww..." Christina couldn't contain the instinctive cry that broke free.

"What's wrong?" His rough voice filled the air.

"My wrists hurt." She reached carefully for the bedside lamp, gasping as the pain hit again. Once she turned the light on her heart stuttered in her chest. "Oh God!"

"What is it?"

She knew the instant he saw the marks, his eyes widened and he sucked in a deep breath. "We have a very big problem." He slumped back on the pillow, covering his eyes with one arm.

"What?" Her stomach dipped precariously. How much worse could it possibly get?

"Your nightmares have spilled into reality." He lifted his arm from his face and she saw fear in his eyes.

The instant he saw the jagged tears on the tender skin of her wrists, Vasya knew the truth. She was slowly being dragged into a nightmare world where she was vulnerable and unprotected. Where he couldn't protect her.

"Vasya?" He felt the fear in her voice and he yearned to make it better. But right now he was lost.

Would he have to battle the demon for her soul? He had no training... Panic rose suffocating him. He had to fight it back, looking for the balance he'd always treasured. The one that lay deep inside himself.

"I'm going to need help, Christina. Contacts. Then perhaps..." He left the sentence hanging. What could he say that would explain the situation adequately? *Hold onto hope and once I have the information, then, maybe I can help you?* He didn't have any idea how long it would take to get the information. Or even where to start.

His ascension had never taken place and now, he understood why. Since Christina had been smuggled away, there had been no need to learn how to control the power within him. Until he could fly, he couldn't tap into his abilities. His parents had made that fact clear on that long ago evening.

"Christina, I..." He stopped unsure how best to describe his thoughts and the situation.

He didn't even know who to talk to about how to get his future on track again. He pulled her tighter against him, realizing she had dipped back down to sleep. His stomach clenched.

Perhaps if he stayed awake he could keep the demon at bay.

The fingers of dawn crept slowly into the room as he dozed off.

❄

"I need to find someone who knows something about Sky Flyers and the myths surrounding them." Vasya's voice startled her. She looked up from the bowl of cereal in front of her.

"What? Oh..." She blinked, waking her mind from the fugue she was lost in. "Perhaps Phil might know who to talk to."

She watched as his face tightened. Christina dropped her spoon into the bowl filled with the soggy mass and eased away from the table with a moan, feeling the slight sting as her wound pulled.

"Are you okay?" His voice surprised her, the way it cut through her self-absorption and she wanted to grin at how real it made the situation seem. She smiled away his concern. She certainly didn't intend to let on that last night's love making had left her a bit sore.

"Yeah. I just need to go..." She moved away from the table, indicating with both her hands over her shoulders and thinking only to grab her mobile phone.

"Christina?" The concern she could hear dragged at her.

The sense of someone worrying about her, hit hard. In the past, she hadn't had to answer to anyone for anything. Except at work... Had he seen the flash of discomfort on her face?

"Yeah. I'm good, Vasya. I'm just not..." Christina breathed deeply. "I'm not used to having anyone watching over me." She shrugged away the concern. "I'll ring Phil." As she hurried off in the direction of her purse, she caught a glimpse of sadness on his face.

When Christina reached the hall, she grabbed at the small bag and dug within looking for her phone, but once she held it in her hands the reality of her situation coursed through her veins.

For a moment, Christina squeezed her eyes shut and focused on breathing. As her heart rate settled, she opened them again. Pressing the buttons with shaking fingers made it hard to dial, but she got there in the end.

"Phil here."

"Hey Phil. It's me. How's everything going at work?" She heard her voice, and nodded. Just the right balance of bright and bubbly.

"I'm so glad to hear from you Christina. We have a bigger situation than we thought. The Alvonian's are on the warpath. Seems someone got three dangerous criminals out of the country in the last few days. Two brothers and one of their wives."

Her stomach curdled at his words. "I... I may know who you are talking about."

He harrumphed down the line. "Thought you might. Anyway, the situation in Alvonia is ramping up. There's been a spate a Search and Seizes. At least eighty of our target refugees have disappeared in the last four days. The teams are working overtime trying to find safe houses for those most vulnerable and their families. We're just not moving them fast enough though. Something is happening at the upper end of the hierarchy to cause this sudden increase of activity."

"Do you need me in there?" Her mind whirred into action, considering her contacts.

"No. You're better where you are. Out of sight for now."

Christina rubbed her forehead. "I can call in some favors—"

"We might need your contacts later if this gets worse. But you rang me. How are you feeling?"

For a few minutes they made small talk, then she steered the conversation back to the reason for the phone call.

She closed her eyes. "I need your help."

The silence on the line was unnerving. *Are my actions inappropriate? Does he think I'm taking advantage of the situation?* She tried unsuccessfully to still the questions in her mind. "Don't worry Phil. I'll sort it."

He stopped her. "You've never asked for anything before. It just... I'm a little surprised. Tell me what you need."

"It's okay, really. I'll find—"

"Christina, just tell me what you need. I can spare a minute or three for you."

She gulped. "I need information. I need to learn about Sky Flyers and their myths."

On the phone she heard the intake of breath. "I'll need to ask around. How soon do you need the information?"

"As quickly as possible, Phil." She waited a minute then inhaled deeply. "Look, given everything else that's happening, maybe this is an inopportune moment."

"Leave it with me." Christina heard the scratching sounds as he wrote something down. "I'll get back to you as soon as I can."

"Yeah." She paused. "Phil?"

"What Christina? Is everything okay, otherwise?" The earnestness in his voice surprised her and she smiled, feeling the muscles at the side of her face stretch.

"Sure. Yes. I just wanted to tell you how much I appreciate you."

"What?" He sounded surprised again and she grimaced.

She'd always focused on getting her family back. That had been her mission for so long, to the detriment of any kind of interpersonal relationship. "I really appreciate that you have been there for me. I'm just... I'm glad you're my friend."

"You don't need to say that, Christina. I would do anything for you." With that he disconnected the line and Christina stood there cradling the small phone against her ear. *What did he mean by that?*

A sound surprised her and she jumped with fright. When she looked around it was Serina. "What's going on?" When her gaze dropped to Christina's wrists though, she blanched. "What happened to you?"

Christina shook her head, trying to head the discussion off at the beginning. "Not now Serina."

It was obvious her sister wanted to demand information leaning in towards her, but with a small scowl she shook her head. "Okay. Don't tell me now. But I want to know everything, and soon." Once more Christina marveled at the woman standing in front of her. Her sister was a woman of strength and determination. "Very soon. Preferably without leaving anything out."

The concern and anger in Serina's voice warmed Christina and she smiled, but it slipped away as she turned.

CHAPTER 15

"*D*amn!" Christina swore under her voice as the vegetable peeler slipped for what felt like the fiftieth time. Her wrists burned. Serina had offered to help, but Christina had ordered the other woman to rest.

If none of this had happened, would she and Vasya have children by now? She knew it was more than likely. To know that Serina has achieved something Christina had longed for...

Christina shook her head at the jealously laden, self-defeating thoughts. Gregori and Vasya were outside attending to something and she shrugged inwardly as the peeler slipped again tumbling backwards and grazing her tender flesh. "Oww..."

"I offered." From the other room she could hear Serina calling.

"Yeah, I know. I don't cook much these days..." Even she could hear how weak her excuses sounded.

A long-suffering sigh emanated from the other room followed by the sound of movement, then Serina stood beside her. Smiling. Holding out a hand but Christina shook her head again. Wisps of hair escaped her straggly ponytail.

"You're supposed to be resting." She said. But in all honesty she was pleased to have help.

Her sister clucked her tongue and carefully took both the peeler and the tuber she was working on from her hands. "Why don't you deal with the meat?"

Christina nodded, feeling useless as she retreated. She opened the door of the cooler and pulled out the meat. Thick slabs of steak would be best for the men and Serina. For herself, there was a smaller portion. It wasn't like she needed to eat a lot—after all, she was either much smaller or not feeding a growing baby.

Her gaze settled on the spice bottles, her one real luxury. *Spices... hmm.* The thought of coating the meat teased but she decided not to this time. Right now, it was better to keep with plainer foods and gradually introduce Serina, Gregori and Vasya to this fare over time.

With an inaudible sigh, she turned away from the rack of condiments and picked up the skillet then placed it on the small stove and lit the gas ring. The meat sizzled quickly once in the heated pan, the scent of cooking filled the air.

"We must really be putting a dent in your life. You haven't spoken to anyone except that Phil guy since we've been here. Where are your friends? "Serina's question caught her off guard.

"I don't..." She stopped and waited.

"What? You can't expect me to believe you... Christina, you've been here over eleven years! You were always so bright and social..." Her sisters' voice trailed away and she looked at her, horror spreading over her face. Christina wanted to turn away, but she wouldn't.

"I focused on finding a way to get you all here." She

mumbled, hearing for the first time the words that described her life.

❄

*V*asya looked on every shelf, in every box. She had tools, but none of them of decent quality and nothing that he could use. No stray bits of wood, chisels or carving knives. He'd left all his equipment behind in the rush to leave. For a second, a seed of frustration rose at the loss of his tools. Many of them handed down from father to son.

"We will need Christina to take us somewhere to purchase quality tools and suitable woods." In his mind, a mental list started to form, while Gregori just grunted in agreement.

It had always been that way. He planned aloud while Gregori silently agreed. Knowing the way his mind worked, Vasya was aware that he'd soon need some kind of occupation otherwise he'd be like a caged bear in a circus, prowling and snarling at anyone in his path.

He glanced outside and noted the lengthening shadows.

Night was creeping in and he'd not yet figured out a way to protect Christina. He thought back to the dangers of her dreams and the scrapes on her wrist. The white marks on her arms and back.

"Will you tell me what happened to Christina? I know you would not harm her so, but she is injured." Gregori's quiet words had him turning.

"The demon, Zuor? The one she feeds? He is stalking her in the Night Realms. He's taken her prisoner and she escaped, only to be captured again. Her injuries are a manifestation of those dreams—and a punishment."

The horror on his brother's face surely mirrored his own, he thought. After all, while they were both Sky Flyers, though neither had ascended, they both understood the importance of what Vasya was saying.

She was in danger every time she dreamed. Zuor, the demon that fed from Christina was slowly dragging her into his world and they had to stop it, otherwise she'd be lost to them. *Again.* This time likely forever.

With a curse he stepped away from his brother. "I have to stop it. I will not allow him to take her. Not now. She's mine and I will not relinquish her."

"I agree, but what can we do?" He heard the intensity in his brother's words and he spun away as the fire burned in his gut. He would find a way to protect Christina.

"I will guard her during her sleep. Be there during the night hours. We will find a way."

The clasp of a heavy hand on his shoulder reassured him. Reminded him that he had a fellow soldier in the fight for Christina's soul.

"Tonight..."

He nodded. "I will hold her while she sleeps. In the morning hopefully this Phil will have some answers." It wasn't enough. Not by a long way. But it was a start.

*P*ain rippled through her and she cried out. "Nooo..." Somehow the cold metal bonds tightened around her arms and legs as if they knew she had come to. Spikes within the cuffs bit deeply and a coppery tang filled the air.

Blood.

Nausea rose and she fought it off, all the while wondering where the blood was coming from. The warm trickle over her skin answered the story, stealing her breath.

Shuffling movements and scurries left her whimpering. She could only guess what was down at her feet but she refused to look.

Blood rats would eat the flesh off anything, including a corpse. She'd seen their handiwork before in this nightmare world.

"I will not look." Her voice broke on the last word as a chill swept over her naked body. The cold uneven masonry behind her caused jagged scratches on her back, but any movement of her feet, to shoo the creatures away, increased the sting from her bonds. It also made her bleed faster. She didn't want either outcome.

"Zuor! You bastard! Let me go!" The echo of her feeble shout was the only response and she slumped just a little. Alone. In the dark—with small bitey critters nipping at her toes.

Cold.

Nothing warmed her, except the stinging hot tears as they trembled on the edges of her lashes. He'd caught her trying to escape and this was his revenge. He'd never let her go. Forever would pass while she was hidden in the gloom.

Even while restraining her, his cruel hands had traced over her body, roughly touching, scraping and squeezing at her flesh. Bile rose in her throat, bitter and acidic. He'd touched her as if she was some kind of slave. As if he owned her.

True she owed him a debt. But she never thought he would take payment like this. The only consolation was he hadn't fed from her. Or done anything worse—so far, anyway. The memory of the last feeding left her shuddering. He'd been so rough as he thrust his teeth into her flesh.

"I have to get out of here." She heard the weakness—and the loss of faith—in her voice.

She had to face the truth. No one knew where she was or how to reach her. The thought left her with little more than fading hope.

Last time there had been a glimmer of light—a spark to light the gloom giving her a reason to try. This time there was none. No one would come and save her.

If she were going to escape it would have to be on her own.

She really wasn't sure if she had enough energy to make it happen again, though.

"Vasya... I just wanted to save you."

A chink, no more than a sliver of light pierced the gloom once again.

The sound of a door, being thrust open caught her attention. "I banished you last time!" Zuor's voice boomed in the darkness and she swallowed an instinctive cry. He surged forward and for an instant her heart stuttered in her chest.

But instead of the light dimming it grew, filling the darkness.

She noted how the blood rats hurried away as the light advanced, changed and took form. A man... or a warrior, lined by the white light. His face and body perfect and she saw the resemblance.

"Vasya?"

The bonds loosened a little and she pushed against them. Each time he came, he brought hope. Was it the hope that gave her the strength to break free?

"You are mine!" Zuor's voice boomed again and she turned, just a little.

"I am no one's. I am mine alone, Zuor. Release me!" She panted, the exertion of twisting and turning, together with the fright, cold and possibly blood loss draining her. But she wouldn't give in.

"Release her!" Vasya extended a hand, and she gasped as a sword appeared before him. It glowed and pulsed. She tugged

away from the shining blade as far as the ties would allow, giving this warrior version of Vasya room to move.

Zuor sprang quickly, dodging under the movement of the blade. "Ha! A little new to this, aren't we? You're too late though. She's mine. In every way that counts!"

Vasya grunted with what she was sure was fury as he grappled with Zuor, his sword clanging to the floor.

Her lungs started to burn and she was sure that all the oxygen in the room was being consumed by the warring men. Pressure bloomed in her chest and she fought for breath. Black dots appeared before her eyes and no matter how hard she tried to focus, they grew, obscuring her vision. Cries and thuds filled the air, but she was beyond caring as she slumped in a dead faint.

CHAPTER 16

*H*e started awake, heaving as he breathed. The dream had been hideous. Visions of a naked, and defeated, Christina in a dim cell, her wrists and arms bound by dark metallic cuffs. She'd shivered while tiny rivulets of liquid trailed down her body. Anger had coursed through him.

A sound intruded. Broken sobs and he looked over at Christina, realizing she'd curled up in the bed while he'd been lost in the horror of his dream.

"Christina." He launched himself toward her, anger at himself and the world beat at his senses. He'd been so sure, if he could just stay awake... But he hadn't and once again she'd paid the price.

He slipped his arms around her, feeling the chill of her body. "Hush Christina, I have you now." She didn't respond, just wept harder and his gut roiled.

How was he supposed to deal with this? How was he supposed to protect her when he couldn't even stay awake? He castigated himself for failing his task.

The crying jag gradually tapered away and she lay spent in his arms.

He turned to switch on the light by the bedside. "Don't." She whispered with her voice husky, and he stilled.

"Why?"

"Because I don't want you to see…" She shuddered. "The dreams have become real. And what you'll see…" She heaved in his arms. "Let me go sort myself out."

He knew he couldn't allow that to happen. She'd faced this alone for far too long and it was time for him to show her that time was over. "No. Lie here and I'll bring a cloth."

She stilled and he sighed, turning back towards her. "This is not your fault, *dushka*. You've done nothing wrong. We will defeat him. I won't let this continue."

She smiled, a wobbly little flash of movement. His heart nearly broke at realizing none of the smile shone in her eyes. *She doesn't believe anyone can save her.* The thought punched him in his chest, stealing his breath. The mask she'd worn when she'd first saved them was once more firmly in place.

Without conscious thought, he pulled her into his careful embrace, noting the bruises that marred her skin. Trails of blood marked her arms and the angry red spots where something within the cuffs had bitten into her flesh. He shuddered realizing that if she passed in her dreams… she'd be gone in this reality too. He hoped she hadn't made that connection herself.

"I will find a way to free you, Christina. Even if it takes the rest of my life."

Christina's head throbbed, as did her wrists and ankles. Thankfully the wound at her side was healing well and long sleeves and pants helped cover the worst ravages. "I'm not really sure how much longer I can hide it from Serina or Gregori."

"Did you say something, Christina?" Serina popped her head into the small room and Christina pasted on a smile and shook her head.

"No. I was just thinking out loud." She didn't think Serina actually believed her but apart from a dark frown she didn't say anything.

The small cell phone rang and she gripped it, feeling the tug and burn of protesting muscles.

"Christina Alward."

"How's it going? I have news." *Phil.* She sucked in a breath. Hopefully something, anything that could sever Zuor's hold over her.

"What?"

"Well, I've found someone to talk to you, but they are a little... uncomfortable meeting outside their own home. Can you come to us?"

Christina sighed heavily. "We would, but there's a small problem..."

"What?" There was distrust and something that sounded rather like anger, in Phil's voice.

"I can't drive at the moment." She sighed heavily. The less people who knew the truth right now, the better. Besides which, if she didn't have to tell him, well, then she wouldn't need to cope with the fallout later on. "There's a lot more to this Phil. Stuff I can't tell you—at least not over the phone. Even if you see it, you may not actually believe it." She laughed, her tone bitter and harsh.

"You'd be amazed what I know. Look... I'll see if I can talk Dravens into letting me take him to you. But you need to be prepared. He'll probably ask for some special things to be done first. Okay?" That piqued her curiosity, but years of experience told her Phil would tell her what she needed to know when the time was right.

"Sure. Whatever I can do. Just let me know, okay? Now what's the situation in Alvonia?"

His grunt told her it was bad. "Look, I can ask some questions, maybe hunt down some more to assist."

"It's not going to be that simple. Word on the ground is that the last few days, with so many disappearing, the natives are getting restless. Nothing much is getting through the blockade—"

"What blockade? Phil, what's happening?" She gripped the receiver harder, willing him to tell her more. The work she'd done over the last few years was being exposed and she desperately wished she were at least in her office over-seeing the planning and strategy. "I can come in."

"No. Not right now. After you got through, they closed their side of the border. We were able to smuggle enough operatives in. Look, I didn't want to tell you while you're recuperating, but not just our teams but others have been put under pressure."

"But—"

"You're my backup if things get much worse and I have to get in there to assist. I need you recovered. That's best done if you're at home."

Christina gritted her teeth. "Fine then. But keep me in the loop."

"I will." He hesitated.

Overnight she'd come to realize that part of his reticence to have her there, injured, was because maybe he felt an attachment she couldn't share. She needed to lay that to rest, now. "Phil, I..." She broke off, uncertain about saying anymore.

"Don't say it. Christina, don't say those words." There was a harsh quality to his voice as if he understood what she'd been about to share. It wasn't going to be an easy discussion down the track but for now, maybe she should leave it.

"Phil?" Silence then the disconnect signal filled the air and she understood he'd hung up.

Christina laid the phone on the coffee table and slumped back in the lounge chair. She worried at the necklace she wore, a nervous habit she'd tried many times over the years to break, and was glad Vasya wasn't there to see.

Gregori and Vasya had decided to walk to the nearest hardware store so they could see what tools they had for sale. They'd been gone maybe half an hour and Serina was lying down in the next room, while she sat here with a book in her lap. One Christina had wanted to read, but never found time for. Instead of devouring it, she looked at the pages, saw the words but couldn't focus.

The phone rang again and she jerked, scooping it up. "Christina."

"So I've spoken to him. Later today... It'll probably be around five'ish if that works best? He prefers to travel in daylight and has some other things he needs to do first." There was a brief hesitation and Christina frowned, waiting for Phil to continue. "He wants you to choose the brightest room in the house. Wear pale clothes and only the four of you. Don't tell anyone else that he's coming. You need to agree so I can reassure him of that. Christina?"

She waited for a minute, memorizing the terms he had

set down. "Yeah. I'll make sure we're ready for him." Christina closed her eyes, rubbing her fingertips over her brow where it ached.

"Good. And Christina? If you need help, please ask me. I'd do..." He stopped, feeling the sense of growing unease.

"Ah, yeah. I appreciate that, Phil."

She heard his breath catch. "Okay. I better go. I'll catch you later."

As she hung up the phone, things she didn't want to consider occurred to her. Things that would change the way she would work with him forever. Things that once acknowledged could never be forgotten.

CHAPTER 17

"Where's Serina?" Gregori spoke to Christina in his usual harsh manner and Vasya restrained his instinctive reaction.

On their return from the store, he and Gregori had seen a pensive looking Christina sitting on the seat in the small lounge. It would take time for everyone to really deeply trust each other, and for all that Christina had done for them, Gregori still harbored doubts about her story, as he termed it.

"In the lounge, resting. She was tired."

Gregori moved towards the door but Christina held out a hand. "Uh, before you go in there, we have a visitor coming. Phil is bringing someone to talk to us about the... situation. He has made some specific requests, so Gregori, if you'll listen for a moment then tell Serina?" She went on to explain the light clothing, light room and not telling anyone. By the end Gregori was nodding, said he'd tell Serina then he left the room.

Vasya felt distinctly uncomfortable with the restrictions. It wasn't about the not telling or wearing light clothes and sitting in the brightest room in the house. It was more about the fact that he knew next to nothing about his own genetic inheritance. He needed the information this man could share, but it also highlighted how badly his choices had failed Christina.

Once he gave his agreement, Christina visibly relaxed. Pleased that she'd settled, he moved towards her and she rose. "I should start getting organized..." Christina started to inch away but he stayed her.

"Wait." He reached out with his hand and she looked up at him. In her eyes he saw longing, fear and something he hoped was love.

It really was too soon, he told himself, but he hoped and prayed.

"What?" She frowned and it reminded him of the damage done to her soul in the years apart. Her experiences with Zuor had profoundly changed the girl he'd married.

She now wore a brittle and thin veneer of sophistication, which she'd lacked in her youth. Undoubtedly she'd been successful in her work and preparations for them, but beneath that lay a lonely woman.

Her gaze roamed his face, the mask firmly in place and he blinked. "Nothing. It's not important."

Instead, he trailed behind her into the kitchen, watching as she set about opening every curtain and window, turning on the lights and wiping down sides. "I can help, you know?"

Christina looked at him, startled. "I umm... I need to do this by myself."

"But..." He reached for a cloth but she snatched it from his hand, her face turning a funny pink. For a moment they were young and carefree. He grinned.

"Come on, *dushka*. I've helped you before." Her face paled at his pet term for her.

"No. I can do this." Accepting for now that he'd lost the battle, Vasya settled himself on the chair to watch.

From time-to-time, she cried with pain. He winced every time she stiffened and raised a hand to one of her many aches. He sighed. Finally, he stood, encircled her waist with his arms and she stilled. She held herself rigid before releasing a breath.

Vasya maneuvered her to the chair and made her sit. "I'll get you a drink. Just tell me what you prefer."

She gazed at him then smiled. This time the light caught in her eyes and he couldn't help himself, swooping in to steal a kiss from her lush lips, tasting and teasing until she moaned.

Heat sizzled between them. He pulled away, the unmistakable desire evident in the uncomfortable bulge that now pushed against his jeans. "I wish we could go on."

She giggled and his heart lightened.

The sound of knocking at the door caught her attention as she looked to the clock. "Oh... That should be..." Her words died away as the sound of Gregori, Phil and another voice intruded.

"I'd say he's arrived."

Phil came up the hallway first, wearing the black suit Vasya remembered from before, his black hair slicked back and the gold-rimmed glasses firmly in place. Vasya could see the tense set of his mouth and the way his gaze darted to and fro until they settled on Christina. Then the look softened slightly.

Vasya felt the primal urge to push the man out the door, but calmed it. He could understand the man's attraction to her. She was both a beautiful woman and a gentle natured soul. Everything he could ever ask for.

Besides which, she'd chosen to be with him. Even during the time apart and the heavy secrets that continued to impact them, she had chosen him. Kept herself for him. He didn't even attempt to contain the grin that crept over his face at that thought.

The man following Phil caught his attention. He'd obviously been a big man in his youth, but now age had caught up with him, as he bent forward, heavy jowls bracketing his face. His eyes were quick and alert, moving up and down, checking the room. He grunted his satisfaction as he shuffled in and pinned Christina with a glare.

"So it's all your fault, is it girl?" Then he reached out with a gnarled hand and lowered himself into the seat. "Well, you better all sit down and get started, before *they* realize we are here."

Vasya bit back an instinctive rebuke and settled into the chair beside Christina, who had now retreated within herself. The light that had shone before in her eyes dimmed and he wanted to curse the old man for his thoughtless remarks.

"So, what do you want to know?" The older man turned to him and he forced his mind to whir into action.

"We need to know how to beat a Demon, how to Ascend and lastly, why the demon, Zu—"

The old man held up a hand. "Don't say his name. It calls them you foolish boy. Didn't anyone teach you anything?"

Vasya curled his fingers into fists. "If they did, do you think I'd be sitting here questioning you?" Even as he said the words he wanted to curse, but the old man just laughed at him.

"Excellent! You do have a spark. I was beginning to wonder when you didn't react to the first jab. It just could be what keeps you alive." He leaned forward in his seat. "It's obvious you haven't been schooled in the ways of the Flyer, have you? So we start at the beginning. In normal talk, we would call you land based angels: Those that watch over the feeders. The ones like her." He indicated with a quick flick of his eyes and jerked out a nod, but he groped for and gripped her hand when she gave an almost silent groan.

"You can tell? I mean, looking at Christina, you know what she is?"

The man cocked his head at Vasya's question. "With practice. Usually because they're pale, withdrawn. Inherently damaged, some would say."

Vasya stiffened. He'd thought pretty much the same thing about her over the last few days.

"Beating them isn't easy, but it can be done. You must be committed to the path, prepared to make many sacrifices and lastly, be strong in both mind and body." This time when the man looked at him, he felt a punch of connection.

Within him rose a sense of power, unlike anything he'd ever before experienced, while his back itched. He twitched uncomfortably on the chair, wondering how the man was manipulating him. "I'm committed but I need to know more. I need to learn how to fight." He poured his anger into the words, infusing them with decisiveness and urgency. "I need to protect Christina. And I need to know why she's a target."

A grin split the old man's face. "She is a target because of her blood." He turned and pinned Christina who blanched, slightly. "He feeds from you, direct from a vein?"

She nodded wordlessly and the man chuckled. "You have a woman with abilities of her own."

He started in shock. "What do you mean?"

"Way back in the history of her family, there will be a supernatural ability or bloodline. Call it an inheritance in her blood. These demons prefer to have those who have strong but hidden skills."

He turned to Christina. "Do you have any natural affinities? Woods or water?"

She shook her head, eyes wide in startlement.

"There is usually one child that is dominant and any further are carriers of a recessive gene. It is rare for there to be more than one Dominant in each generation. Where this occurs, there is a need either to continue the bloodline, some kind of danger or..." He lounged back into the seat with his fingers steepled. It was clear he wanted them to consider what remained unspoken.

"No. See, he, Zu...the demon, has never showed interest in my sister. At least..." Christina rose with a jerk and stepped away, he made to rise, but she fluttered her hands at him.

"Your growing thin though, aren't you? You would have been a naturally happy and open child. He would be drawn to that. He feeds on emotion as much as the blood. It sustains him. As you become more negative, he is less able to draw the positive energy that keeps him alive. Usually that is found in those with some kind of magic ability or skill. Or bloodline, as I suspect is your case."

Christina ducked her head, wondering what on earth would make this old man think that she was anything special.

"Oh they really only feed from those with the dominant abilities. When they target the carrier of the recessive gene, it's usually some kind of discipline. In my experience, the feeder is made to watch and suffer. He'll be wanting you to feel guilt and helplessness so you try harder, look for more experiences as you come to understand what he requires of you." Christina gave a tiny sound of distress.

"You didn't realize they feed not only on your blood, but also your emotions, did you? Positive ones are stronger, so they prefer those, but even the negative ones will give them some kind of charge, but so much weaker that they require more regular feeding."

Christina shook and Vasya's heart ached for her pain.

"He invades your dreams?"

Christina nodded, poured a glass of water and drank deeply. "Yes."

"Are they dark? Do you feel strong emotions?"

She nodded her answer and the old man closed his eyes.

"Is there any light? Something that happens? Any action that triggers him?"

Christina started to shake her head and then stopped. "Yes. There is. I saw Vasya last night. In my dream, he shone. A sort of white-blue light surrounded him. The demon..." She drew an unsteady breath and the man nodded, encouraging her to speak. "He didn't react well at all. They fought and I... I woke. Sort of..." She turned away and in his gut Vasya felt a twisting pain.

The old man smiled. "Then your man has already begun his ascension. It's like opening a portal to his powers. He can only achieve that once he has found his mate. Your brother? Has he experienced the same?"

Vasya looked at his brother who shrugged. "Yes. But only since we have been here. Before that..." Gregori shrugged and the man grunted with satisfaction.

"Phil here, has told me where you came from. They treat the waters, and they call it pesticides or fertilizers, because it keeps supernatural abilities muted. While there you could never have experienced the full range of skills."

The old man reached into his pocket and handed something to Christina who closed her hand around the item. The small silver disk with a tiny blue stone in the center was threaded onto an old tarnished chain.

"Wear this at all times. It will give you some protection from the dream realms. But... once he realizes, you will need to take swift action. He'll be angry and ready to fight for what he covets." He closed his eyes, his lips moving silently. When he reopened his rheumy blue eyes they shone. "Maybe it is time to take a stand and end the Darkness, but... It is something you will need to consider, and, I daresay, it will take all of you to prevail." On those words, the man rose, pushing his hand flat against the tabletop.

"Phil will bring you all to me tomorrow. I will begin training you Vasya and Gregori. And the ladies I will arrange some meetings and we shall see what eventuates. There's going to be a fair battle ahead and you will need to prepare."

Then he left the room and headed for the door. But the silence where they remained was deafening.

Phil rose. "And now, I'll take him home.

"*R*eady for bed?" Vasya moved in behind her, running his hands slowly up her arms, igniting her senses with flickering eruptions of lightning. Christina lost herself in the sensual thrill that rushed through her.

"I don't know... Probably." Her stomach quavered and she clutched the small stone centered charm in her hand.

"Would you put this on me?" She uncurled her fingers, feeling Vasya's hot breath slide over her shoulder.

"What's on it?" As if reminded of the item, his voice carried a question.

"I don't know." She dangled it from the old silver chain. It spun madly, catching the light and sparkling. A pale white-blue stone sat in the middle. She hadn't been able to make out the inscriptions on the surface. The old charm was worn away and she swore she could feel something of the previous wearers in the metal. The item was warm to the touch and she hoped it would offer some protection from the nightly terror of Zuor's world.

"My mother had one of these." Vasya's quiet words had her turning quickly.

"Really? What happened to it?"

Vasya shrugged. "When she died, Father refused to let them take it from her. I think it was buried with her."

Sorrow seeped through her. She hadn't been there for the death of his parents. It was yet another injustice that she carried on her conscience. "Vasya, I..."

This time, he took the necklet and slipped it over her head, the action so intimate, she nearly gasped at the feel of him touching her. "Not tonight. Tonight I need to..."

He stopped as she laid her fingers against his lips. "I know. I feel it too," she whispered and then moved her fingers away, slowly touching her mouth to the same spot.

The electric thrill spurred her on and she raised her hands, cupping his shoulders. Feeling the strength of sinuous muscles beneath her touch. She used her thumbs, tracing small circles and felt him relax beneath her caressing hands.

"Your body has changed so much. In so many ways." She shifted her fingers, tracing a path up his strong neck. "So much muscle and so many things I missed. Things I should have been there for."

"But we're together now." She felt the vibrations of his words and marveled that they were, as he said, together.

"I couldn't imagine being with anyone else the day we married. You looked so handsome standing there, waiting for me. And I felt so special knowing you had chosen me to be your wife."

She carried such a burden in the mixture of grief and pain. The urge to share it spurred her to tell him everything. "Then I was taken away. But I mourned your loss. Every day, I mourned for the life I planned to share with you." She reached up on her toes, pressing kisses on his cheeks. "I see what Gregori and Serina have, and I feel so angry that it was taken from us."

He settled his hands at her waist, pulling her firmly against his body and she burned. She knew what she wanted. "I wish we could begin again. As if this was our first night. Knowing we have forever stretching between us."

"We do. It can be. What came before? It was a mild emotion—the love of children. Now, we can start fresh, renewing the promises and vows we made then, knowing that we're ready as adults." He lowered his mouth to hers and she felt the kick of intimacy. The way his lips moved over hers drugged her senses.

His hands slipped down, covering the curve of her backside, molding her more firmly against him and she felt his erection through the layers of clothes. She arched away, dragging her mouth from his, warmth curling up within her again, just as it always did when he kissed her.

Christina moved her hands, splayed them over the hard muscles of his chest and inching towards the buttons that kept her from his skin. The need to touch urged her onwards, seeking his heat.

The hard plastic button brushed her fingertips and she slipped it through the hole and continued down his shirt until it gaped open.

Vasya hissed as she laid her hands against his chest but they didn't still. "I want you naked, my husband. I want to kiss every inch of your body." She trembled as she spoke, feeling a ripple of pleasure. Her nipples had budded tightly beneath her bra and moisture pooled inside her panties.

"I want you too. I want to throw you on the bed and show you all the things we've missed. I want to suck your breasts, to lick my way down your body and to swallow your cries as you come apart in my arms. I want to watch your body stiffen as the pleasure of our loving overwhelms you."

His husky words ratcheted up the tension deep inside her, while his hands burrowed down the back of her trousers, pushing them down until they pooled at her ankles. Vasya shifted his hands back up to her shoulders where he pushed on the lightweight cotton top and it gaped under his ministrations.

She made to lift her hands, to push the material away, but he stopped her. "No. I need to do this."

She waited for him to continue, each second making her yearn for more. She shivered as the molten pool of want licked its way through her body.

With care he dragged the material up. It caught on her distended nipples and she cried out at the light scraping sensation shattered her senses.

Finally freed of the restricting material she reached for his belt and made short work of the buckle and he chuckled. "You obviously need this as much as I do." She glanced up and noted the way his jaw was tightly clenched. *Oh yes, they needed each other.*

She hurried to divest him of his clothes, fingers stopping now and then to simply touch the miles of skin she bared. Desire grew within her, a raging fire of need. It was as if she was empty and the pressure low down in her belly, the coil of passion expanded. Her fingers felt fat and unresponsive and she muttered as she finally pushed the heavy denim down his long muscular legs, feeling the rasp of hairs across her sensitized skin.

Finally he was naked before her. His gaze travelled over her and she waited for him, the fire in her belly growing white hot. "Vasya, please." She pleaded, needing him.

He leaned in and this time, when he took her mouth it scorched her. Rapacious as he nipped and sucked at her lips and tongue. Noses bumped and she didn't care, all she wanted was him.

His hands on her.

When he moved to her jaw she arched her neck, sensations exploding and she gasped, blind with longing. His hands cupped her now heavy breasts, fingertips caressing her nipples. "Vasya, please!" she moaned.

Christina slid her hands over his flesh, feeling the strength in the flanks of his legs, the densely packed muscles of his backside and the length of his erection, where it pushed against her belly.

Without conscious thought she widened her stance allowing him to strip the panties from her, shivering as the cool air caressed her exposed skin. He started pushing them down her thighs. "Come. Come now, Vasya!"

He lifted her, the pooled garments falling away and the softness of the mattress beneath her welcomed their combined weight. His skin connected with hers and his mouth roamed over her shoulders, licking and nibbling his way down to the buds of her nipples. Here he stopped and feasted, sucking each in turn, flicking his tongue against the distended flesh, the touch setting off explosions of pleasure-pain deep within her.

She writhed beneath him. "Vasya," a long wail of hunger interspersed with mindless needy movements. The tug of nails biting deep and an arch of her spine demanding more and harder.

Christina hooked her ankles around his back, gripping his hips and stopping his progress down her body.

"No more?" She opened her eyes and sucked in a ragged lungful of oxygen. "Oh God, no! I don't think I could survive much more." She panted heavily, feeling the rapid thrum of her pulse at the thought of what they were about to do.

He laughed and the rumble of his chest set her nerve endings sizzling.

Slowly he leaned in toward her and fixed his mouth to her lips in a questing feast. Their tongues mated then he settled himself in the cradle of her thighs while Christina wrapped her arms around his neck, sinking her fingers into his hair to anchor herself.

She felt him position himself against her intimate flesh. Felt the slow slide as he thrust deep. Vasya pulled away and groaned as he slid home again, seating himself to the hilt deep inside her body.

The sensation of fullness left her whimpering her need. "More. Give me everything." Her hoarse demand must have pushed him beyond all thought because he rocked against her, sliding forward and back, the slick movement hard and fast. She met his thrusts, the slapping of flesh and the panting all wreaking havoc on her senses.

Faster they moved, harder and more deeply. Both

needed the connection and release that could only be achieved together. "Vasya! Please."

He groaned unintelligible words against her temple as he shook.

Finally the pinnacle drew near and she tightened her grip, the ripples starting deep in her womb. The orgasm swept over her and she gave herself up to it. He stiffened against her, filling her with his seed.

Their bodies stilled, while around them the scent of sex filled the air.

"I never wanted that with anyone else, Vasya. Only ever with you."

Tears welled in her eyes and he rolled, pulling her with him, held firmly against his chest. "That's a good thing, because I can never let you go."

Tears leaked, tracing burning tracks down her cheeks as they washed away her pain.

*H*olding her close, he gloried in the sensations and feelings she roused in him. He loved this woman. Had never really stopped. He'd just lost sight of how important she was to him in the haze of pain that had wrapped around him. The shock when Christina came back into his life, hurrying him and his family into her car and away, had blinded him to the truths he'd buried.

Now lying in his arms, resting in the aftermath of passion he knew he had to tell her how he felt. "Christina..."

She snuffled quietly and he knew she had fallen asleep. He'd seen how tired she was and the dark shadows which stained the skin beneath her eyes. Still, he hadn't quite expected her to doze so quickly. He thought over the few facts she had shared from her dreams the night before. He hadn't told her that he too had been in the small cell. He'd been fighting Zuor when she woke, her waking pulling him from the realm of pain and despair.

"I need to sleep." He tested the words, weighed them and knew it was the best option. Tomorrow they would go to meet with the older Sky Flyer and learn more. But for now, the best thing he could do for Christina was sleep.

He settled himself pulling the covers over her nude body and said a quick silent prayer that they would sleep deeply and dreamlessly.

Sleep eluded him for a long time and he reached for the blinds and opened them, watching the stars twinkle in the dark sky. If he ascended, he would be able to fly. Perhaps even take Christina with him. "She'll enjoy that."

Finally able to clear his mind he relaxed the muscles of his body, closed his eyes and felt consciousness slip away.

The next time he opened them, the sun shone down and the bundle of warm woman in his arms stirred restlessly.

The blinds were still open so he extended his arm and slipped them closed just as she opened her eyes. "Vasya? Did we sleep the night through?"

He smiled. "We did. You slept well, didn't you?"

Christina nodded, her hair like billowing clouds of silk and he had to restrain himself from hooking it behind her ear as she beat him to it. Instead he pulled her closer to him.

"We'll have to rise soon." Her answering smile warmed his insides.

"We probably should, but I have this idea I'd like to try out first." She dipped closer and kissed him.

CHAPTER 18

*T*he sun was high in the sky as Phil pulled into a farmlet some distance from town. The green trees swayed while the breeze blew fresh and Vasya smiled. Perhaps, if Christina was amenable, at some later point—when their situation was more settled—they might find somewhere like this for themselves. She'd always appreciated wooded areas.

They parked under an old shiny tree and climbed out. Visions of small children running and laughing in meadows, gathering wild flowers hit him hard—his and Christina's. Perhaps also Serina and Gregori's child would join theirs in games. He'd noted that the two women were talking without the stilted behavior Serina had exhibited when Christina had found them in Alvonia and pleasure filled him.

Knowing that Christina and her sister were working on repairing their relationship gave him peace. She needed her sister, now more than ever.

The old man rounded the house as they arrived and he

saw a motley collection of others. Dravens, the old man they'd met the day before, indicated they should join him and as one, the group moved slowly toward the building.

Women and men milled and Christina grabbed his hand. Hers shook. In his mind was pleased that she was willing to share her fear with him, but his heart hated that she had to live through this experience.

"It'll be fine, *dushka*. We need to know as much as possible so we can beat him."

"I know." Her words were strangled but she clenched his hand, squeezed once then let go. Christina would have moved away but Vasya caught her close and dragged her back against him. Wordlessly lending her his support. "I want to be free of him. I don't want him to *own* me anymore."

Vasya understood. She needed him to meet the others and his chest swelled with pride, yet both concern and respect warred within him at the way she overcame her terror.

"Well, come on boy! We haven't got forever." The crotchety man's voice made him grin. The *starik* probably thought he had him cowed, but Vasya stifled the snort.

"I've asked members from a range of clans to join us today, so we can work out what skills and abilities your women hold." He indicated to the motley crew of people gathered around. "Since I was unsure of exactly where to start, I reached out to as many as possible. These are the ones who could come on short notice. We have representatives from a range of communities including the fey, sirens and even nymphs. Then over there..." He waved in the direction of a group who didn't mix with those seated, "the were's and others." He squinted at Christina and Vasya stiffened, ready to react. "Until we know what you are, we can't exactly plan for contingencies."

A young woman stepped forward. No doubt in most circles she would be considered eye catching, but to him—with her blonde hair and pale blue eyes—he felt nothing. It was as if she were somehow faded beside Christina. In his mind, Christina glowed with fire and passion.

Dravens waited as the woman took a seat beside him. "This is my grand-daughter, Jelena. She is one of the strongest warriors we have in this region. Once your Ascension is completed, you will be placed in one of the legions." The old man's lips twisted in a half smile.

The woman eyed him, her glance raking over him and he burned with discomfort. That he didn't know enough and that she was deciding what he might be capable of, while clearly not meant to unman him, was nevertheless frustrating.

Dravens gave a cold laugh and Vasya resettled his eyes on the man. Dravens peered closely at him. "I'm guessing you aren't planning on going anywhere?"

"No. As long as..." He let the words hang. Christina had built a life here and he wouldn't drag her away from that. Not unless she wanted to be somewhere else. She'd been forced to give everything up once. He wouldn't ask her to do it again.

With a sigh, the man shrugged then turned to introduce them to the gathering. The Were's took an uncertain sniff of the women before stepping away to mutter amongst themselves.

One, carrying an air of leadership stepped forward, cleared his voice and waited for the throng to quieten. "These women are not of our world." With a respectful bow to Dravens and the others gathered, they formed a phalanx around the speaker. "Lord Dravens, we consider ourselves released from further discussions." He spoke softly but with undeniable firmness. Vasya made a note to ask about that later.

Dravens spread his hands and gave a short nod of assent. "You are free. I thank you for your attendance." As if the words opened a portal and freed them, they made for the woods without a sound.

"It's a ritual?" He heard Serina but didn't look back as Phil hushed her, with a "not now."

The same act of stepping forward and either touching Christina or silently sniffing continued. Each time, her face blanked a little further, but the squeeze of her hand became stronger.

The sirens nodded sadly and melted into the woods, other beings gave their pronouncement.

It was both awe-inspiring and fantastical to realize the stories his parents had shared were based on fact. It amazed him further that they coexisted peacefully here.

Time passed and the sun rose higher in the sky. Finally only the fey and nymphs remained, watching in the silence.

The fey stepped forward and then turned. "He is fey. Court fey." They pointed to Phil who scowled.

"You were not supposed to be considering my parentage." His angry tones left Vasya confused.

"Then you should not have cloaked yourself in the guise of a human as you came before us." The glance of the faeries gathered hardened.

Vasya opened his mouth but Phil's headshake stopped him. "Ask no questions and I won't need to tell you truths you do not wish to hear, Vasya." His words chilled Vasya to the core, imbued with some form of deep and powerful magic.

Phil stood, eyes glittering with anger and the outspoken fey stepped back. "You must choose your path. Come with us now." Leaving him no opportunity to evade their hands they marched him into the middle of the meadow. Once there, their hands moved as they talked

The nymphs stepped forward, their eyes soft as they gazed on Christina and Serina. The women were loose limbed, with long flowing hair of every imaginable color, but it was the young one, standing before Christina who spoke. "They are of us as we are of them. Come sisters, we will walk and share the stories of our kind."

"What?" Christina squeaked, and she glanced in his direction, a question shining in her eyes. He too felt so much had happened quickly.

"Go with them. I'll be here when you need me."

"Serina?" Christina extended her hand, which Serina clasped. Then without another word she followed the speaker to the meadow.

He watched for a moment before Jelena spoke. "Your Ascension is well progressed for one traveling this route alone. Your body will be preparing to expel your wings. Once that happens your ascension is complete."

Wings? His parent's hadn't mentioned them. He raised a hand and forced a cough, letting himself take a second to regroup his senses. She watched as he looked at her.

"You don't have any." His words accused her and she laughed.

Her smile broadened. "Not that you can see. Not at the moment, anyway."

Jelena snorted, and he watched as she circled him once and indicated to her grandfather. He simply smiled as Jelena took position behind him. She swiped her nails across his back and he growled. "You're almost ready. There will be more pain before they emerge, though."

His stomach roiled. "How long?"

She shrugged. "Hard to say. Could be in the next few days, though." She followed through with the same actions to Gregori and nodded. "Both of you should soon complete your Ascension."

She turned as if to leave. "Jelena... show them the rest."

She stopped and turned back. "Grandfather...!"

"No. You will show them." Their gazes clashed in a battle of wills that went on for ages. His faces hardened and she hissed, before glancing away.

"Fine." With an angry jerk she removed her shirt, another lighter top sat below—a leather vest of black fastened with silver and blue clasps. It was well worn with wide straps that crisscrossed her shoulders.

Jelena grunted and suddenly a whooshing sound filled the air, while two enormous white wings appeared from wide gashes in her back. Now, her body glowed so bright that Vasya cupped his hand over his eye —unable to look away from the sight in front of him. A shake of her hand and a large curved sword appeared, in her hand.

"Grandfather?"

The old man held out a fine piece of fabric. With a swift movement she took it, before giving a quick twist. The blade cut through the material as easily as a spoon through melted butter, the forgotten cloth floated to the ground.

Vasya leaned forward. The sword itself was deeply scribed and glowed with the same blue sheen that encompassed the warrior woman standing before him.

He took a single step forward even though the proximity stung his eyes, unable to glance away from the vision in front of him. "This is...?" His mouth was too dry to speak anything more. He gulped.

"When it is done, this is what you will learn among many other things." Then she sprang up and took flight, moving in what looked to be effortless dips and glides. Vasya watched while hunger for this grew in his belly and need gnawed deep within him.

That will be me soon. I will fly. Then I will *defeat the demon.*

CHAPTER 19

The scent of grass and flowers floated on the air and the sun warmed Christina. "Umm, forgive me. But how could I possibly be a nymph? I mean aren't they some kind of immortal beauties who take a myriad of lovers?"

Christina stopped, realizing her words might be considered an insult. The woman, no she reminded herself, the *nymph* in front of her merely smiled and Christina released the breath she'd held onto.

"Well, that is a common misconception. But we decided long ago that it rather suited our ends to have people believe those facts to be accurate. Come... Let us walk together." Christina followed her. "Your name is Christina, isn't it? Your sister will wait here with Erina and Naiea."

She indicated with a soft hand toward the center of the meadow and Christina followed the dark haired woman, mesmerized by her graceful movements. *How can I possibly be a nymph? I'm nothing like this woman.*

"You no doubt have many questions, but let us begin with my name. I am Galene and the elder of the nymphs locally. My great great-grandmother, also Galene, was believed to be the daughter of Nereus and Doris."

Christina blinked unsure who this Nereus and Doris were. The silence grew and Christina wondered what Galene was thinking.

"I'm sorry, but I… I don't know of these people." Shame filled her. Should she know this? Was this one more thing that should have been learned during her childhood? Schooling in Alvonia was basic at best and she'd had to learn so much already.

Glancing at Galene she was surprised by the soft smile. It was as if Galene was revisiting old but happy memories. "They were minor Gods, although mythology also says that she could have been a love child of Zeus and some minor river goddess. My family isn't exactly good at sharing information." Galene chuckled drily. "Besides which, not only was it rather dangerous to own up to being his child, even if she was…" the woman shrugged and confusion filled Christina.

"I don't… I know of Zeus but how could anyone know if the child was his. I mean Zeus wasn't particularly loyal, at least according to what I learned." She gulped, knowing she was treading on dangerous ground.

"It is true, he took many lovers and begat many children. I suppose we continue to believe and share that truth because we know the original Galene chose to give her children a portion of the immortality that they would have usually inherited from their father if he'd acknowledged them."

"Pardon? Why a portion?" Christina regretted the question as soon as she said it.

Galene however laughed. "We don't know. Not really. Anyway, that's why, while we enjoy a longer lifespan, we are not immortal. The immortality was something the original Galene banned. But I'll explain that later, once the immediate danger has passed." She turn and kept walking as she spoke, running her hands along the tips of wildflowers that filled the field.

"Your man will also have a longer life span. Most fliers live for hundreds of years, so at least neither of you will be alone at the end of your lives." When Galene halted she turned and speared Christina with a piercing glance. "That was one of your concerns, wasn't it?"

Christina stopped. She hadn't really even thought that far in advance. But now, the thought crashed through Christina's mind as she also attempted to process the facts that Galene had just shared.

"My sister?" She stopped and Galene did the same. "Will she enjoy the same lifespan?"

"That I can't be sure of." Christina's heart dropped into her belly. Would she have to watch Serina age and die? What about Serina and Gregori's child? The knowledge was sobering.

"When the original Galene—my great great-grandmother—shortened our lifespan, she also sought help from her father in limiting how many of her offspring would be able to use their abilities. She wanted surety that her children and children's children would be able to blend into humanity. After all, so many were afraid of us already, and the skills we carried..." The nymph looked into the distance and a small frown creased her forehead. "Those of us who retained our gifts assumed roles as protectors of the weaker among us as well as the water courses. That is, those who have been able to embrace their gifts. The ones the demons haven't irrevocably damaged, anyway."

If Serina couldn't access this gift, then what would that

mean for her sister and Gregori? She'd seen the closeness between them and now she feared his reaction if the worst case eventuated and Serina took her place as a feeder.

Multitudinous questions crowded her mind and all without answers. She breathed deeply hoping to clear the fog that settled in her brain.

"You should not worry, my dear. When they petitioned that second and subsequent children couldn't access their skills, they set in place a failsafe. It was a..." She cast around as if lost for the correct term. "Consider it as a fallback position. In case something happened to those with the dominant abilities then those with the recessive skills would be able to access them."

"So you mean, if something happened to me, then Serina could use the same skills?"

Now Galene's face screwed up as if unsure how much negative information to share. "More or less." Her shrug discomforted Christina. "In some situations, both the first and second child are able to access the full range of abilities. However, only those with the dominant abilities can pass their abilities along to their children." Galene shrugged her slender shoulders again. "As I am the only child of an only child, it is difficult to know the true lifespan of those with recessive abilities. Never before have we needed to collect such information."

"The situation in Alvonia, though. Is it placing stresses on you and your..." Christina hunted for an appropriate term.

"Ahh, that is entirely another thing. That is because of the ruling class and the corruption of darkness. I fear there is far more to learn about that, yet."

Galene laid a gentle hand on her shoulder. It was soft and reassuring. "You have a path to follow. That of protector while your sister will have to walk her own path. Your future could be a long and lonely one, and you must find that strength within yourself."

Fear seized her. *Protector? I'm good at hiding people, organizing teams but that doesn't make me a protector.* She thought hard, framing the words in her mind before she spoke. "How can I be a protector? I'm not a warrior. I have no great skills and I don't know how to protect anyone." A cold laugh erupted. "I couldn't even protect *myself.*" The self-loathing she'd hidden for years gushed out and she moved away, balling her fists.

She'd let her grandfather spirit her away, instead of staying and fighting. "I was weak, Galene. I didn't stay with my parents, or my husband. I ran and I hid." Churning sickness rose and the bitterness of bile coated her tongue and she spun away. Galene touched her shoulder.

"Christina?" She glanced over her shoulder as Galene spoke, this time there was steel in the grey eyes that gazed on her.

"You are a nymph and we are protectors. But you needed to grow into yourself. Before you were weak and young. Unprepared. Without a true understanding of your nature."

Pain assailed her. "But I ran away."

Galene tensed as if frustrated at Christina's intransigence. "*So?* It wasn't the right time. Now it is. When Dravens contacted us, we asked questions about you. In your own way, you are a warrior fighting for the weak. Your work, rescuing those from Alvonia gives them a chance at freedom. You move whole families who've been targeted by the secret police."

Christina heard the words, but shook her head. "No. I have teams who do that. I haven't done that in years."

The smile Galene bestowed on Christina blossomed

with understanding. "If you hadn't put in place the people, the resources, they would have no future. In your own way, you ensure their protection."

"But—"

Galene raised her hand, stopping her argument. "Your own family required your help and you planned and brought them here yourself. Not someone you sent in."

"But they're family. That's different."

Silence met her outburst and Christina wondered if she'd gone too far

The quiet stretched between them, then Galene started walking again, leading her further into the meadow. "It's not. Once you have them safe, you work through channels to help them build a life. Christina, that's your protective side."

Galene stopped and dragged her close, enfolding her in a hug. "You are truly a gifted nymph."

"Even if I accept what you're saying, which I don't, I still have to have some kind of a part of nature, don't I?"

Christina locked her knees waiting for Galene to answer. The silence stretched out, tearing at her nerves. "We just need to find out what your affinity is. Nymphs are associated to watercourses. They can be rivers or lakes or streams. And that, my dear, is going to be the easiest part of all this. Tell me, where do you feel the most comfortable? By a river? Near a lake...?"

Christina closed her eyes, breathed deeply and relaxed herself, seeking where she'd been at her happiest. By the river, the day Vasya had asked her to marry him. He'd also kissed her for the first time beside that river...and done a lot more.

"There is a river near our home in Alvonia." She smiled. "Do you think...?"

Galene nodded. "Then likely you're a river nymph and do better living near rivers."

An instant of darkness crossed Christina and she looked up, sucking in a deep breath. "Oh my!" The sight of Jelena, the granddaughter of Dravens flying overhead while her blonde, silk hair trailed behind amazed Christina. Her heart pounded. Someday, that would be Vasya. She couldn't visualize it though.

"They are truly amazing, aren't they? But flyers need to be able to move quickly, to strike where the enemy is and when it appears in its many guises."

Knowing that Vasya'd soon be able to protect himself gave her strength. She welcomed the knowledge—along with the information that one day she'd be able to help him. "But why would Zu... Ah... the demon, want me? What makes me so special that he has singled me out?"

"It could be anything Christina. Maybe he feels threatened that you are fighting him. Or... it could be because there is something about *you*...perhaps your natural affinity or strength. Or it could be sexual. Most demons are basic creatures. They want basic things. Sex and power rank highly for them. But it's important to remember that at the heart of it, just like us, they have their weaknesses. They can be overcome."

Christina made to open her mouth to explain, but Galene stopped her. "No. You know not to name him don't you?" When Christina blinked Galene's face took on a hard mask.

"Uh yes. Dravens explained why." Christina snatched one last look to the sky then glanced back to Galene.

"Then the first step to your schooling is to know never to say his name. Each time you do, it's like summoning him. Say it enough or demand his presence strongly and he will materialize before you. The next time you are in his realm you need to find out what his affinity is."

Christina frowned. "You mean like mine is probably a river? Is he likely to share it?"

Galene snickered. "As a river nymph, his will be complementary. It could be fire or rock or any one of thousands of things that impede a water flow. Once you have that knowledge, you'll be able to fight and possibly defeat him."

Understanding dawned and Christina dragged her hand through her hair. "Once you have that, contact me here." Galene shoved a piece of paper into her hand.

Frustration welled. How on earth was she supposed to learn what his affinity was? "But how will I know?"

Galene smiled. "When you find it, you'll know. Now, you can contact me anytime. Let's head back to the others." It was clear from Galene's final words that the discussion was finished, so Christina mulled over the information she'd gleaned so far.

Her experience in conflict was solely based on her escape and work, yet she was preparing for a battle of greater proportions. One that included supernatural beings, magic and heaven knew what else. The task ahead was immense and she worried that she wasn't strong enough.

I'll just have to be.

※

"I need to go back to his realm." Her bold words shocked him to stillness. The air in the small bedroom grew close as she rolled away from his embrace. Exhaustion still hung from her frame, and he had agreed to lie down with her while she rested. He could understand her fears, but with the medallion, surely she could chance a rest in the daytime hours? She'd fought him, but he'd stood toe-to-toe until she finally agreed.

Even though he'd expected her to rise soon in order to prepare the midday meal he'd been surprised by her quiet words. "No." Every muscle in his body locked. "You can't. It's too dangerous."

Christina lifted worry filled eyes to his. "If I don't, he'll do something. I'm fairly sure that whatever it is, it won't be pleasant."

His gut clenched at the determine set of her lips. He held her close. "Christina... I need to protect you but I don't know how. *Not yet.*"

Powerless. He knew that right now there was not much he could do to protect her and he wanted to rage against his inability to act. She's *mine! I should be able to protect her.* He gritted his teeth. "No."

"Dammit Vasya! I have to. I need to see if I can find out his weakness. What his affinity is. Galene and I talked about it and she was right. Once I know what his weakness is, we can use it." She slipped her hand over his cheek, thumb tracing small circles over the hard planes. Nerves jumped and danced below her soft caress. "I'll be careful, I promise. And if it helps, you can watch over me. Okay? But I can't see any other way. I need to do this...for me." She flung her arms out. "I need to do this for us."

Much as he didn't want to face the truth, they needed every possible fact and skill they could amass and she really was the only one who could give them the knowledge. It didn't mean he had to like it though. It smacked too much of endangering her. And giving in to her went against every instinct. "Perhaps..."

Maybe if he spoke to Jelena, she might be able to help him find his way. "I need to talk to Jelena. See if she can come up with any kinds of safeguards." He leaned forward, folding his arms around Christina and soaking up the warmth of her body. "I gave you my promise and I'll see it through. I'll protect you any way I can."

"Phil might—"

"No. I know Phil is your friend but he'd like to be so much more." Christina's face screwed up.

"I know. I don't know how to tell him that we can only ever be just friends."

Vasya's chest expanded and he grinned. "I think he's starting to understand."

"Oh dear." Christina worried her lip and Vasya breathed in her scent, the light floral fragrance he now associated with her. A thin and high scream echoed from the back of the house.

The hair on the nape of his neck rose.

It was Serina, he was sure of it. Pushing off the bed, they ran. His heart beat wildly in his chest. The door between them and Christina's sister was locked. He jiggled the metal latch but it didn't give.

"Serina! We're coming!" Christina cried against the wood, her eyes wild as she caught his gaze. Gregori bounded in their direction, a tense expression on his face.

He gave the door a dark look before raising his head, lips tight and fire in his eyes. Christina moved away and the two men backed up then rammed it, the wooden frame shuddering.

Serina's cry tapered off beyond and the adrenaline in his system pulsed with every anxious beat of Vasya's heart. His sister-in-law was facing danger. Alone. Each cry sliced through his shredded nerves, leaving him cold.

The door creaked and groaned and they charged it again. The door quivered. Once more they backed up, and as they hit, the wood shattered, chunks of the laminated surface flying into the air.

On the bed, Serina lay slumped in Zuor's embrace. The demon lifted his head and Vasya had the impression of coal black skin and widely flaring nostrils. Serina looked so pale, her face white, while blood spattered her shirt. The sight of the jagged feed marks on her arm left him reeling.

It was obvious she'd passed out from the shock. The need to tear at the creature, to drag him limb from limb had him snarling.

Control! In his mind Jelena's words chorused and Vasya curled his fingers into his palm, feeling the sting, he fought the fury within himself. The creature still held Serina, his eyes glowing red, before pushing her away like a discarded doll. She fell to the bed and Vasya turned away from her, scanning the creature in front of him. The stink of sulfur mixed with the copper of the blood dripping from his chin.

For Serina and the child's sake, he needed to concentrate on his actions. "You are not welcome here!"

Zuor gave a chilling laugh before he turned, his coal-black skin glittering in the dim light of sunset.

The grin on his face grew wider and he glared at Christina, "I warned you I'd seek retribution of one kind or another."

Her face blanched. Her gaze ran over the demon.

Vasya knew the moment the truth dawned on her, the way her eyes widened when she noted the blood dripping from his incisors. She swayed and he wanted to reach out and support her. He couldn't though. Instead he hovered close, ready to engage the enemy if he took another move toward Serina.

As the demon lifted a sharply tipped nail in Christina's direction, he growled, "You're mine. You made a bargain—

one you haven't yet fulfilled. Someone must pay the price, not that I care who it is. That's the bargain we struck."

Vasya blocked out the sound of her ragged breathing, railing against the fate that left her at the demon's mercy while Vasya stood guard over her sister.

*C*hristina couldn't look away from Zuor. She loathed the way he'd just taken what he wanted, it caused fury to score her soul. Vasya made to grab the demon, but his movements were ungainly and Christina felt like she was watching the action through a tunnel—everything took on an unreal air.

Gregori punched past her and dropped to Serina's side as one of Zuor's ugly barks filled the air, then he waved his hand in a quick motion, disappearing. All that remained were the trailing wisps of black smoke and the stink of sulfur.

Her gaze dropped back to Serina, settling on the scarlet trails; the only sign of Zuor's visit. That and the destroyed door, her mind added. A hysterical laugh rose in her throat but she cut it off before it escaped.

Gregori gathered his wife into his arms, and his eyes, when they settled on her, were distant and cold. "You must pay the price Christina. She and the child..."

Christina closed her lips tightly knowing the wrong words now would ruin everything. He was right. She needed to pay, and soon. Before it was all too late.

"I know. I'll fix this." Then she turned and left the room, her shoulders hunched and arms wrapped tightly around her middle.

"If you weren't my brother, I would kill you for that comment."

Vasya seethed. Right now he wanted to hit his brother. Pound him for the look he'd just seen in Christina's eyes. The guilt he knew she felt had become a heavier load.

The sight of her retreat would be burned into his mind forever, but for now, he had to say his piece to Gregori.

"This is my wife and my child. I will protect them anyway I can." Gregori kissed Serina's hair gently, wiping the tears trailing down her face.

Even as he looked down on Serina, Vasya felt an instant of terror... She was pale and still. But the rise and fall of her chest told him she still lived.

"You should cleanse and bind that wound." Now wasn't the time for grand gestures or angry words. Christina had been shattered, the small fragment of comfort she'd managed to amass, the sense of camaraderie that had been forged would be strained and she needed him more than Serina did.

"I need to find Christina and make sure she understands it's not her fault, no matter what you say." Gregori glanced away.

With a quick movement, he spun and left.

CHAPTER 20

Christina huddled on the bed, thoughts of what could have been chased madly around the inside of her mind.

Gregori was right, of course. The price had to be paid and soon. Maybe then she could discover Zuor's weakness.

Her nerves were stretched taut—the knowledge that Zuor had hurt Serina left her ill and shaky. "I won't let him do this again. No more. It has to end." She swiped at the tears on her face, before standing quickly. Her bag and keys were in the hallway and she took the chance, sprinting through the house, to grab them.

At the table, she stopped, her fingers creeping up to the necklace around her neck. Slipping it off only took seconds and she hurried to the kitchen. The bottom draw contained envelopes and she grabbed one from the top then scrawled Serina's name on it before dropping the necklace inside.

Vasya would throw a fit if he knew what she was going to do, but there really wasn't an option. She made for the front door and opened it with a snick. Christina thanked the fore-sight of keeping the barrels oiled as it closed softly.

The car sat in the driveway and she got in. Her body ached, though not as bad as the day before and she silently thanked Phil for driving them to see Dravens. That had given her a chance to heal sufficiently, and allowed for her to move more freely than she had since the accident.

Christina slipped the key into the ignition and the engine sparked, she wasted no time reversing into the empty street. Christina saw him run to the road as she accelerated off. It's the only way echoed in her mind.

"Oh God…" She moaned knowing she needed help to achieve her outcome. She drove for a few minutes until she found a quiet park and pulled the car over fishing around her bag for the phone. Hands shaking as she dialed. More than once she had to disconnect as her stomach roiled with fear. The blur of tears stung her eyes. Blinking furiously banished them.

She dialed again.

"Phil." His groggy voice filled the near silence.

"Phil? I need your help. Please?" Her throat tightened, knowing she was mad to attempt this so far from Vasya, but what other choice was there?

"Christina? Where are you?" His voice was tight.

"I'm at the park on the north side of the village. Not far from home."

"What the hell are you doing there? Where's your… Where's Vasya?"

She flinched at the mention of Vasya's name. "Look, I really need to see you. Tell me you can meet me."

"Okay, just give me a minute to write down your location." Through her phone came the sound of scratching. She imagined him writing down the details, and calmed herself.

"Stay there. I'll get to you as soon as I can."

Her stomach jittered as fear assailed her. *What the hell was I thinking?* If Zuor came upon her before she was ready he could drag her to the realms and this time she might not be able to break free. *I really didn't think this through, did I?* But going back wasn't an option because Vasya would watch her like a hawk now.

"I just have to hope Phil is strong enough to get me through." The words didn't inspire confidence though.

Day turned to night by the time she noticed the headlights piercing the darkness. Her nerves skittered like leaves on a blustery day.

Through the windshield, Christina watched as Phil parked the car. She watched as he climbed from it, his angry stalk as he moved towards her, but she remained seated in the car. This had to be on her terms.

Christina wound down the window and peered out.

"What the hell are you up to, Christina?" His voice mirrored the anger on his face.

" Zu... The demon attacked my sister. When I spoke with Galene, she suggested there might be a way to find out how to beat him. Vasya and I talked about it, but he said it's too dangerous. Now, Gregori... Gregori blames me for the attack on Serina." Her voice broke and she turned away, the despair she'd felt—a sense of being out of step with everyone who was dear to her—rose up again.

The gentle touch of his hand on her shoulder bolstered the fragile calm she managed to muster. "I need... I need somewhere I can sleep. Then I can slip into the realms and hopefully gather enough information to finish this. I can't just go to a hotel, though Phil. I need someone to help me. Right now, only you can do that." The words tumbled out and his face betrayed his shock.

"You're joking, right? After this demon has been

attacking you for... How long exactly?" His voice conveyed his incredulity at her request.

Christina looked away, shame rolling over her. "He hasn't always been like this. Just lately."

"Christina, I can understand why Vasya said no. It's dangerous. What if he holds you there and you can't get away?"

She'd thought of that already. "Then you call Vasya, or arrange for him to get to us." He looked stunned, surprised and more than a little shocked at her words.

"Look, we need information. The type we can only get if I can get back into the realms. The last few times, I've come to know a bit more about how the realms work. They feed on negativity. The more pessimistic or tired or negative I am the more damage he can do, right? So I have to feel good to carry out my plan." She reached out and grabbed the sleeves of his jacket, exerting enough pressure that he looked down into her face. "Please Phil. If I don't do this, he'll kill Serina. Or do something even worse. If we can defeat him—"

Phil's eyes closed. "He's involved in what's going on in Alvonia too. We could all do with the information, but you're taking a huge risk, Christina. I'm not sure we can keep you safe while you hunt the information that's needed."

"I know we can do this. I just need you to keep me safe." Vasya might never forgive her for asking Phil, but he'd already stated adamantly that she wasn't to take the risk. There really wasn't any other way as she saw it. If it also helped with the situation in Alvonia... She let the thought drift away. "I thought we could drop the car on the road verge outside the house then we could find somewhere I could sleep. That way Vasya will have the car if necessary, right?"

Phil looked unconvinced, but finally nodded. "If this goes wrong, I want it made clear to you and Vasya… I tried to talk you out of it."

He sighed as she gripped his fingers.

"Good. I'll follow you back to your place and leave the keys in the car." She'd already planned the next stage while waiting. She wouldn't leave the keys in the ignition, but she'd make it easy for him to find them, but by the time he did, they'd be gone. "Once we reach the house, you need to ring the home phone number. We can wait around until someone comes out of the house, so we can be sure he finds the keys. Then you drive off with me. Quickly. Right?" She gripped her fingers together, felt the sting of her nails on the palms of her hand.

"Whatever. At least that way the car won't get stolen." He gave her one last sour look. "You're sure I can't talk you out of this?"

"No"

"Fine." He stalked in the direction of his car and she waited for the roar of the motor before turning the key in the ignition of her vehicle. Rolling past him, she kept her eyes averted. The trip was swift and at the house she turned off the car, watching in the mirrors as he parked behind her. She fumbled for the keys, dragging them out of the slot before throwing them into the glove compartment.

As she headed to Phil's car he was dialing the house phone and the shrill ring cut the air in the quite street.

"What?" His tone was terse and she felt bad for putting him through this.

She grabbed the phone. "Vasya, the car is out the front. You need to come get the keys. They're somewhere in the car." Hanging up, Christina climbed inside and closed the car door.

The light flared above the door as it opened, Phil pulled smoothly out of the way and she looked back to see Vasya run onto the lawn. She disconnected the call and drove into the night.

CHAPTER 21

Phil's house was only minutes from hers, something she'd never known.

"Phil, why did you take so long?"

He grinned expansively. "I was elsewhere."

"Oh." His words and the half smile told her she didn't really need to ask the rest. He'd been busy. *With someone.*

When he offered her a glass of wine she accepted it, her hands shook so much she had to place it on the small coffee table or else splash herself.

Time ticked by and her anxiety grew as she mentally prepared to attempt this stealthy mission.

"You're sure you can do this?" Phil slid his hand over hers and pressed. She accepted the touch for a moment before drawing away.

"Yes. Whatever you do, don't wake me. Let me wake myself. Unless..." She sucked in a shuddering breath. "If I don't wake up in say three hours, then ring Vasya. You have the number."

"Why wait that long?"

His eyes narrowed and she ploughed on. "Because if it takes that long, I'll need his help."

Phil paled at her words.

"You're a good friend, Phil. I never knew how much until now."

He grimaced and her stomach knotted when he closed his eyes. "I would have been more if you'd let me."

Now it was Christina's turn to grimace. "Phil, I never…"

His eyes opened, his face soft and somehow sad. "No, I know. You never promised and I never asked. But I would have. I care…" He cleared his throat and she felt ashamed. How could she have never noticed before? "I care deeply for you Christina, but you've only ever wanted Vasya. I can see that now. But if you ever nee—"

She smiled and nodded, cutting off his words before he could say something they'd both regret. "*I know.* I wish I could have wanted you like that Phil."

She took a moment, enjoyed the last sip of the dry white wine, and thanked every deity that he took the hint. Sliding the glass on the table she closed her eyes, settled her emotions. "Time to get started. I'll just go to the bathroom."

In the small room, she splashed her cheeks with cold water, hoping to soothe the burning sensation stinging them.

His declaration hadn't been a total surprise, given she and Vasya had already deduced his attachment to her. Regret filled her. Phil was her friend and she never meant for him to think she wanted anything else.

"I never would have called him a friend before this. Maybe an acquaintance." She looked at herself in the mirror. Her critical gaze scanning her face, seeing the stark angles and deep shadows, her eyes weren't anything special

—she certainly wouldn't consider them piercing or any single color.

Her dark hair usually hung straight, though right now, tufts sat up. Christina dragged her fingers through it. At least it was long and healthy, she thought. Her single claim to beauty was probably her full lips, but she couldn't help thinking they weren't enough to make two men want her.

With a shrug she turned away.

"I just hope his infatuation melts away soon. That he finds a good woman one day." Truly, he was a kind and caring man, though she sensed loneliness in him.

A vision of Draven's blonde granddaughter entered her mind. She smiled, remembering his look when he'd seen Jelena... Christina shook the image away. *I'm not exactly brilliant at this wife thing, so I really shouldn't be meddling in anyone else's affairs.*

Pulling away from her thoughts, she sighed. Time was passing and here she was wasting time best employed getting into Zuor's realm.

She rested her hand on the bathroom door to steady herself. It took a tremendous effort to clear her mind of negative thoughts, but finally she was ready.

Christina opened the door and headed to the lounge, where Phil waited.

During her time in the bathroom, he'd been busy, pulling up a coffee table and placing a small bedside lamp on it and a glass of water. He'd even put sheets on the seat and a pillow.

She sniffed back the tears that rose, feeling deeply touched by his thoughtfulness. "Oh, Phil! You've done a marvelous job."

He smiled wanly and indicated to the reclining chair

beside the lounge. "I'll settle in here and keep watch. I have a book and the phone to keep me company."

Christina bent to remove her shoes. "You're okay with this? Me being here and entering his realm?"

"Yes. We can't leave you alone while you do this." His words had Christina stilling, one leg raised. But when he didn't say anything else, she shrugged and continued divesting herself of unnecessary clothing.

He retreated to his seat as Christina slipped back the top sheet, remembering the other times this had happened and how she'd ended up naked.

That thought left her stomach flip-flopping. "Uh Phil? Sometimes, I'm..." She gulped, embarrassment spearing her. "I... uh... wake up naked. It seems to be something to do with the crossover between the nightmare realm and reality. I'm not really sure how it works. I suppose it's some kind of magic."

"Oh..." The single word spoke volumes.

"Could you find a robe for me? Maybe slip it over the chair?" She couldn't look him in the eye for a moment.

He rose and she followed him with her gaze. Phil blushed and she giggled. Like that, the discomfort melted away.

When Phil returned to the room, he had a black silk robe hooked over his finger. She raised an eyebrow but she didn't say anything until he settled back into his seat.

"One last thing. If you do need to call Vasya, ask him to bring me some clothes." Then with heated cheeks she lay down, snuggling slightly to find a comfortable position. "Night Phil"

"Night Christina."

She closed her eyes and waited for sleep to overtake her.

It eluded her.

She moved—turned and squirmed.

Breathed deeply and tried to clear her mind.

The silence was un-nerving and she turned again, plumping the pillows and missing Vasya.

"Are you okay?" Phil's voice was strained.

"I'm fine. Just need to find the right spot." She kept her eyes closed, if she didn't know better, she'd guess a barrier had risen between her and sleep.

A yawn surprised her and she stretched once more, but sleep remained elusive.

Suddenly it occurred to her that maybe Zuor had worked out her plan. Was he strong enough to stop her sleeping? "Phil?"

He answered her whisper with a quiet, "What?"

"Do you think he…"

"Worked it out? I doubt it. You just need to relax."

Easier said than done, she thought sourly. Another thought taunted her: What if she never slept again? Panic rose and she had to swallow the frustration and fear. Beat it back with calming thoughts. Her mind replayed scenes from her childhood. Interludes that calmed her mind and gradually her body relaxed.

Finally, she dropped like a stone into the depths.

The ground was wet and cold and she had entered a different location. Normally she came to manacled and attached to the wall. Something she'd need to ponder later. Christina took a step and felt the sharp bite of gravel beneath her feet. As she gazed around, surprise filling her.

The soft drip drip of water echoed in the depths and she looked around, willing her eyes to grow accustomed to the dark.

This was unknown territory. She was somewhere she'd never seen before, although the gloom was the same—dark and perva-

sive. The air froze the moisture on her skin and she rubbed her arms to generate some heat.

"Come on, Christina, time to look around." She moved towards the wall, feeling the rough edges until she realized it was stone. A grotto?

Which way to go? Left or right? She tried to visualize the area but couldn't. She vacillated momentarily before deciding left was as good as anything.

Christine moved, sliding her feet along the rough surface. They hurt as she trod on sharp-edge stones but she refused to cry out, instead biting her lips.

This time she had the upper hand and she had to hold onto it.

Step-by-step she moved until finding an aperture. With careful fingers she inspected it. The large opening was higher than where she stood. A doorway? She peered carefully around the corner but couldn't see anything. "Nothing ventured, nothing gained."

She stepped through. The entrance gave way to a low-lit room. Statues stood in every imaginable position and she would have dearly loved to examine them, but time was short. Once he knew she was here, the danger would become extreme and she just knew he'd work it out sooner or later.

If in fact, he didn't already know.

That thought had her stomach clenching hard.

Christina scanned the room hunting for another doorway. It took precious moments to locate, then she debated whether to head straight across the open expanse or inch along the walls. After seconds of internal debate she scurried quickly to the next doorway, the whole time seeking a weapon to keep her safe. Nothing obvious caught her eye.

This time the room opened into a long corridor. Doors dotted its length and the chill, more extreme than before, froze her to the marrow.

The floors changed from rough stone, which pleased her. The surface now resembled uneven slabs of rock and stone. "I have to find my cell." *Her voice echoed slightly and she winced.*

She didn't know why, but instinct told her this corridor hid many secrets. She looked in doors, peered around corners and only stopped every now and again to remind herself she needed to be thorough but quick.

One door remained in the hallway and she peered within. Finally, she was sure this was the original cell. A large glasslike viewing platform took up an entire wall and she stepped forward.

"So, you've returned. Of your own volition, too. Excellent!"

Her heart stuttered at the voice. Zuor. Dear God! What have I done?

He laughed and the sound bounced off the walls while the hated manacles appeared at her wrists. A force propelled her backwards against the wall and she hit it with a thud, the breath whooshing from her body.

"I'm so pleased you could join me for my little show."

This time the glass shone as the daylight view burned her eyes. She spied flames and the scorch of heat licked at her once more naked body.

Sounds of screams filled the air and she wanted to cover her ears. To block it out.

Only one positive thought occurred and she grabbed it, letting it settle the knot that again formed in her belly.

His affinity was fire.

"You can't hold me Zuor. I'm not your servant." *He stalked closer, leering in until she could smell his fetid breath.*

"You were mine since before the cradle."

She swayed, unwilling to let him see her growing fear. "I'm free of you. You don't own me. Let me go."

He laughed and she quavered. Lord, what have I done in my arrogance? *It was too late to regret her actions, all she could do was deal with the situation at hand. To free herself from the prison she herself had entered.*

"You were promised to me before your birth. Before the birth of you mother even. Generations of your family belong to me. A contract made centuries ago, that you should enter servitude. You fought me all the way—never wanted to submit to my will and for a time that amused me. But no longer. Now you pay the price."

The metal encircling her wrists bit tightly and she cried out. "Let me go, please Zuor! I beg you, let me go." Desperation colored her tone.

He laughed loudly, before screwing up his face. "No, I shall never let you go." He spoke in a parody of her frantic tones. "I need you and your blood. The refreshment I obtain from your blood makes me feel good. But now you're here, you can watch your sister. She's mine now too, along with the brat she carries within her womb."

Through the window, Christina spied Serina, her eyes wild. Beyond a profusion of creatures, wiry and scaled, with skins of mottled orangey-red advanced in Serina's direction. Their claws extended as if ready to carve her flesh. "No Zuor! Please don't. Anything! Anything you want. Keep me if you must but release her!" Panic rose. The suffocating sensation nearly stripped her mind of the last shreds of sanity.

His answer was merely to extend one finger, the nail elongating before her gaze. The sound of her sister's screams battered her senses, but she ignored it. She had to make Zuor agree. If she gave him what he wanted, perhaps he would release Serina.

His nail grazed her skin, sliding over her. She couldn't contain the whimper of fear.

Each time she glanced in her sister's direction, her chest tightened further. Serina was pleading with the creatures, a shaking hand covering her belly and the tiny life growing there. Christina redoubled her resolve. For Gregori, Serina and their unborn child, she would accept this price.

"Say the words then Christina. Tell me you will submit to me."

"Please Zuor, I will, just release Serina first."

He growled his displeasure. "Say the words then I will decide."

Her mind froze. *He wasn't going to promise. I'll take any chance to see them safe.* She gulped down the lump of fear, her eyes settling on the scene before her, knowing that would lend strength to her conviction. "I will submit." Her words echoed in the tiny room.

She shivered and he smiled, a spark of red glinting in the dark. "And now you are my consort. Forever."

She flinched as he leaned in, his incisors lengthened before her horrified gaze before he punctured her chest above her breast, drinking deeply.

The suckling seemed to go on forever. Lethargy filled her, her knees trembled but she fought the blackness. *Whatever Zuor wanted, she would give him.*

Tears trickled down her face as he pulled away, this time with more care. "That's good my pet. Now you will rest."

Zuor straightened up and moved away, his body changing, fining down until it became human-like. The muscles rippled and grew, dark hair covered his head and she cried out. Before her stood Vasya. Or a facsimile that stank of sulfur. She nearly retched there and then.

"Serina? Release her. I'll do anything you ask, but please..." She pleaded hoping now he'd fed, and now that she'd agreed to his bargain, that he would give her this one boon.

"Not yet, my pet. You must still be punished and I can think of nothing more fitting. However, I will not kill her. Or the child."

He flicked some invisible lint from his shirt and she wanted to scream, "I didn't sacrifice myself for nothing! Please!"

She restrained the urge, knowing that to do so would anger him. Something she couldn't afford with her sister's fate hanging in the balance.

His voice changed too. "You are mine. You always were." *Then he left her there, in the darkness.*

Hot, scalding tears dripped down her face while she looked through the viewing window. She could still see Serina, fighting, screaming, while the creatures fed.

"I'm so sorry Serina! I never meant for this to happen."

As if she could hear Christina's words Serina lifted her bruised and bloodied face. Serina gazed directly at her and on her face Christina read cold hatred.

It pierced Christina to the soul. The cold finally surrounded her heart and she closed her eyes, unable to watch anymore.

CHAPTER 22

asya paced. Anger rode him hard. "Where has she gone? Why?" His hands clenched and unclenched as he scoured what he knew.

"I didn't think. I never meant..." Gregori's face flamed.

"Just—" He wouldn't look at Gregori, otherwise he'd regret his outburst later. "Not now, Gregori." Accepting Gregori's apology wouldn't be enough because he had a suspicion of what action she'd taken. Christina had left with Phil, hard on the heels of his brother's outburst. He'd seen the pain and sadness and knew it would be eating away at her.

Each jerky length of the room paced, saw him run a hand through his hair. Serina watched him quietly, her eyes shadowed and bruised. "She'll be okay. I'm sure of it." Her voice wavered and Vasya stopped.

"I don't know that she will. We thought everything would be fine, but she wanted to enter the nightmare realms to find a way to defeat him. To look for a weakness and I was going to watch over her. Keep her safe."

"She wouldn't do something like that, she's not stupid."

But Serina's words lacked conviction and he saw the shock and horror on Gregori's face.

"She felt guilty about the attack on Serina? Because of my words!" He clenched his fist and swallowed convulsively. "If Zuor finds her, we don't know what he'll do."

He turned back to Serina, noting the blaze of pale blue fire at her neck. The necklace had been left in an envelope, addressed to Serina. The only armor they had to keep Christina safe. "That's why she took that off. To protect Serina."

He curled his hands, searching the clock face. Three hours. She'd been gone long enough to enter the realms, to be in danger: For Zuor to find her and take his revenge.

"What about..." Serina stopped and he turned back to her. "What about if you slept? Could you help her?"

The thought stunned him. He didn't know and it was too late to call on Jelena or Dravens for information. Perhaps he could take the chance.

There wasn't much else he could do right now. He nodded with a jerk and made for the seat while Gregori watched with lips compressed. Serina screwed up her face, her eyes sheened with welling tears.

"If I don't wake in an hour by myself, wake me." He settled himself willing the tension to leave his body.

He thought positive thoughts. He remembered Christina telling him she thought that was part of the key, while he hunted for a modicum of relaxation. The clock ticked in the quiet room and he focused on the rhythmic sound.

The more he tried to settle, breathing in and out, the further away sleep crept.

Panic rose in his breast. *What if I can't reach her*? He breathed slowly, counting in his mind each exhalation until the numbers became laborious.

The sound and movement jarred him and he fought to keep from opening his eyes.

He needed to focus and settle. He'd be no good to Christina if he couldn't control his reactions.

An itch settled in his back and he tried to ignore it, refused to rub his body along the seam of the chair.

It didn't go away, but grew stronger.

Fury rose and he snapped open his eyes, Gregori and Serina watched him, hands clasped together. "I can't sleep."

Serina wailed and Gregori patted her on the back. "What have we done?" He groaned and Vasya restrained his angry outburst. It wouldn't help now.

An argument wouldn't solve the problem. Without thought, Christina had been pushed into a dangerous corner, one where she was desperate enough to take her chances with Zuor.

Bile burned his throat. He stilled himself, until that too subsided.

The phone rang, breaking the spell and he hurled himself from the chair, snatching up the receiver. "Vasya? She won't wake up. She told me to ring you if this happened." *Phil.* Vasya closed his eyes. "She said also to bring clothes."

He grunted and hunted for paper and pen. "How do I find you?"

Phil gave rapid-fire instructions, which he wrote down.

"I'll be there as soon."

Gregori stood and so did Serina. "We'll come with you." He turned away, savage emotions warring.

He couldn't face them right now, so nodded and moved to the bedroom, opened the cupboard and wrenched jeans and shirt from within. Next, he rifled the drawers finding underwear, shoving them into a bag.

The rage deep inside told him the wrong words right now would only inflame things further. Without a word he pocketed the keys for the car and house then marched to the front door.

Serina and Gregori waited silently, and he was grateful for that small mercy. He felt brittle, cold and yet almost incandescent with rage. She had taken this step to protect their siblings and neither of them understood the enormity of the risks she had taken, again.

He did.

He'd seen the cell, the way she had been naked and bruised. Zuor didn't just want her blood, he wanted her body. Something Vasya refused to let him have.

Gregori and Serina followed him out to the car and he jerked the door open without a word. They climbed in, the silence colder than he ever before experienced. The gulf between him and his brother was wide and deep.

The car swayed as they slammed the doors and he turned the key in the ignition, before reversing down the drive. Vasya accelerated, paying careful attention to the instructions Phil had given him.

He'd memorized them, but knowing one wrong turn would cost time, he checked them again as he drove through the night, searching for the building at the edge of town.

Ten minutes later, he pulled up outside a small stucco house. The street around them was quiet, and for an instant a thought flashed. *This is what Christina deserved. A house in a safe street. Somewhere to raise children.*

Unless he could reach her, none of those things would happen.

Only one house was illuminated. He knew at once, it was the right place when Phil stepped onto the porch.

In the man's stance he read concern and worry and his

gut tightened further. She was in danger, and he couldn't help her. Not yet.

He hurried out the car and up the path.

*V*asya dropped down by the chair, his heart nearly stopping when he laid eyes on her. She was pale and cold to the touch. A hint of blue ringed her mouth and eyes. He chafed her hands while every now and then a slight shiver racked her body.

"Christina? Wake up!" But she didn't and he knew he would have to find a way to enter the realms.

"How long?" He stared at Phil.

"Over three hours now. I noticed she was cold probably about two hours ago."

Vasya grunted. So far she wasn't thrashing about. That was probably a blessing. "I need the chair. I'm going to try to go in and get her."

Gregori nodded as if understanding his plan and pushed it next to the lounge. Vasya lurched into it. This was the only way he could think of. "If I sleep, wake me within an hour. No longer." Then threading his fingers through hers, he closed his eyes, willed himself to be still, searching for a way into the realms.

He dropped down, into the silence and darkness, casting about for which way to go. Vasya moved silently. Power vibrated through his body and he knew he was stronger than the last time he'd been here.

He waited in the darkness as his sight adjusted to the gloom. At least the room was empty—a small mercy. This was not where she was though. He'd need to find her quickly.

A doorway lay just across from where he stood. He scanned

the room before moving. The skittering noises around his feet turned his stomach, knowing what he had seen last time... The small rat-like creatures had been heading towards Christina's blood.

A long passage stretched out before him, it was barely lit by the pale glow-baskets stationed intermittently on the rough-hewn walls.

He didn't check anything on the walls or floor too closely.

Christina was alone here and he had to find her. That was now his entire reason for being. A premonition of danger urged him on. Sounds filtered from beyond and he scanned the small rooms around him with quick movements, fearing discovery. If anything saw him, then Christina would be lost. Unacceptable.

He found a corner to hide behind as he saw a chuckling Zuor wandering slowly down the hall, a male slung under his arm. At least it wasn't Christina and for a second his heart lightened.

The man struggled weakly and as he watched, Vasya's eyes picked up facts that nearly turned his stomach. Welts, old and bloodied crisscrossed the man's back, his hair limp, lank. The greasy locks dragging on the hard cold floor. Ribs and his spinal column clearly outlined under skin that sagged.

The weak struggles and cries of "No. Please don't hurt me," died away and the burn of bitter bile rose once more in Vasya's throat.

Had Christina been subjected to this? How long had passed for her in this horrific subterranean world?

Vasya swiped a shaking hand over his face, sweat slicked his skin, it stung with a chill that invaded his body. Once he was reasonably sure that Zuor was too far to see or hear him, Vasya straightened and proceeded cautiously.

At an intersecting part of the corridor, he peered carefully to the side.

This was one he was sure he remembered and he moved as

silently as possible, his skin prickling. "Where the hell is she?" He hadn't realized just how big the dungeon actually was.

I could look forever and never find her. The thought stole his breath, filling him with a fear he'd never before experienced. Worse even than when she'd disappeared eleven years ago. At least then, her parents had warned him she was safe. This time he had no such intelligence to rely on.

A door lay open and he peered within, his stomach turning. This time the sight before him pierced him...

A viewing window had opened and he could hear and see something that looked like Serina and she—it, he corrected himself— was surrounded by hundreds of ugly creatures. They appeared to be feeding from her.

If he hadn't left her safely in Gregori's care, he would have believed it was her.

The Serina-creature's hand carefully covered the curve of her belly. The sight sickened him.

A whimpering sound caught his attention and there she was: Christina was once more naked and chained to the wall. Her body scored and bleeding.

"Christina." He breathed. She didn't raise her head. Not even to acknowledge him. "Christina, it's me. Vasya. I've come to take you away."

Her eyes were dull and downcast. Her skin bruised and scraped and at her breast he saw the dry crusted blood that showed Zuor had fed from her.

"Oh God! What has he done to you?" He lurched forward, ready to free her from her bonds when a large booming laugh filled the air.

"You think to take her from me?"

Vasya stiffened. "She's mine."

Zuor materialized beside him and pointed to Christina. "Wake slave!"

Christina lifted her head and he saw the emptiness. The desolation.

It felt as if her soul was shriveled to a pinprick. He wanted to howl as rage spewed.

"You can have her... If she agrees to leave."

What? What game is Zuor playing? *But he could and would take her. She would want to come home.*

"Christina? I've come to take you home."

She shrank against the wall, moving her head from side to side with a jerky motion. "No. No I need to stay here." Confusion filled him.

"Christina? Dushka, I have come to take you home."

She moaned and dropped her eyes. "No. I have to stay here. Leave without me. Go home and forget I exist. Please." She breathed the last word and closed her eyes.

"No! Christina..."

Zuor laughed. "She will not go with you. Now leave, flyer. This is not your realm but mine."

Anger coursed through his veins. "No! I will take her."

"You cannot, weakling. She has spoken and you must leave." Zuor waved his hands and he felt a stirring in the air. He started to dematerialize, as Zuor fought to eject him. Vasya used every ounce of willpower, forcing himself to stay in this place, but it only worked long enough for him to hear Christina's words.

"This is for Serina. Then he'll let her go..."

The room shifted into focus and he panted. The others gathered around. "Why hasn't she woken?" Serina reached for her sister and he grabbed her hand, his body sucking the warmth from her skin.

"No!"

Serina jerked away from his touch and he turned, back to the woman lying on the seat. "Christina!" He gripped her hand, alarmed that it seemed even colder than before. His chest heaved as he looked to Serina, Gregori and Phil hovering.

"We're going to need more help to free her." He stood, wobbling. "She refuses to come back."

He gathered every bit of strength before looking into Serina's eyes. "He has one like you and she believes you're in the realm." Serina paled.

"But you can make her believe it isn't Serina, can't you?" Phil's voice was hoarse as if he'd spent hours screaming.

His mind flung up the view of the Serina-creature. "It's not... She's seen..." He couldn't bring himself to describe what he'd seen. The emotionally destroyed Christina he'd left behind. "We have to make her believe it isn't you." He rubbed a shaking hand over his face, playing everything over in his mind while his stomach roiled.

But while his mind called to her, all that answered was cold silence.

CHAPTER 23

*M*orning came slowly, while he paced and worried. Step, turn, look at Christina then ball his fist. He had to fight to release the tension before retracing the action again, until the first fingers of dawn crept over the horizon.

At some point, Gregori shoved a hot coffee into his hands. He'd drunk it without thought before he noticed the empty cup in his hand.

It felt like a symbol.

Right now, he was sure his heart was empty, broken by the sight of Christina in that dark cell: Beaten and cowed.

"She'll be alright, Vasya. She's stronger than you give her credit for." Serina's voice broke through the silence. He turned and attempted a smile, but all that emerged was a brittle grimace.

"Serina, if you could have seen her. The things he showed her." His mind shied away again. "The trick he played on her mind to get her to agree to stay was cruel. He'd showed her what could possibly be her worst fear." He had to turn away the horror of the view fresh in his mind. He couldn't possibly convey the sight...

"He's been feeding from her, you said?" Gregori spoke slowly and he nodded.

He looked over to where she lay. Serina had kept a vigil over her, tugging the blanket the few times she'd moved. Her chest rose and fell in small increments. Until she was released from her bonds, he knew she wouldn't regain consciousness. She'd given up the fight for herself.

Fresh bruises bloomed on her flesh, purple blue and orange.

The knowledge that he'd failed her tore at him, scratched its way through his emotions, tearing at his psyche and he wanted to scream and rage.

If he could get hold of Zuor, he'd make the bastard pay.

"I'll kill him. I promise you... I'll tear him apart." His voice was raw, and his head ached.

He began pacing again.

From the corner of the room, Phil watched. He was the only one who hadn't spoken while Gregori attempt to placate Vasya. Vasya was aware of the way Serina tried to keep Christina warm. As the sun crested the horizon, he rose and checked his watch, then walked to a small table against the wall and lifted the handset from the telephone cradle, passing it to Phil.

Exhaustion fogged Vasya's mind. "Dravens? This is Phil. We have a problem and need you and Jelena."

Vasya straightened and a rush of adrenaline surged.

Phil listened intently. "Yeah. Maybe ten minutes?" Vasya waited, every muscle in his body tense as Phil nodded at the phone, then hung up.

After Phil broke the connection he turned back. "Serina,

you need to stay here and watch over Christina. Do you still have your amulet?"

Serina nodded and Phil turned to Gregori and Vasya. "You two need to come with me."

Vasya felt torn. He needed to get Christina out of the nightmare realms, but it meant leaving her with only Serina to watch over her. He didn't want to leave. "What about..." He indicated to Serina but Phil just shook his head.

"Dravens said she should be fine while she wears the amulet. Zuor can't hurt her at the moment and he won't touch Christina here as she's in his realm."

Vasya shook his head. How had it all become so damned complicated? All he'd wanted was his wife and a life together.

He knew the truth now that their lives had always been compromised and would continue to be so while Zuor lived. It was too late to unlearn what he knew and he didn't want to. If he didn't do this, he wouldn't be able to help Christina. Vasya sighed and followed Phil from the house and into the car.

The drive was quick, and he paid little notice to the road, focused on his internal struggles.

When the car stopped, he shoved out of the vehicle. Dravens and Jelena hurried towards them, their faces drawn in the early morning light.

"What the hell happened?" Dravens demanded, and Phil quickly explained while Vasya's stomach tumbled at the memories. Jelena looked at him.

She pierced him with her gaze. "You need to ascend now."

"What? And just how am I supposed to do that?" The anger he'd reined in broke loose. "My wife's imprisoned in some alternate dimension cave and you're telling me I need to ascend? You said this would happen once I'd found my mate. It hasn't yet."

Jelena raised her hand as if to halt the spewing rage-filled words. He spun around, ready to walk away, when a foot was thrust out, tripping him. If not for Gregori he would have hit the floor and he gave a furious snarl, throwing himself from his brother's hold. Vasya made to turn but once more she tackled him, scraping something along his back.

Vasya cried out, bearing his teeth while feeling a rippling pain spread through him.

The sound of tearing flesh filled the air and he screamed. Vasya's body convulsed, muscles and sinews tore. He contorted against the pain slicing through his body.

His concentration narrowed as torment filled his mind. "What. Have. You. Done?"

Once more his spine bowed while tears coursed down his face.

Vasya heaved and retched, falling into the dirt.

Lost in a world of constant torture that seemed unending, and the tearing of his back had him writhing in agony.

Then finally the pain stopped, receding as quickly as it had overwhelmed him.

A voice, Gregori's muttered "Oh my God!"

He lay supine, his body limp and wrung out.

Jelena's feet filled his view. "Get up Vasya."

He willed his body to move, but his balance was off and he dropped forward, reaching out with his hands to brace himself, scraping his knees.

"You can't just lie there. Get up. You need to save Christina." He wondered if Jelena would attack him if he laid still.

He refused to give up and dug his fingers into the dirt, shoving upward 'til he regained his feet. His arms wobbled and his legs felt like limp noodles but he finally faced the woman who'd done whatever this was, to him.

This time he felt light. Not just lightheaded, but his entire body seemed disconnected from the ground.

When he looked to Gregori and Phil, it was to see their stunned expressions. Dravens and Jelena just looked smug. He snarled and dove forward but Gregori moved, cutting off his path.

"Wait, Vasya." Gregori's eyes looked over his shoulder, his face pale and shocked.

He pushed Gregori aside and made his way toward Jelena but she stood her ground, a grin splitting her face.

"You'll do."

He snarled again and her smile broadened.

"Now you ascend. Warrior, it's time to begin your training."

He stopped. "Ascend?"

She nodded. "You didn't think that pain was for nothing, did you? It was certainly faster than any wing birth I've witnessed, but quite impressive. Most men would have passed out from the pain."

Ascended? Wing Birth? What was she talking about? He caught a flash of blue and grey as he turned. The flash moved with him.

"You've got wings now, brother." Gregori's words stunned him.

"Wings?"

"Yeah. In grey and blue."

His heart beat fast in his chest. "You're joking, right?" But in his soul he knew.

Ascended. Oh yeah. Now he had a chance at beating Zuor. He grinned and the way Phil stepped back, he knew it was cold and scary. *Perfect.*

CHAPTER 24

*V*asya snarled. What looked simple for Jelena wasn't quite so easy for him. Sweat poured off him and he stank from the hours of exertion under the heat of the sun.

Each hour that passed he grew angrier. He let that anger feed his strength. He did this for Christina. She was still there. Alone and unprotected in the frigid depths of her own personal hell.

Once more Jelena goaded him. "You won't be any good to her if you can't summon your sword." He glared at her. *Does she think I don't know that?*

He knew the words were meant to urge him on, instead they just angered him and he bared his teeth. "I'll get this even if it kills me!" The longer he was gone, the more danger to Christina.

Sucking in a deep breath he resumed searching deep inside himself, seeking the blue light. Just as he'd done countless times before today, he closed his eyes and a flicker caught his attention. In the distance lay the spark of blue fire that would banish the dark.

He reached out with his mind, calling the flames to him just as Jelena instructed him to do. They swelled and grew larger before his entranced gaze. Not quite corporeal, but he could see it—feel the heat and hear the crackle of sound. The flickering movements wavered in and out. He strained, just a little further his mind stretching, and they settled and assumed a more solid form.

In his hand lay a sword, molded to his grip. He grinned.

I've done it! He wanted to roar in triumph. *Now I can defeat Zuor!*

The sword wavered in his hand and he grunted, an empty pit opening in his belly.

The metal weapon disappeared.

"No!" He bellowed, his anger reverberating through the woods. "What the fuck happened?" He opened his eyes and Jelena scowled at him.

"You have to be one with it. Not see it as a blade to exact retribution. Try again." She stabbed a finger in the air, pointing to him. He growled, closing his eyes.

This time the light was there, waiting. *Ready for him.* He focused and the sensation filled him, he breathed out. The simple act steadied him. He let the tension flow away from every part of his being.

Then it came: The warm flow trickling down arms and legs, his skin goose-bumping in reaction.

This time when the sword appeared, it wavered once and Vasya blew out, releasing the thoughts of anger and hate. He could feel the weight distributed evenly through his grip.

He opened his eyes slowly and Jelena smiled. "Much better. Now send it away again."

Vasya blinked and it left. "How?"

"You have to make it go. Imagine it disappearing from

your hand. That is the way to control the magic. You have to command it."

He willed it gone and it shimmered, before winking out of sight. His body reacted to the loss of the powerful tool.

"It will become attuned to you. Now bring it back without closing your eyes."

"How?" Desperation colored his voice, the sun was directly overhead and he was drenched with sweat.

"Concentrate on the sensation, warm, heavy, prickly... Whatever is your trigger?"

Warmth... He listened and concentrated, not looking with his eyes but his senses. A breeze... He focused, letting the cool wind brush over him. The hairs of his legs and arms stood on end while the warm rush invaded his body.

Vasya embraced it. This time the sword didn't waver at all, it settled in his hand and he welcomed the weight, his eyes scanned the glowing pommel and blade. He clutched it, the warm handle molding to his grip.

It balanced beautifully in his hand. It felt perfect, like an extension of his arm and he moved slowly, letting the blade slide gracefully through the air. Sunlight flashed over the elaborately detailed guard. Along the blade, the scrollwork was dotted with pale blue stones and he grinned dazzled by his achievement.

"Right. I could show you any number of moves, but the most effective ones we sky flyers use come without any conscious thought. After all, it's not like learning any tradi-tional swordplay. These swords are part of us—a physical manifestation of our power. We don't plan our moves, they are..." He watched as she hunted for the word. "I guess they're instinctive. We're born to be warriors. However, there is one more gift I can give you."

Lightning swift, Jelena turned, striking Gregori across

the back with the flat of her sword. He moved swiftly while the blue orbs glowed brightly against Gregori's skin. His mind churned even as he went to block her unwarranted attack on his brother.

Jelena reached out her hand, stopping him.

Where she'd struck his brother on the back, small slits appeared and grey green tips poked out by Gregori's shoulder blades.

The fight in Vasya melted away.

Realization dawned as the slits widened, droplets of clear liquid seeped and feathers peeked out. His brother had slumped to the ground writhing in agony.

Vasya remembered the pain, his stomach twisting, but it was necessary if Gregori hoped to Ascend.

"Hang on, Gregori. It will soon be over." His brother howled and scrabbled at the dirt while the wings emerged, slowly at first, then speeding up as his skin tore to allow the wings to emerge. The intricate feathers were wet at first but once they had fully exited his brother's body they unfurled and dried in the sunlight.

He looked at Jelena as his brother cried out in agony and noted the smile of satisfaction on her face.

"We don't have time to teach him everything yet, but if you show him the use of his power, he will be able to stand guard over his wife." She glanced down at Gregori who lay quietly on the ground. Then she gripped Vasya's arm hard and he winced. "You'll have to make it quick, though. Based on my experience, I'd say time is running short for Christina. You'll have to be quick to save her."

Jelena released him, and he crouched beside his brother. "Next time you come to me though, I will teach you how to fly."

He nodded soundlessly. Gregori rolled over looking pale

and unsteady. Vasya gripped his shoulders. "We have to hurry." Gregori grunted and met his gaze with narrowed eyes while Vasya hefted him to his feet.

"Now, pay attention and hold out your hand. Make a cup of it." Gregori did so, but nothing appeared and he snarled.

Jelena crowded him, her voice stern. "Vasya, project your sword." This time, without conscious effort it appeared and Jelena reached out. She grabbed one of the blue stones from it, holding it in the sunlight so it sparkled.

The sword vibrated and a glow began where the stone had been removed. The metal heated, jerking in his grip, then as quickly as it had started, the movements ceased and in the spot where the one had been removed, another had taken its place.

"The stones contain some of your essence." His eyes narrowed and even as he framed the thought, Jelena placed the single stone in his hand. "Give it to Gregori."

The look he gave Jelena must have been uncomprehending because she sighed. "By giving it to your brother, you can communicate between realms. Gregori, curl your hands around the stone." With an angry look he did so, growling slightly. "Cup it in your hand."

A bright blue bubble shone in the sunlight and, against his will, he was intrigued as to what would happen next. "Vasya, you do the same."

A twin globe appeared and he could see himself. Hell, he could see what Gregori could, he surmised. He smiled. He'd be able to show Christina exactly what Gregori could see. He could reassure her.

"I won't teach you how to fold your wings. Too much time has passed. You need to hurry and go get your mate."

❄

uor appeared in front of her. This time she could barely summons a grimace. Her body ached and she was cold... So cold. Through the barrier she could see Serina resting against the rocks. Christina had honestly thought, and hoped, Zuor would have released her sister, instead he'd taunted Christina with the sight of Serina feeding the creatures. The horrific view tore at her psyche until no more tears remained. Now she felt empty. Spent.

She remained tense, with her arms stretched above her head accepting her punishment. Her muscles and tendons screamed in pain, and she bit her lip, the coppery taste of blood filling her senses.

"So, little slave, you have finally learned not to fight me." He grazed her skin with a sharp edged claw. Christina was sure he had other indignities planned for her, but she no longer cared. How long had they been here? There'd been no day or night to help her understand how much time passed, all she knew was watching the creatures with her sister left her aching with regret and anger.

At least they seemed sated. For now.

Her stomach cramped with hunger but she ignored it. Two of his ugly creature minions had brought her food, but the sight of it had left her feeling nauseous. When she had complied with Zuor's demands that she eat, it had left her retching.

Her bladder stung with the need to empty itself and this time she couldn't contain the moan. "Zuor, please... I need..."

His eyes sparkled at the pleading tone of her voice. "Soon pet. Right now, you have one more lesson to learn." He licked his lips and she shuddered. What could he possibly still wish her to learn that she hadn't already? He'd taught her that he gloried in causing her pain, in watching her distress. That he was brutal and evil.

In his mind, it was clear he saw her as his slave, to do with as he wished. The only thing he hadn't done was...

"No." *Fear pulsed. He was going to rape her and she was tied to the damned wall. She'd agreed to whatever, not realizing he would go quite this far. She tugged and pulled against the metal restraints.*

"You are my pet," *he jeered.* "You will do my bidding!"

Slap!

The brutal blow to her face left her senses swimming, her cheek stinging and tears leaked down her face. "Please Zuor. No! Not that!"

Her mind screamed in denial. This time the graze across her skin wasn't gentle. He raked her left breast, leaving her crying out in pain. Blood flowed, warm and tangy in the dank cell.

What have I done to deserve this? Which Gods have I angered?

"*I have waited for you. Showed you what will befall your sister should you not cooperate, when I should have killed her and taken you as I wanted. But was I not merciful?*" *He laughed ominously, stretching his arms wide in a parody of evangelical showmanship.*

She'd feared his civility was little more than a fragile veneer, but now she added insanity to her list of worries. It seemed her denials had pushed him further to the edge. "Now you shall know the pleasures of Zuor."

He gripped her breast and squeezed hard. "Every inch of you, your flesh and your blood belongs to me." *His hand trailed down her body, over the plane of her stomach toward the curls at the apex of her thighs.*

"No! You can't! Please Zuor! Anything... Just not that!"

"I will, because you're mine. You gave yourself to me! Remember?" *The memory burst into her brain making it throb and pulse. She fought the intrusion and he swore viciously.*

Zuor raised one hand and a long dark whip appeared. Bile rose in her throat and she stared horrified at the swishing leather in his hand.

He swung it with a crack.

She screamed as pain exploded down her side.

She jammed her legs together focusing on her bladder, hoping it wouldn't release. That would be one indignity too far. The whip swung again and she cried out once more, the pain biting deeply.

A light flashed—shimmering blue in the darkness.

Surely it was a figment of her imagination, giving her some relief from her fears before she passed out? How she hoped for that! Only that could be a truth in this place of horror and subjugation. She would accept almost anything to escape.

She could barely breathe, her pulse thrumming wildly as the blood in her body surged, driving adrenaline to every tiny nerve ending. She tugged one last time before her legs collapsed, the only thing holding her upright was the manacles' attached to the wall.

The light grew and Zuor stopped mid-strike, arm pulled back and whip quivering with readiness. Fear crept across his face, for an instant a seed of rebellion grew in the pit of her stomach, but it died away at his snarl. "You're mine, slave. Remember your sister will pay for your indiscretions!"

Christina choked back a cry as he slammed his hand against her face, each claw tearing at the flesh of her cheek. Warm blood dribbled over bare skin and tears leaked from aching eyes.

The light grew, large and bright until she could see Vasya— once more surrounded by the glow.

His gaze settled on her, shocked before he turned with an angry roar, baring his teeth to Zuor. "You will pay for your actions!" This time, there was something different about him. She wanted to cower away from the light.

It stung her eyes and showed every inch of her humiliation.

The urge to cry rose, but there were no tears left. Instead, she moaned as the muscles of her overstretched arms protested.

Determination etched his face, he extended one arm and a shining sword appeared, dotted with small blue orbs.

"She's mine!" Zuor roared but Vasya didn't retreat.

Instead, he advanced on the demon who hurried away from the light and the now extended weapon. "You cannot take her. She agreed!" He flung the words at Vasya who stopped, as if a wall had risen between him and Zuor and Christina.

"You lied to her. You made her believe that was Serina."

Zuor grinned. "You cannot prove she isn't. She won't believe you."

The sword disappeared and Vasya cupped his hands. An orb appeared and Zuor looked dumbfounded. "No! It cannot be!"

Christina could see herself and Phil. Her eyes closed, her face battered while beside her Serina crouched, crying. Her sister was calling to her. Pleading with her to come home. "Serina." The words were low and weak, and a flicker of doubt grew in her mind. Could it really be? Was Zuor tricking her?

As if he could read her mind, Vasya gazed at her, pain and regret filled his eyes.

"They are waiting for you Christina. That..." He jerked his other hand to the viewing window, "That isn't Serina. It's a creature called up by Zuor. But it's not real. Serina is waiting for you, tending you. Can't you feel her warm touch on your brow? How tenderly she leans forward to kiss your forehead?"

A sensation wavered within her. She could feel it: The touch of her sister caring for her body. "A trick?" Her mind stretched, seeking the truth. "Serina isn't here?"

"She's waiting for you, worrying. Can you feel her touch?"

Zuor roared in anger but Christina closed her eyes accepting Vasya's words.

"Vasya? Take me home." The well of strength that had kept

her upright fled and she collapsed. Vasya raced forward, the shield between them dissolving.

Everything Zuor had told her, and everything she'd seen was nothing more than a lie.

No longer was she bound to Zuor in this horror-filled dungeon. She could leave. She gathered the tattered remains of her pride and smiled at Vasya hoping and praying he was right.

The last sound she heard was Zuor screaming at her that she was his...

Christina came to with a rush. She shuddered and shook in reaction while her body screamed in pain. "Vasya?" The weakness in her voice reminded her of the terror she had felt in the nightmare realms.

Her eyes stung with the unfamiliarity of the bright light, but she could clearly see Serina. "You're here... Not there? He doesn't have you?"

She made to rise, her body protesting even as she noted her nakedness. Every muscle screamed and ached; her face itching and she lifted a hand, swallowing hard as she noted the blood on her fingertips.

Vasya sprang forward, and she let him fold his arms around her, scorching her with the heat of his body. "You're safe now. I'll never let him take you again."

He spoke roughly, folding her close and tight. The pain receded as she welcomed his careful embrace. The tears flowed—she needed to let the pain and terror go before it overwhelmed her. Vasya held her tight, his warmth filled her, along with his love.

Gradually she settled lying back against the cushions making a mental assessment of her injuries. She was damp.

Her body covered in grime and blood. "Uh Vasya? I need to go shower." Embarrassment filled her. What had they seen? Heard?

He grunted wordlessly, pulling the bedding tighter around her and lifted her against his chest. She gasped as pain wracked her.

"Stay still. I'll attend to your wounds in the bathroom." His words helped her cling to the fragile shell of failing sanity.

Memories washed over her riding her hard. Zuor had touched her. Had tried to violate her.

What would Vasya think? Her stomach dipped. She wanted to shrink from Vasya's touch before he could show his disgust of her. He wouldn't want her now. The conviction broke her heart and she bit down heavily on her lip.

In the bathroom he dropped her legs to the ground and she turned away. "I'm sorry you have to see me like this." She wished a hole would open up and swallow her. Humiliation stained her skin with heat.

"Christina, you did nothing wrong. You only wanted to save your sister. You were prepared to give up everything so she and her child had a chance at a future. You were willing to surrender your life. In my eyes that makes you special. There aren't many people in this world who would give so selflessly."

Despite his words, she refused to look at him. *How can I ever face him again? Or myself?*

A soft finger curled under her chin and tugged her face up. "Never be ashamed of doing what you felt was right. No one in that room was disgusted by you, or your actions. The only negative emotion they felt was anger that you had to endure Zuor's torture."

She gulped again. "I really... I really need a shower." She tried to pull away. "Could you just..."

Vasya shook his head. "You won't get rid of me that easily." He tugged her close as she fought him.

"Dammit Christina, let me help you." His muttered words made her feel worse. Now she'd angered him too.

Fool! "You can't want me after..." The words were torn from her mouth and the look he gave her filled her with horror and shame.

"Not want you? Christina, I would walk into hell to find you. Nothing you did was shameful."

"But he..." She choked on the words. "He touched me. He was going to..."

Understanding shone in his eyes and his lips flattened. "Did he? Did he rape you?"

Hair flew as Christina shook her head. "He was going to, when you..." She shrugged, rising up on wobbling legs and moved away from him.

Strong arms reached for her, pushing away the stained bed clothing. "Even if he had, I'd still love you." Strong emotions echoed in his voice as he pulled her close, kissing her tenderly.

"How could you love me, still? Look what he did to me. To us."

"My love isn't weak or dependent on how you look, Christina. I see your heart and the strength of character that allowed you endure his torture. I love you more each day." The words were a balm to her soul and she sighed, wanting to accept them at face value. "Let me show you."

She searched his face, but there was no hint of disgust, just the strain that flattened his lips and narrowed his gaze. With a tiny nod of assent he let go of a shuddering breath.

Slowly he removed his clothing, his eyes never leaving hers, before carrying her to the shower stall. It closed softly, a barrier between them and the outside world. Vasya wrenched on the taps and glorious warm water sprayed down on her.

The heat invaded her body, melting the ice that had settled around her heart.

Cuts, slices, abrasions and the whip marks stung but she hung on to Vasya. Heat flowed back into her body, washing away the scent and blood that clung to her.

She'd attained some measure of understanding of Zuor, and his dark ways, the lies and subterfuges as well as how to defeat him. It was clear it took the blue light and Vasya's abilities to accomplish that. But there had to be more.

The one thing she'd gathered during her time in the dungeon was her knowledge of his affinity. It had been evident with the brimstone scent he left behind. The shroud he surrounded himself in, just like the sulfurous scent that he carried wherever he went. Fire was his weakness.

They would need something cold to douse the flames within him. The ones that fed his abilities

Vasya gently rubbed soap on her body, then washed it off, stroking away the memories and pain. Finally done, he slid strong arms around her waist and tugged her close. Christina wanted to melt into him, to take every inch of emotion he offered.

"I'm so sorry you felt you had to do that alone. I never wanted that."

She felt him swallow convulsively and she closed her eyes. Deep wells of pain and love warred within her. "You came for me."

"I promised you I wouldn't let him harm you. I failed again. Not much of a protector am I?" The pain in his voice cut like a knife.

"Don't you dare take responsibility for his actions. I made my decision. I was sure I could find out—" She swallowed, remember how hurt she'd been by Gregori's words. How she'd ached at seeing Serina so still while Zuor held her in his grip. The pain lashed at her, but she'd made the choice. She had to trust Vasya otherwise she'd be a hollow shell forever. "His affinity is fire."

He kissed her forehead and she frowned. Maybe he hadn't heard her? "Fire. We should be able to fight him with your sword and water." This time he nodded then rested his chin on the top of her head and rubbed his hands carefully up and down her spine, the only place that was unmarred by Zuor, though it was scratched and aching.

She shivered, her mind screaming with terror. She needed to pull away, before anyone could hurt her again. She had to protect herself, but confusion clouded her mind. This was Vasya. Her husband. Not Zuor. He'd never beat her to make her submit. Her stomach curdled. "Vasya?"

"I heard you. But right now, I'm just soaking up the fact that you're alive and here with me."

She moved away and hissed as her body protested.

"Let me." He reached over and turned off the taps then carefully lifted her into his arms and carried her from the stall. With a quick movement he jerked two towels from the rails and slipped it around her as best he could, single-handed, then threw the other over his shoulder.

*H*e felt her in his arms, as he laid with her on the bed. Her skin torn and bruised and he couldn't escape the reminder of the chances she had taken. Pain lanced him. She'd suffered so much. More than any woman should have to bear.

He traced a scar, probably from a brutal feeding, half healed with the redness fading to a dark pink. Her flesh was adorned with half healed bruises and it gutted him. Yet, even now, she was trying to tell him the weaknesses she'd noticed in Zuor's realm. Thankfully Phil had passed him a medical kit after he'd dressed and slipped out to the kitchen to get her a drink of water.

"Let me take a look at your injuries." He kept his voice calm and even, but inside, he wanted to scream and rage. Welts, cuts, and scratches dotted her skin. Her face bore mottled reminders of her imprisonment and cuts had begun repairing themselves. He had to remind himself that after this was done, he would do everything to make it up to her.

She lay still, and he smoothed antiseptic creams over the grazes and cuts. The ones on her breast concerned him. "When did he do this?"

Christina turned away and he stopped the outburst that sprang to his lips.

Keeping his touch gentle, Vasya careful checked to make sure the shower had removed all the grit and dirt in her wounds. He had no intentions of letting her contract something that would make her ill. Next he went to work applying cooling gels to her face. She hissed as it worked and he waited, gripping her hand.

When the tension eased, he leaned forward dropping a careful kiss on a tiny bit of unmarred flesh. "Better?"

"Yes. Thank you."

The last marks were the worst. He applied ointment to the broken skin but though she stiffened, she remained silent. He was only partly thankful, yet it also concerned him. He applied bandages to the wounds, winding it carefully, the material a stark white against her pale skin.

He carefully stood and backed away. On the chair in the corner were the clothes he had brought with him. "If you get dressed we can go home."

Christina stood, stiffly. He balled his fists wishing for the power to smite the demon right now.

"Yes. I'd like to go home." She reached for and dressed. He watched as she tried to balance herself long enough to step in to the panties, wobbled precariously.

Her herded her to the bed. "Sit on the edge and I'll help you."

Christina sank down. The bed squeaked beneath her and she blushed.

"I wonder what the others are thinking." He smiled and hoped the joke would break the fragile aura that surrounded her.

She smiled. It was only a ghost of one though. A bare uptick of the corners of her lips, but it was a start and he felt his mood lighten. Within minutes he had her dressed, and heading for home.

In the doorway, Christina swayed and Vasya gathered her close while Serina and Gregori watched silently. "You should rest."

She shook her head, and he could see she was pained, her face tight, and fine lines had settled at the edges of her mouth. "I don't want to."

"Christina..."

"No. Please, not now Vasya." She turned away, and the action gutted him all over again.

CHAPTER 25

$\mathcal{V}$asya scooped up the phone and found the number for Dravens and Jelena.

"Hello?" Jelena's voice was cautious and for an instant he thought something was wrong. Then he reminded himself, she was the leader of the local warriors.

"Jelena, we have her safe and sound, but I don't know how to protect her from returning to the realms."

She laughed lightly. "Remember the orb? The blue stone we took from the sword? That is what the amulets are made from. See if she has a necklace you can set the stone into. This time, though, make sure she doesn't remove it. It will give her protection from the demon."

"Of course." He thought back to the necklace his mother wore and now he understood how important it was. If only they'd known, then he could have protected her. It hadn't been the way it worked out, he reminded himself and to keep harking back on his failures wasn't going to help.

"Come out tomorrow if she's up to it, then we can sit down and decide how best to move forward."

"Thanks Jelena. For everything."

They hung up and as soon as the connection was broken, more questions invaded his mind. Never mind, he would have to ask them tomorrow. Right now Christina needed him.

He moved back to where she huddled in the lounge. During the trip back, she'd retreated into herself. He couldn't and wouldn't allow that, so he grasped her by the hand. "Do you have an old necklace I can pull apart?"

She looked at him, with searching eyes and then nodded. Once more anger rose at the careful way she moved, regret for his previous careless words and actions crashing down on him. Then he brushed it aside. He couldn't afford that emotion right now. *I need to focus on helping her find some peace.*

"Gregori? Go find pliers. Serina, make drinks. We have an important task to attend to."

Without waiting to see if they followed his direction, he trailed Christina into her bedroom. She yanked open a drawer and pulled out a small jewel case, thrusting it into his hands. She didn't ask the question he could see in her eyes.

"Wait and see, *dushka*." He smoothed his hands over her cheek, noting the way she jerked initially then settled into his caress. He knew she needed his gentle touches and understanding so didn't push for any further intimacies.

He dropped his hand to hers, lifted it and pressed it to his mouth. She watched with wary eyes, which hurt, but instead of saying anything, he made a show of leading her back to the kitchen

Gregori waited, pliers laid out on the table and he was pleased to see there was a range of sizes.

Vasya settled Christina in a chair. "Wait 'til you see this." He summoned his sword. She gasped when the blue light shone and he smiled broadly before winking. He picked a small stone from the blade, waiting until another formed in its place. She eyed it with interest and he smiled before dismissing the sword. He laid the stone on the table and grabbed the pliers. "Choose a necklace."

Christina blinked. "What?"

"Pick a necklace. One you like, because you'll be wearing it a lot." He gave a small laugh and she gazed at him for long moments before reaching out, choosing a small silver piece. At its heart lay a dark green stone. He took it from her and carefully peeled back the prongs holding the glass bead in place until it popped onto the table. He smiled and slid the glowing stone into the setting, inspecting it as it sat proud on the arms.

He waited as she gazed at the stone's pale-blue glow. A sense of contentment and pride filled him. It was his magic that created the stone that would keep her safe from Zuor.

Vasya pushed the stone into place and started to carefully close the prongs around the orb. "That will do for now. We'll get a better mount for it later on. One that will last." He lifted the cheap necklace and placed it in her hands.

She cried out, "It's hot!" Her eyes rose to his and he saw the question there.

"Yeah. It's magic. Now you need to wear this—all the time. Don't take it off. With this on, he can't touch you."

A grin stretched across her face. He caught a glimpse of happiness in her eyes, the one that had been missing since he'd saved her. Then the smile melted away.

"You're sure? Because if he comes after me again, I don't think I'd survive." Then she whirled away, moving swiftly towards the bedroom while he watched her go.

❄

 he knew the instant he decided to follow her, as she settled herself on the bed. "Christina?"

"I'll be fine. I just needed..." She waited for the jumble of emotions, fear and anger to pass.

"I will protect you." His voice was rough and she chanced a look at him.

"I know you will. You'll do your best and then some more." She sighed. "I just feel like I'm so needy. I hate this. I'm not a crier or a complainer. I don't retreat from hurts, so I can't understand what's going on in my head."

"Whatever you need, you only have to ask."

She closed her eyes at his words and barked out an uncertain laugh. "I've already taken so much. How much more do you have to give?"

Vasya laid his hand over hers. "As much as you need, when you need it."

She sat back up and nodded, accepting his promise before looking to the necklace. "Put it on for me?"

She hoped he understood what she was saying: That she wanted and needed him to protect her. She knew it hurt him to have to keep telling her. She damned herself for the mess she was making of things. Just because she was dealing with both the physical and emotional damage didn't mean she had to drown him in it too.

When Vasya rose and took the light chain she sighed. The cold metal slid over her skin and she covered the pendant with her hand, touching the tiny stone that warmed her skin. Vasya fastened the clasp then his mouth settled over it, sealing the action with a soft kiss.

"I will always try to protect you, Christina, because I love you."

CHAPTER 26

Christina's first reaction was to question his declaration of love. Just a short while ago, he'd been cold and uncommunicative, and now he offered her the heaven she'd dreamed of for eleven years. The to-ing and fro-ing of emotions left her feeling like a yo-yo.

Instead, she swallowed the angry words that rose in her throat. What use was there in asking why? If he truly loved her, then how could he be so damned stoic? Heaven knew, she wanted to rage at the way Zuor had tricked her... Christina stopped the negative spiral of thoughts—they could only make things worse and she needed something positive to cling to.

Maybe it was time to change the habit of a lifetime? Meeting his gaze she smiled, her mind seizing on one aspect they'd always had in common: *Intimacy.* "Show me."

For a moment a frisson of alarm shot through her as he stared. Slowly, a grin crept over his face. "Are you sure?"

She nodded wordlessly.

"Then let me just go..." He pointed to the room beyond and she nodded, understanding what he meant to do. Until now, she'd always gone out to bid Serina and Gregori goodnight. Vasya would do that for her tonight. He left the room and she lay there, staring at the ceiling.

A stray thought captured her. What if the amulet didn't work? She dispelled her worry, looking for peace in the storm of emotions. "Vasya will keep me safe." The door creaked and she released a sigh.

"So... Still waiting for me?" His quiet words were careful, as if he expected her to change her mind.

"Why wouldn't I?"

The bright smile on his face fled and before her now stood an uncertain man. "Because of Zuor. What we do..." He extended both hands to her, encompassing the bed and room. "What we do here is an act of love. Not a way to forget." It was a subtle reminder that he wouldn't allow her to use it to make her feel better.

Shame clawed at her. *Isn't that what I was planning on?*

Even as her subconscious questioned her motives she shook her head. "No. What we have means something Vasya. It always has. Years ago I loved you like a child loves the boy of her dreams. But now...?" She stopped, steadied herself before continuing. "Today, I can sit here and tell you I love you with a woman's knowledge. As only a woman can love a man."

He moved forward before stopping at the end of the bed. He watched as she slowly rose off the mattress. "I love you more than I did the day we married. Not because you saved me. Not because you will protect me."

Inside her was a passion and need. It wasn't hers to keep though, it was meant for sharing. "It's because without you, I can never be whole. You are the other half of my soul."

She crawled to the end of the bed on her knees, slid her hands over his face and kissed him softly on the lips. As she pulled away, she whispered, "You are the light to my dark."

His arms fastened around her and she quivered. Needing the sensation of his soft touches. This time, she pulled at her shirt, tugging it over her head. His eyes shone in the light, but he stayed still.

The night air caressed her skin. Her fingers shook and nervousness ran through her. The bruises and cuts hadn't yet faded. She accepted them as reminders of her time in the realm.

"Vasya? Tonight I need you. The heat and strength of your body as much as your heart and commitment." The emptiness of her core also reminded her that she needed his body filling her. His hard steely length.

"Love me Vasya. I need to burn in your touch."

"Then you must take the lead." His gravelly voice was a vibrant thing, caressing her mind, body and soul.

Christina raised her hands and undid the clasp of her bra, feeling the sag of her breasts before she threw the scrap of white material to the floor. Deep inside her belly the emptiness of need grew and fire licked at her soul.

His gaze roamed over her, causing her pulse to jump. She moved her hand to the band of her underwear; hooked it under the elastic and pushed downwards. Her fingers skated over aroused sensitized skin and she couldn't contain the moan that rose.

Christina rocked back slightly, material pooled at her knees on the bed. "Like what you see?"

She knew he did; the shining light in his eyes the only answer she needed.

Vasya's reached for the buttons of his shirt. Slowly he unclipped them and bared inch after inch of broad shoulders and lean flanks. The shirt hung open, and she reached out, softly dragging a finger down the center of his chest. She loved his bronzed skin, the warmth of it. The way the muscles indicated years of hard work. And she adored how they rippled under her touch.

"Please take it off." Christina moved into a reclining position. Vasya smiled but the flare of heat in his eyes promised a wild erotic journey ahead. Slowly he shrugged the material away. It fell with a soft sigh to the floor.

His fingers moved to his belt and damn if she didn't grow hotter!

Her secret recesses were damp now. The scent of her musk filling the air already redolent with sounds of passion.

Vasya moved faster, belt unbuckled, jeans unclipped then he toed out of his boots and stripped. Socks and pooled fabric went flying. She had to swallow, as the sight of his fully erect length caught her eye.

"You're sure?" Unable to form a coherent answer, she nodded reaching out to him.

Vasya stepped forward, grasped her waist and lifted. Her breath caught at his swift action, her senses skittering wildly. Now she stood before him. Naked. Skin against burning, hot skin.

"Ahhh..." The cry tore from her throat and her nipples budded into hard points of arousal, grazing against his chest.

"Vasya?" He knelt and one large hand touched her calf. Encircling it with tenderness. Crouching, her looked up at her. Nerves jumped as he stroked her skin.

"Only love will hold you now." With great care he rubbed where the manacles had bitten into the flesh, caressing and loving her with his soft touch, then his hands skated up, feathering over her calf muscles and finding her knees. They slipped behind, gliding over the tendons that weakened her.

The view was utterly erotic: this huge naked man, running his hands over her legs while wildfire lapped at her, melted her knees. Christina locked them together, hands splayed to the walls either side of the bed. He traced the dimples at her knees with his tongue and damn it, she was already prepared to explode in a white-hot conflagration!

His exploration continued upwards, achingly slow as he cupped her thighs skittering close to the juncture between before sliding away. His breath teased her and she tensed, her sex clenching against his sensual assault.

"Vasya." Her moan filled the air.

"Not yet," he said pulling away. "I want you to know how much I love you. How much I am prepared to pleasure you and give you everything before I plunge within your delicious body."

His thumbs traced circles on her inner thighs. Instinctively she widened her legs.

Vasya laughed, the rumble of his breath fanned the flames as he moved his fingers over her mound, twirling lazy circles that left her gasping. She closed her eyes, lashes fluttering together, unable to cope with any further call on her senses. She was lost in a sensual haze as his fingertips explored her body, yet never invading.

She danced in the fire his touch ignited.

The sound of movement caught her attention, pulled her back from the precipice of pleasure. Her chest heaved and she opened her eyes, her lids heavy with arousal.

Vasya had risen up like some ancient god-like warrior, His face taut and all edges, his eyes glinting with fire and his hands now lightly held her still, just under her breasts. He clasped her ribs, electricity arced everyplace their bodies touched.

"Please?" She yearned for him to do more, to cup her aching breasts. She wanted his mouth to close over the buds and to suckle. As if reading her, he leaned forward, the tip of his tongue glancing over one and she bucked.

With exquisite slowness he shuffled her back to the bed and laid her down. She watched him through slitted lids as he loomed over her.

Gently, Vasya reached down, parting her legs once more while his gaze captured hers befor dropping to her breasts. "Beautiful." The words shook her as his breath once more teased its way down her belly to center between her legs. His tongue flicked her folds and she reacted, gripping him with her thighs.

"Not so hard, *dushka*." He laughed before latching on and suckling.

She mewled and arched. Rocked and bucked. The pleasure of his hot mouth teased and coaxed her onward, into the spiral of growing hunger.

Mindless need pulsed, the invisible wire within her drawing tighter and tighter. She twined her fingers in the sheets while he continued his erotic torture until finally, she stilled.

Her breath caught.

She splintered.

Time stopped as she let the maelstrom sweep through her. Cleansing her.

Awareness returned slowly. Her chest heaved. He hadn't even kissed her and she'd blown apart in his arms! Christina felt no shame though. Instead she knew she needed to return the favor.

His skin was flushed, rosy; he was more than ready. As

he crawled onto the bed beside her, she grabbed his shoulders, pulling him against her and kissed him, mouth wide open, inviting his tongue.

The taste of her on his lips goaded her. Roaming her hands over his hot skin, Christina sought the length of his erection. When she found it, she curled her fingers around him and gave an experimental pump.

Vasya groaned, pulling away from the kiss and she smiled. "My turn." She let go and placed her hands against his muscular chest, giving one good, hard push he fell against the softness of the bed. It creaked and shook beneath the movement.

"What?"

Christina crawled on top of him; her lips finding the firm pectorals, grazing her teeth over his flat nipples while her hands explored. Cupping his sac she carefully ran a fingernail over the engorged length. The muscles quivered beneath her playful touches.

"Where did you learn..." His strangled tones had her laughing.

"Sometimes I read magazines. Amazing what you can discover." He grunted his pleasure, before she decided that too wasn't enough.

Hunger pushed her onward and she kissed her way down his chest, feeling the muscles of his stomach contract until they were hard beneath her caresses. The groans she wrung from him urged her on, feeding her own burgeoning desire.

She reached his length. Hot and ready. Christina looked up and saw him watching, his face hard with need and she dipped her head.

"No!" His hoarse demand left her smiling.

"Why not?"

"Because..." He stopped and she dipped closer, blew on the flesh that jerked. He hissed, muscles quivering.

She opened her mouth, flicked it with her tongue and he bowed, spine arching off the bed. "Oh God!"

"Do you like that?" She already knew the answer. His skin was sheened with sweat, his chest rising and falling rapidly. She swiped her tongue over him again. "Well?"

"More than..." He gulped, and exultation swamped her. "More than you could guess."

This time, she tongued the tip, paying careful attention to the slit, tasting his saltiness. Then she slid her lips over him and lowered her mouth, taking in as much as she could.

He groaned and rocked beneath her ministrations, while she bobbed up and down. Firm fingers stilled her.

"No more. I need you. I need to be in you."

Suddenly raging fever swept her away, her sex clenching once more at the thought of him embedding himself deeply within her and she backed away.

Vasya moved but she gripped his shoulders. "No. Like this." She straddled his lap, fitting herself over him before carefully sliding down. He frowned as she let her body take every inch, seating him firmly.

"This is what I need." She leaned in and kissed him.

Her careful rock led to yet another moan, this time from her. Their rhythm sped up so that they moved faster and wilder. His fingers caught her hips, raising her and she moved with him.

Each time they swung together, it was deeper and more magical than the last. The link between them grew stronger with each successive thrust.

"More!" her cries echoed in the shadowed room.

His fingers found her breasts, gently caressing the uninjured flesh as she threw her head back, exposing the line of her throat.

She closed her eyes, gasping and moaning.

When his fingers found the nub between her legs she exploded with a wild cry. The milking sensation worked on his body until he too erupted, his seed spilling into her.

Their panting the only sound in the otherwise silent room.

Sensation returned. Christina opened her eyes, the effort nearly sucking her into sleep, and she slumped forward against his chest unable to move further.

His chest rose and fell as his arms circled her. "I'll never let you go."

His words washed over her, calming her. Then sleep descended.

She woke and cautiously stretched. The nightmare she feared hadn't come to pass. Vasya's rough hand smoothed over her cheek and she could feel the warmth of his body against hers.

"I love you Vasya." She knew she'd never spoken anything truer.

He rolled her onto her back then slid deep within. Her body, already on fire for him, welcomed the intimate embrace. The rhythm swelled and changed as they linked their hands together. Then the passion overtook them.

Christina waited for the beat of her heart to settle as she snuggled in Vasya's arms. "We need help, don't we?"

His arms tightened just a bit more. "Yes. But I think I have an idea."

"What? Can you tell me?" She pulled away but he shook his head.

"Not yet. But I know who can help work it out. I need to organize for us to meet with Jelena, Dravens and I think we need the nymphs there too." Her stomach churned. "Don't fret. You gave me the idea." He smiled at her and she returned it, though not sure it was as full-bodied as his

"When did I give you this great idea?"

He smiled and tapped her cheek. "Last night. In the shower."

She frowned, but nothing came to mind. She mentally shrugged. He had a plan and she was more than willing to trust him. "Okay then. We'd better get up and do something about getting dressed."

Once more, Vasya caught her close. "You frightened me yesterday. No matter what, don't ever take that kind of chance again. It nearly destroyed me when I couldn't reach you."

She turned away—the raw and naked pain in his voice shamed her. "I just wanted to—" He slid an unsteady finger against her lips, stopping her words.

"I know. You're the most giving woman I've ever met. But I love you far too much to lose you again. Please? Christina, promise me?"

She nodded. Anything to relieve his remembered anguish. "I won't do it again."

He sighed unsteadily. "Thank you." With a kiss on the top of her forehead he pulled away. "We better get up and dressed then."

They hurried and soon headed to the kitchen seeking coffee and breakfast. Serina waited at the table.

"I was telling Christina we need to go see Jelena and Dravens again. We'll need the nymphs there too, because last night Christina said something that sparked an idea." This could be the beginning of the end or the beginning of the future.

Neither outcome was clear and that worried her.

Silently she drank her coffee and hoped she could ignore the uncertainty for a little longer.

The nymphs, Dravens and Jelena were waiting in two discrete groups as they pulled up in the vehicle. For the first time, Phil followed them in his own car. He'd argued that it would make the journey easier and decidedly more comfortable. It left Vasya wondering what else he was up to.

Since coming here, Vasya'd faced shock after shock. He'd heard of many of the races, nymphs, fae and even shifters. They were all creatures he'd previously believed didn't really exist.

Then had come the knowledge his wife was a nymph, an acceptance of his status as a sky flyer and her friend was actually fae. He'd met were's and sirens and who knew what other races.

For a moment Vasya wondered if Christina's parents knew of his and Christina's heritage as well. They'd obviously known something, because her mother and grandfather had been feeders.

The car stopped and Christina looked at him. "Is everything okay, Vasya? You've been very quiet on the way here."

"I've been thinking. It seems odd that we have arrived here, and all of a sudden the demon has increased his attacks. Add that together with how little you know, and the secret police in Alvonia. It's just overwhelming."

Christina blanched. "Do you think someone is feeding him information?"

"No. Not necessarily, I just think the coincidence is a little odd though."

She stared at him and he patted her hand reassuringly. "Come on. The others are waiting."

Christina nodded with a jerk and got out of the car but he kept tumbling the thoughts over in his mind, unsure if there was a connection or not.

Galene stood and inclined her head toward him, and Jelena stood unsmiling. Dravens indicated they should settle at the long table before the small house. The nine settled themselves and waited.

"We need to make a plan; one that deals with this demon while ensuring the best possible protection for all. I can only speak for the flyers, but I've had enough of seeing innocents terrorized." Dravens eyed everyone at the table and Vasya found himself nodding along with the others.

Galene lifted her hand. "That's true, but before we go any further, I must ask some questions."

They all looked at her. Galene speared Serina with a look. "Where did that lock of white hair come from?" The other nymphs waited quietly.

"I—I woke up with it." The sound of indrawn breaths told him this was an important fact.

"What does that mean?" Vasya's demand was met with a glare and Jelena hushed him.

One of the nymphs rose, her eyes flashing. "You don't talk to an elder like that."

Galene rested a hand on her arm. "He has the right to ask." The nymph shot an angry look in his direction before sitting back down.

He bowed. "I meant no disrespect Galene."

The nymph nodded, accepting his apology. "You don't know our ways and time is short. I will forgive it. But as to what it means, I hypothesize that your nymph genes have been activated. I understand you were attacked two days ago by the demon?"

"Yes. He attacked me in Christina's home. So she left me her pendant while..." She touched the necklace at her throat and Galene turned to Christina.

"What happened?"

"I went into the realm to find his affinity. I thought if I could find that, then we could use his weakness." Christina avoided Galene's gaze.

Dravens interrupted. "Who wears the necklace?"

Christina blushed. "I gave it to my sister after the attack. Then... Then I entered the realms." She turned away and Vasya reached for her hand.

"Jelena showed me how to call an orb. Now they both have protection." Dravens raised an eyebrow, then shrugged. "While there, she found his affinity. It's fire."

All sound stopped as eight pairs of eyes turned in his direction. "You're sure?" Dravens leaned in closer. "Absolutely certain?"

Vasya returned his stare. "As sure as I can be. The smell of sulfur follows him, his realm is cold I think to balance his internal heat..."

Christina cleared her throat. "And the world he showed me..." She shivered and he grabbed her hand, lending her support. "It was desolate and hot: Lots of flames. And there were these scaled creatures. Things that need heat to exist."

Dravens nodded at Christina's words. "Then I would say you're correct. But if he's a fire demon, no one of you is strong enough to defeat him. In fact I'm not even sure that the two of you together would be enough."

"Dravens, I wonder." Galene stood up and wandered around to Serina. "I believe that with your powers activated, that you too are a water nymph, which would make sense given that you are sisters, then we have two sky flyers and two nymphs with an affinity to water." Galene twirled a lock of hair around a finger as she thought. "Jelena, does Vasya have an affinity."

"Not really, but there's been so little time to delve into his skills."

"Water can douse flames and it has always been my experience that affinities tend to be compatible. I wonder, Jelena, when we are done, could you explore his ability with ice? It would make sense to have a water nymph connected with an ice affinity sky flyer. Their powers are compatible if that's the case and they'll be able to work together most effectively. Given the speed with which we've had to push their powers to emerge, it's no wonder you haven't had adequate time to investigate their abilities. Yet they are younglings and there's plenty of time to learn how to manipulate what they have." Galene leaned in closer, making her point. "Yet, it's even more curious, that the demon chooses not to use his powers. I wonder if they've somehow been diminished?"

Vasya frowned. The words sounded encouraging, but still, all they had were suppositions and half-guesses.

"So what do we do?"

"I think I can shed some light on that. Phil, tell them what you have found out." Dravens' voice caught Vasya off guard.

When Vasya swung back to look at the man... no the *Fae* seated beside him shock rippled through him. Phil's hair glowed in the sunlight and his face had sharpened subtly. In fact Phil looked like himself and yet more... *refined* and glowed with an internal fire.

"I made some enquiries last night, after you left. There are places here that I can go to ask things no one else could answer."

Phil smiled and Vasya felt his eyes narrowing, while he waited impatiently for the fea to continue. He jiggled his feet and had to control his fingers.

Phil looked at him and smiled. "It would seem our demon friend has an entrance to this world at a wooded glade nearby. I know it, though not well, yet it never occurred to me that he would have a portal there. But it seems to make sense if his power is waning, he'll need another way to come and go easily from his underworld."

"And how can we trust you?" Gregori's words were a deep growl. "You want Christina."

Vasya turned but Phil answered before him with an irate expression on his face, "You mean after I was there for Christina? After I picked up the pieces following your outburst? How about since I put you in contact with Dravens, here?"

Each comment was spat with the force of a bullet. Vasya watched the embarrassed red glow shine over Gregori's face. He would have pulled Phil up on this but Christina's future and his was in the balance and Gregori had spoken out of line. "It could be..." He shrugged, knowing he didn't have the words to explain.

"Thankfully for you, a Fae can't actually lie." Jelena's tense voice cut through the silence.

"Really?" Vasya eyed the man who faced him with ice-cold eyes.

"I think you wish to hear the rest of what I've learned?"

Dravens rolled his eyes. "Get on with it. You can sort out

whatever personal dispute you have later, once we've dealt with the abomination.

Phil cleared his throat. "His underground access is close, but guarded day and night. His minions could be a source of problems. They are Jinn—or at least half Jinn. We aren't sure exactly what else. Whatever it may be, I think it's the cause of their reptilian features. We've ascertained that like the demon they serve, they can't attack anyone wearing a sky flyer stone. But you'll have to get through them before you can battle the demon."

Phil shook his head, as if sharing the information was painful. "I also agree with Christina's assumption. They're creatures of the hot realms, making them perfect for working with this demon. Whatever their mix of ancestry is though, it includes a fondness for human blood... if we take what you saw at face value, Christina."

Vasya looked at her. She was wan and she clung to his hand. "But what I saw wasn't real."

"No, but Jinn are masters of trickery. There could be some true Jinn in amongst them. In which case, my brothers, sisters and I will deal with them when you clean out the realm. Get them out into the woodlands and let us do what we can."

So much information. So many variables. "How?"

"To beat them, we must work together. We four together while Phil clears the glade." Christina summed it up and Dravens nodded.

"Yes. But to do that, you my girl, must learn more about your powers; like how to use them. And Jelena must drill the two men if we are to defeat him."

Christina looked at Galene. "So what exactly can I do?"

They had walked back into the meadow, the one they had been in before. She looked around, but her sister had gone in the other direction with another nymph. She wished Serina was here, but focused when Galene touched her hand.

"Come sit with me." They sank to the ground, among the wildflowers. "Today I will teach you the basics. Believe it or not, these are the skills you will need to defeat the demon."

"What do you mean?"

"You can make water respond to your command. Water is, after all one of the strongest elements imaginable. It can carve a rock, quench a thirst and take away life."

Christina listened to Galene, but her words confused her. "I get that, but how will it help me to defeat Zu... to defeat the demon?"

Once more Galene grinned at her, and Christina was filled with amazement at the sheer beauty of the woman and her smile. "You must learn to control it on a cellular level. Agitate those molecules correctly and you can cause a flood. Even with just a small amount, you can drown somebody in a desert. Several well-placed drops can give life to a dying plant. Water can give life and water can take it away."

Christina mulled over the words. "So I just need to learn to control it with the power of my mind?"

Galene smiled. "At the beginning it's hard to understand."

Christina wasn't sure she was convinced even though it sounded so simple. "What about Serina? Will she be able to do the same?"

Galene shrugged. "Probably, though it is unlikely that she will ever do so with the same level of dexterity. She is a *reformed recessive*. She was never meant to learn how to use the power, so the magic will not be so easy for her to control. Now stop worrying about your sister and concentrate. Your path will be rocky enough without taking on her problems too."

The information left Christina wondering exactly how they were going to use Serina's skill then, if she wasn't going to have the same strength Galene insisted she would have.

Sitting back in the sun she was more than happy to embrace any advantage they could get. Christina watched the grass swaying in the light breeze, the scent of flowers filled the air as Galene pulled a flask and a dish from the bag she had carried. "You do understand about molecules, right?"

Christina nodded.

"Good, that makes it easier. Water is a made up of molecules that can be agitated. What you need to do is envision them, make them jump and bounce."

Christina stared at her. "Jump? Bounce? How am I supposed to do that?"

Galene sighed heavily. "Think of them as balloons or grains of rice or even balls. The water calls to you, right? You need to call back. See it in your mind, with a label. See the labeled molecules bouncing up and down." Christina giggled at the thought of grains of rice bobbing up and down. Galene's smile looked far more forced than before and Christina had to control the urge to roll her eyes.

The first hour passed slowly, as Galene tutored her in imagining the individual molecules. She looked at the water in the bowl, but it didn't move. Not even a drop. The whole time, she was aware of Galene's eyes on her, searching for a sign of movement.

Perhaps, she thought to herself, if she couldn't see anyone watching her she would have greater success. So she closed her eyes.

I have to get a handle on this.

With a force of will she imagined balls. Blue round balls with their symbols tagged on them. Two balls labeled hydrogen and one oxygen. It took a while until she could visualize them. When she finally did, she made them jump and bounce. Each move was higher than the last.

Galene laughed. "Stop, otherwise you'll make rain!"

When Christina opened her eyes, fat plops of water dropped on her head. "It's already raining."

"No it isn't. That's the water you just made bounce."

Christina gaped at her. "Really?" She checked the bowl, it was half empty and a trickle ran down her back.

"Yes, really. Now let's see if you can do it with your eyes open."

So she sat on the floor of the meadow, repeating the exercise over and over again—sometimes she was more successful than others. Then Galene made her create strings of water.

The first time she did, she was surprised that it looked like a long blue ribbon. "That's amazing."

Galene didn't answer, just simply gave her something else to learn.

CHAPTER 27

The journey home was silent. Perhaps they were all lost in an introspective cloud, she couldn't really be sure. After weeks of ups and downs, the air was fraught as they prepared to defeat the monster who had ruled her life for so long.

She pulled the car into the driveway and while Serina and Gregori wandered in, she and Vasya sat in the car, soaking up the silence.

"I'm scared." She looked at the door to the shed. Her mind whirled. "I mean, what if this goes wrong? What the hell happens then?"

Vasya, reached for her hand. "I don't know. We can hope to get it right, but that's all."

She spun in the seat, so she faced him. "Vasya, Serina's pregnant, I'm a wreck and you and Gregori..." She released a shuddering breath. "You're having to pick up the slack. I feel like I have nothing to offer right now." Fear and exhaustion, her constant companions, beat down on her. Her eyes ached and rubbing them was like scratching them with sandpaper. Tension coiled deep.

Vasya reached out to her again. "Chris—"

"No Vasya. Facts are facts. They can't be ignored. I feel like I'm a failure. Or at least broken." Her voice cracked on the final word and he gathered her close.

"You do the best you can. That's all we can do, Christina."

Silence stretched out as she mulled over his words. *You do the best you can.*

It didn't seem enough. But for now it would have to do. "I guess you're right." She waited a beat and then looked at him. "We should go inside. Get ready, eat and rest." She released the breath she'd held. "I think it's going to be a long night."

He pulled back, and Christina moved to get out of the vehicle, but he gripped her shoulder. "We'll do our best. Hopefully it will be enough."

She sighed and slid out the car. Guilt weighed her down even as she entered the house.

The meal was cooked in somber silence. Conversations started then petered away, it was as if everyone understood the risks.

Christina worried about her sister and the child she carried. She fretted for Vasya, who wouldn't have been involved but for her, and Gregori who was only here because he'd married her sister and was brother to her husband.

The only fact she was sure of, was that they needed to defeat Zuor. That would set them all free and then real decisions could be made for the future. Whatever it might hold.

When dinner was done, Gregori and Serina hustled Christina and Vasya from the kitchen. "We'll wash up tonight. You go shower and rest."

They searched through their clothes, choosing dark

pants and tops that would be hard wearing. Comfortable shoes, with adequate grip, that allowed them to move as silently as possible.

Afterward they lay together on the bed, resting until the time they had had to rise in order to be where they'd agreed to meet with Phil and Jelena.

An urgent hand shook her shoulders. "Time to wake up, Christina." She must have dozed off.

She stretched and rubbed her eyes, yawning. "It's time?" Vasya nodded and she pushed off the bed. Her stomach rioted as a million butterflies took to the wing inside her.

She hurried for the door, in the direction of the kitchen. She'd planned to carry a small water bottle with her. One of the tricks Galene had shown her started with a small amount of water as a kick-starter for her skills.

Serina joined her. "What are you doing?"

"Getting some water. Here's a bottle for you too." She stopped after thrusting the bottle into her sisters' hand, and cleared her throat. "Galene told me we can use it as a kind of igniter to activate our magic." Serina nodded, as if absorbing the information.

"Look, it's my fault you're in the middle of this—" Serina made to talk but she cut her off. "No. It's true, but whatever you do, don't believe his lies. He's a master of them. You can banish them but only by telling yourself that they aren't real."

Anger, guilt and worry grew. She had to make sure Serina understood how to protect herself and the fragile life she was growing. "Just stay safe, okay? I could never forgive myself if something happened to you or the baby."

Serina smiled at her. "It's not your fault. You tried to protect me anyway you could. I know that now. While I love you for that, you also need to understand you can't protect me forever, Christina. I'm an adult. A wife. And soon to be a mother. I have to make my own decisions and take my own chances. And this time, my decision is to help protect you."

Christina teared up, her eyes burned and she accepted the hug from her sister.

"Everything okay?" Vasya slipped a hand around her waist.

Christina broke away, swiping at the tears. "Yeah. I'll be fine. Let's go get this done."

They climbed into the car, worry battering her. She gave a sniff and straightened in the seat. She needed to take her own advice. Concentrate on the positive and wrap it around herself. They would defeat this damned demon, even if they were only a motley crew of untrained warriors.

They stopped and picked up Phil, who directed them to the edge of forest. So far everything was just as they had planned.

All five crawled out and Vasya engaged the locks, before Phil lead them into the cool dark wooded area.

"Tell me why you and Jelena cannot fight in the nightmare realm again? I didn't really get why you can't enter." Vasya walked carefully, treading in Phil's footsteps as they had all been instructed to do.

"It's a little tricky really. The demon has access to dark magic. As a fae, I can see it dimly. I see the aura of his magic. It allows him to not only mask his realm, but also acts as a specialized security system." Vasya nodded. This was a much better explanation than the earlier one he'd given.

"Unless I'm either invited into his realm or somehow deeply involved in his plan, I can't get through the barrier he surrounds it with. We know where the realm is, but cannot enter. Not even if I was to come with you. That's part of the magic that makes him so strong. With Jelena, it's more to do with the fact that she isn't bound to anyone involved. The four of you are bound together by love and familial ties."

"I get that. But then, why can't I enter via a dream and allow Serina to join me? Then, surely Gregori and Vasya could find us?" Christina's voice broke the sudden quiet.

"Because we know, in the nightmare realms, you're a slave. A prisoner. He knows where you are and prepares accordingly. We've already seen that. I would imagine he's erected more barriers since you escaped last time. And to be honest, I'm not sure it would be wise for you now, anyway. We don't want to make any of this easier for him."

Vasya watched as Phil sighed heavily and Christina, walking a little behind him, fell silent. He wanted to reach back and grasp her hand. Offer her hope. But she was just out of reach.

Then Phil stopped them with an upraised hand, and they stilled. "Wait."

They heard a growling and shuffling that sounded like the beat of a hundred angry horses. The sound grew and swelled before petering away. Vasya's heart pounded in his chest. He didn't want to know what caused the ruckus.

Phil had already explained that these woods were sacred to many of his kind and inhabited by many strange beasts. He'd also warned them not to ask questions about what they saw or heard.

"I can't get caught bringing you in here, otherwise it will bring disrepute on my house for have outsiders in the forest." Phil looked around before nodding to the others. "Follow me and stay quiet."

This time they moved faster, heading for the center of the woods, the eerie silence broken only by their footsteps crunching on decaying leaves.

They moved into the middle of the glade, and there stood Jelena, waiting in the shadows for them.

Her heavy black clothing accentuated the curves of hip and breast, the strength in her arms and the long line of her neck. Her blonde hair was caught up in braids and her eyes burned with the light of what he considered was most likely readiness for battle. If it wasn't for his love for Christina, he probably would have been tempted to consider a liaison with her. As Christina held his heart, for him there was no competition.

He caught a flash of interest between Jelena and Phil and smiled at the way they skirted around one another. *Now here's an interesting mix.* It would be fascinating to see who won in a battle for control between a hardened sky flyer and the fae. He filed that information to share with Christina later.

Christina wound her fingers through his. "It's time." She looked worried, a frown on her face. He wanted to banish it.

"Just stay safe. If I say duck, do it." He leaned in and cupped her cheek with his hand. "I want us to come out on the other side of this with a future together." He pressed his lips to her. The spark of sexual heat was there, but muted by the knowledge that they were about to go into danger.

Their greatest strength lay in the bonds of love and family. Together with their newly discovered skills it hardly seemed enough.

The two women slipped off the amulets and handed them to Phil. They'd agreed that they would cause more issues than offer them protection, given they were both wide awake. Vasya tugged Christina hard against his chest before dropping a lightning fast soul-stealing kiss on her lips.

Jelena pierced him with her searching gaze. "Don't assume your sky flyer form until inside his realm. We can only guess if you will be able to enter in any other form, but experiences of similar locations have always ended with failure."

He nodded silently, watching as the other three checked their small backpacks and prepared for battle.

Phil indicated a cave at the other end of the clearing. "That's the entrance. Be ready for anything. Once you're safely inside, I will summon the others in preparation of the Jinn abandoning him.

"Take care down there." He extended his hand and Vasya grabbed it.

"Tha…"

Phil waved a hand. "Don't say it." His eyes sharpened and Vasya nodded in agreement. With a swift turn he indicated to the others to take the formation they had agreed upon, him at the front and Gregori at the rear with the two women in the middle. They linked hands and headed for the cavern.

Stepping inside the gloomy tunnel a charge, a little like a battery sting, ran through her. "Was that the veil Phil was telling us about? The one that keeps everyone out?"

Vasya shrugged. "Maybe. It certainly felt odd. Like a tingling running through my body." The others nodded.

Christina looked around, taking in their surroundings. Fear ate at her nerves; the dank and smelly underbrush made her want to rush out, but they had to go on. Holding hands, they moved like a human chain.

"Wait!" The group stopped and looked at her. "I have an idea."

Christina gripped the small torch she had pulled from the pocket of her backpack before they entered. "Here, Vasya, hold this." She thrust the metal tube into his hands. "Shine it on my bag."

She shrugged off her backpack and fished around for the length of light line she'd put inside. "Here it is." She held it up and heard a quiet chuckle from Vasya. "If we thread it through our belt loops we can all stay together without getting lost and we regain use of our hands." With quick movements, she threaded it through Vasya's and tied it loosely, then threaded it through hers, then Serina's and lastly handed it to Gregori.

She heard his quick movements and then he smiled. "Done."

She slipped the bag back on, the water bottle clipped to her belt swung madly, hitting her on the leg. She ignored the discomfort.

Vasya grunted and they moved off again, crunching their way through the twisted cavern.

The original tunnel opened into a large cavern and they could see small fire pits dotted the middle. Thankfully both stalactites and stalagmites formed a natural wall along the higher edges of the room. Vasya lifted his finger to his mouth and they silently nodded their agreement. They couldn't afford to be detected, not this early on, otherwise their mission was doomed before it began.

Christina chanced a look through a gap and noticed the reptilian creatures were cooking something over the fire. The quick view nearly turned her stomach and she looked away. Vasya must have caught the look on her face and touched her cheek in understanding.

There were other tunnels, and she spied the Jinn creatures coming and going. One of the passages what clear, with no traffic. Vasya indicated with his arm to the empty one, with a question in his eyes.

She gave the thumbs up signal, and they set off again, with careful steps. Sometimes their steps would result in a crunch as gravel moved beneath their feet. Christina would swallow her fear and wait for them to be discovered. When it didn't happen they'd keep moving.

They turned a corner, checking front and back, left and right. She hoped this was the right direction; she wanted to get out of this horrible place as quickly as she could.

With great care they crept on, finding another tunnel, obviously well used. This time they moved quickly, scurrying up to the light beyond. In Christina's experience of these caverns, there was only light where Zuor kept things he needed to watch—like his prisoners. The jinn could see as well in the dark as the light.

"I've been here before." She breathed almost silent and Vasya looked at her. It was the room she had woken up in. "We need to get to the opposite side to enter the corridors. I'm willing to bet he has a room, or lair, somewhere along the way to the cell where I was held."

Quickly they dispensed with the rope. No need for it here now that they could see and be seen, and speed would be far more beneficial than stealth.

Vasya handed her the rope with a smile and she returned it to her bag, taking a second to bask in his approbation before sucking in a deep breath. "Maybe I should lead from here on in?"

The suggestion wasn't warmly accepted, given the way

Vasya's face darkened and Gregori scowled, so she spoke quickly. "No one else has been here. I sort of know my way around. I can get us to the cell, so it makes sense."

"Christina, it puts you at greater risk." Serina's words had her stomach churning again.

"I know, but someone has to lead the way."

Rather than wait for the argument she hurried across the room and the others followed. She hugged the wall once through the doorway, checking the hall for movement, checking each room with a door that opened easily.

They attempted to check those shut, seeking others lost in this dungeon but time was precious. The third doorway led to another cell, the person within lay curled on the floor in a fetal position, moaning quietly. Christina made a mental note to come back for them.

They wouldn't be safe if released just yet, she argued with herself. But it didn't help with the tense knot of guilt.

The next several rooms were empty, but there was a tell-tale scent—that turned her stomach—of old excrement and who knew what else. Several times Serina had to back out to Gregori with one hand firmly clapped over her mouth.

The third such room left Christina gagging. "I don't know that I can do this."

Vasya wound his arms around her. "You have to, otherwise things will get worse. You know that."

She sniffled and nodded. "I know, but it's so hard."

He pulled her tight against him and for a moment she soaked up the support he offered, then he set her away. "Come on, let's get this finished."

She nodded and headed through the door to join Serina and Gregori in the hall.

CHAPTER 28

The door opened at the touch of her hand on the knob and she gasped. It was the cell where Zuor had held her. The place of her humiliation. On the wall she could see the black manacles that had held her prisoner. And the room stank: A mixture of human waste and sulfur.

Christina spun to see the dark figure behind the door. "He's here!" She screamed the words as the door clanged shut behind the four of them.

Zuor grinned at her in his trademark evil fashion. His eyes glowed in the half-light against his coal-black skin. His long black robes, decorated with silver and gems, glinted in the meager light. He extended an arm, a shot of light careered to the far wall and she jumped away. It almost blinded her. Blinking, she cleared the spots from her vision.

"So my pet has returned and brought friends. Excellent." Zuor rubbed his hands together.

Christina stiffened, terror freezing her in place. "I'm not your pet or your slave!" She spat the words at him but he laughed off her bravado.

As he lifted his hands, a wave of some kind of energy

flowed over her catching her and she screamed. Her body tensed and she lunged for Vasya, but he wasn't there. Instead she was in the cavern, the one she'd seen through the viewing window, with hundreds of the jinn creatures, their skins scaly and red in the gloom, writhing about. The noise, when they realized she was there, swelled.

"Vasya!" She screamed his name and could see him further away, his skin glowing blue as he transformed. "Serina? Gregori?" She cast about wildly, spotting them in other corners of the cavern.

Gregori was batting away the Jinn with his meaty fist, but as fast as he cast one aside another charged at him. Her sister crouched in another corner of the room, eyes wide with horror.

Separated. He'd separated them. Her mind spun and her stomach cramped. Why? *Think!* Did he somehow know about their powers? Their plans? It didn't seem possible that he should know. She shrugged off the thought as a sound caught her attention.

"Since you seem so keen on playing games, I will allow it. Just this once."

Unable to see Zuor, she scanned the large room quickly. It was a flash that made her look up. A rocky outcrop jutting several feet above the floor of the stone balcony was decked out with a large seat. It reminded her of a throne with the way it was decorated with black and red banners. There, seated in the chair was Zuor, his arms curled over the edge of the platform.

Something grabbed her from behind. Long sharp claws tearing at her and panic settled in. *How in hell am I supposed to beat these creatures?*

A fetid wind travelled over her and she knew it was the

breath of a Jinn, hoping to drag her down. It wanted to feed on her flesh and blood.

"You won't take me!" She scrabbled and lunged, aiming a savage kick, hitting the creature in the face and it fell back, clutching at its head. Blood, black and viscous flowed from the wound site. She moved, already anticipating the next attack that would result in the grasp and slice of claws.

Something bumped against her leg and she stilled. *Water bottle.* Her comments to Serina echoed in her mind. "A starter for activating our magic." *Just what I need right now.*

Another creature tried to capture her, but she'd taken control of her wits. Now she was ready to fight, because she had a tool. Something she could believe in; a plan of sorts.

She unscrewed the top of her bottle, moved and kicked another creature then slopped some of the water into her cupped hand. It splashed as Christina whirled away from another creature. Even as she watched, the creature fell upon the floor with a growl.

Christina cursed. This time envisioning the molecules was difficult with the noise and her constant motion.

Tiny droplets of water lifted into the air while she opened her mind, seeking more liquid. Her senses located some in the ground beneath her feet and she called to it. There was an almighty rumble and a fissure opened, splitting the ground into several sections. Water rose into a curtain around her, and more than one creature yelped, springing away.

She rocked back and forth, while the water formed a spout. It was only small, maybe a foot high and the same wide, but it was effective at cutting a swathe in the path she needed it to travel.

Holding the metal bottle in one hand she pushed the

geyser toward the center of the room, noting that Vasya was headed in the same direction.

Triumph roared just as a claw clamped around her arm.

*V*asya roared as he took down another jinn and moved forward. The ground shuddered under his feet and he looked up to see Christina, a serene smile on her face as she moved behind a large waterspout. It gave him heart. "Get them, *dushka*."

Arms with long talons reached for him and he started slashing once again, thanking every deity that using this sword was as Jelena had told him, instinctive. It sang under his touch.

This time when he looked up, Christina wasn't there. His heart nearly stopped in his chest and he opened his mouth to bellow when it started to rain. The water hit the ground, sizzling in the heat and Vasya seethed, looking for her. He began searching in the direction where he had last seen her. Scanning the ground.

Anger pulsed through him and he raised his sword high. A pulse boomed, and the rain turned to ice. Howls of fury rent the air and he watched, mesmerized as the creatures retreated. Christina staggered on her feet. From this distance he couldn't see if she was hurt or not, and he couldn't dwell on that now. He was incandescent with rage and channeling it through his sword gave them both an opportunity to catch their breath.

On the other side of the cavern, Serina and Gregori fended off more Jinn, their numbers looked to be dwindling.

Surely that means we're winning?

As Vasya stepped forward Zuor appeared in front of him,

his arms spread wide and arcs of electricity skittered in the air around him. "Enough!" His voice boomed and the cavern shook, sending rocks and small stalactites crashing to the floor.

Vasya narrowed his eyes at Zuor. The demon's loud bellow catching Vasya by surprise and he blinked as those opposite slunk backwards. *Why?* Zuor had encouraged the fight so why had he suddenly commanded the jinn be still and silent?

Zuor waved his arms and advanced, the scent of sulfur filling the air once more. "I will squash you. I will shred your body and use your entrails to feed my army," Zuor said smiling.

"You know what Zuor? I think you're just full of hot air."

He looked across the chasm to see Christina forming her waterspout once more. Serina was white and shaking but had managed to summon a rain cloud and Gregori smiled at him, as his wings unfurled.

Vasya released his own wings and his sword glowed brighter in the darkness.

It's time to end this.

They hadn't been able to plan their actions but they were ready, each with their powers in play gave them an advantage. One Zuor was unprepared for, Vasya was sure.

They'd all agreed that it was necessary to quench Zuor's fire. What could be better than rain and ice—their two natural affinities?

Christina's waterspout headed in their direction, while Serina's cloud rose. Vasya gave a hoarse battle cry as the rain crossed the divide and headed in their direction.

Gregori raised his sword.

So did he.

Zuor turned and moved unsteadily, before he began

laughing. "You think you can defeat me? You and your sword?"

"I'm not alone."

Now the two women manipulated their water. Everything stilled and he glanced at Christina, her face set in concentration, her hands moving slowly. Fury shone in her eyes as she watched the demon advance. The whirling vortex moved faster, became wilder. Bigger. The spout whirled and dipped gathering momentum.

Gregori raised his sword and Serina's rain became icy hailstones.

An idea occurred and Vasya realized they needed the rain and spout to be in just the right location before he could unleash the storm of pure ice that would put an end to the dark demon. Vasya took a cautious step backwards and Zuor smiled.

"Come on Zuor. You think you can defeat us?"

"Your puny skills are nothing. This is my realm. I am Master here!" Zuor sneered.

Another step. Should Vasya goad him? Would the demon see through the ploy? His brain worked at lightning speed, weighing up the next move. "Sure Zuor. Because you've defeated foes who've entered your dungeons before, right?"

Zuor reacted as expected bellowing and charging. He wasn't sure if Zuor could see it happening in slow motion like he could, but the onslaught was right on him now.

The rain hovered to his left and the spout spun madly in place at his right. He gulped knowing they only had one chance to make this work. "Together now!" His bellow echoed and the twin storms descended.

The rain and spout battered the demon and Vasya raised

his sword. He had to dig deep hoping Serina understood he needed her to freeze the water.

The spout pulled at Zuor's robes while the rain pelted and the sizzle and pop rose from Zuor as he fought their magical storm.

Puffs of white, rapidly cooling vapor filled the air, sizzling as it fought the twin attack. "Gregori! Join me!" His roar was met by his brother's.

A pulse erupted from their swords, rattling the ground and knocking anything in it's path down. Ice formed on Zuor as his minions fell to the ground, the Jinn stunned into insensibility.

Zuor writhed beneath their onslaught, his arms flailing in the air and the cavern grew steamy, like water on hot rocks will often do. Exhaustion clawed at Christina. The need to step away from the suffocating heat intense and fear was ripe in the air. She couldn't, though. To do so would let Zuor free.

He'd unleash a firestorm and destroy them.

She focused harder. Magic and muscles strained by unfamiliar power, the pull on her psyche was draining. There wasn't much left to work with and she snarled, "I won't give up!

"The water agitates and moves, molecules forming into strings that I can see." She spoke aloud hoping the sound would give her enough *oomph* to finish her part of the task.

The need hammered. Pressure building in her chest, and the knowledge that time was running out hovered at the edge of her mind. She thrust it away, aware they needed to keep battling if there was any hope of defeating Zuor.

Her arms ached, her vision blurred.

"Bouncing. Balls. Of. Water." The last whoosh of steam erupted and a black demon stood before her. Diminished but not yet defeated.

Her arms dropped. They shook with fatigue and waning adrenaline—too heavy to keep aloft. Zuor turned to her.

His smile was feral. Wickedly hideous and razor sharp teeth jutted from his black mouth.

Evil.

"You may have stopped my fire, but you can't beat me."

He started moving toward the chasm; heavy pounding steps. The floor shuddered beneath her and Christina moved too. From her angle, se saw that the bottom of the divide was molten lava. Her heart stuttered.

What more can we do? Her gut cramped, then a thought occurred. "Serina! We need to create a wall of water."

Serina launched forward with an unsteady gait, tossing every ounce of magical energy she had left at Christina. Every action was instinctual now. They may not have mastered power sharing, but the touch of magic slid over her like a well-worn cape: Comfortable and familiar.

Christina dug deep, finding a last tiny well of supernatural skill. It flickered like a guttering flame in her mind. She grabbed onto it, forcing the water molecules into a deluge that rained down into the chasm.

She couldn't cool the lava, but hopefully they could form a thick crust of ice. It might give them enough time to complete their task here.

"More!" She screamed demanding every last ounce of her power, as Zuor threw himself toward the chasm. He needed the heat and while it existed, there was no way to defeat him. "Serina! Help me! We need ice now!" Her scream was frantic and high pitched.

One last time Christina raised her arms with a strength born of desperation. Her mind sought any source of moisture in the dry cavern. Shuddering wails and inhuman screams rose: A cacophony of dread that sliced through the echoes of battle.

The water moved and danced for her while Gregori and Vasya battled the few minions who'd risen. Zuor dragged himself over the floor, his ungainly stride reinforcing this was the right choice.

"We'll beat you yet, Zuor!" Her bravado was weak though. She was failing—the thrum of her blood slowing.

Ice lay extended, tendrils of crackling inching over the rocky cavern floor and walls. Christina moved forward, weariness dragging her every step. Would it hold her weight? Holding her breath, she stepped onto the covering. It held and she moved a little toward Vasya and Zuor each step a little faster and surer.

"You ruined everything!" Zuor's petulant roar echoed through the cavern. The huge stalactites that hung from the ceiling quivered. Tinkled. Then with shattering explosions first one then another dropped, crashing to the floor.

For a moment her heart stood still.

"You chose this path, Zuor. Let us go and we'll leave you be." She staggered and almost fell to her knees.

He smiled, bearing jagged teeth and she wavered, remembering each time his long incisors had sunk into her flesh.

He reached out and she knew, if he got to her, fed again the cycle would restart. It couldn't happen. She wheeled, her feet slipping on the wet, icy floor and she tumbled heavily.

A roar sounded, heavy with rage. *Vasya.*

"Stupid!" Angry tears rose in her eyes as she struggled to her feet.

Zuor reached for her, claws finding purchase in her clothes, tearing them. Sharp points broke her flesh, and the scent of copper rose.

Whoosh. The air rippled and Christina spun away from the demon.

A crash echoed and a scream cut off suddenly. "*Vasya?*" She lay there on the ground, spent. Panting as red liquid entered her vision and rivulets trickled past her fingers: Ripe and threaded with black.

Christina gazed up. Vasya hovered, wings spread, his eyes wide with fear. "Christina?"

She moved slowly, turning on her side. "I'm okay."

She glanced over the cavern, her gaze dropping to the ribbons of black-red liquid, Zuor's blood her mind supplied —a poisonous stream mixing with the water. Beyond Vasya lay a body; a large black unmoving mass. Zuor.

They'd finally defeated the demon.

CHAPTER 29

Rumbling filled the air as Vasya hurried over to Christina lying—bleeding—on the ground. His chest tightened with fear.

He crouched and touched her, relieved that she breathed. "Christina?"

She moved slowly, turning on her side. "I'm okay."

The rumble grew louder and her eyes opened wide, looking over his shoulder toward the ceiling. Fear flashed across her face and he reached for his sword. "What?"

"We need to get out of here. Now."

With a hiss Christina pushed herself from the ground and he extended his hand.

Gregori and Serina joined her just as a stalactite crashed to the ground, shattering only feet from where they'd been standing. The floor shuddered at the impact.

"What's going on?" Serina's words were lost as another thud filled the air.

"I don't know."

"I have an idea that this whole realm is dying, along with its creator. We need to get out of here. Come on."

Christina led them to the viewing window, which gave under his and Gregori combined efforts. Their swords shattered the magical barrier and they clambered through.

"Argh!" Christina moaned.

"What's up?" Vasya turned to help her through.

She swiped her hand over her black pants. "Caught myself a little, but it's nothing huge. Come on, we have to keep going."

Now in the cell, Gregori and Vasya surged against the door. It clanged and banged but didn't give.

Vasya grunted. "Try again."

It didn't budge.

The rumble was definitely getting louder and he feared the ceiling would fail.

Serina stepped forward. "I have an idea." She gripped her water bottle and tipped the contents on the floor.

"That just might work." Christina gave a tired grin.

Together the two women joined hands, sharing their powers as they pushed the water toward the wall. The thread curled and climbed before finding a weak spot. There it burrowed within the walls, out of sight.

Christina shook, sweated and vibrated as she used her abilities.

It was working though, he knew it.

"Okay, we're going to freeze the door hinges. You need to finish it off for us."

Understanding flared and Vasya motioned Gregori closer.

"One... Two... Now!" Side-by-side they rammed the door. On the second impact the door quivered. On the third it gave, crashing to the floor with a tremendous thund.

Then they were off again, the women scurrying ahead.

They hurried to the doors they'd marked on their way in, showing the location of survivors and wrenched them open.

"We should leave them." Gregori's voice caught his attention.

❄

"No, they'll die if the dungeon collapses. We have to release them. No one deserves to end their days like this." Christina shook her head.

Soon there was a motley group of people staggering along, some held up by others. The group scrambled through the halls and rooms, out of the cavern and up the tunnel. Cries and groans their companion as they moved.

Beneath them, the ground bucked. Zuor's nightmare realm was in its death throes because the magic that had brought it forward was slipping away.

She wondered if they would make it out in time, but let go of her worry. She breathed in quick snatched pants, her muscles screaming. There'd be time for healing later, after they escaped. Ahead lay life and behind them only death and destruction—if only they could get out. She needed to focus on that.

Christina glanced at Gregori who carried his wife in his arms. That was the future; a bright and positive one.

Long curls of magic swept past her, carrying the signature sulfuric taint she associated with him.

Ahead she could finally spy a glimmer of light. Gregori slowed and she shouted in his direction. "Keep going!"

They had emptied every cell containing survivors and she watched as they scurried up the tunnels. "Where are the Jinn? Have they all escaped?"

Vasya shrugged. "Not here and we should be thankful for that."

She agreed silently, knowing Phil and his forces awaited them beyond.

Somehow, Vasya had managed to reach the mouth of the tunnels before her and she grinned as she hurried up to him. He waved the survivors through, reminding them to wait just beyond the entrance. She smiled at the sight of their hopeful expressions.

Christina watched as the final survivor, an older man, shuffled his way to the exit. As he reached her, he tripped. He shuddered and glanced at her.

"Are you okay?"

Even in the darkness his eyes shone with tears. "I am now."

He turned and moved through the opening and Vasya swung his arm around her waist as he addressed the man. "Anyone behind you?"

The only answer was a shake of his head and Christina took a second to lean into Vasya. "We're the last."

Then she gathered herself, took his hand and together they hurried through the end of the tunnel.

This time there was no frisson or sensation of magic parting.

The glade came into view and as she stepped into the area, breathing deeply. The scent of death still surrounded her.

She looked around, noticing they were surrounded by fae warriors, in bloodstained garb.

She gulped and her eyes sought Phil. He stood to one

side looking not quite smug, but at least pleased with himself.

His clothes had changed too, now he wore a flowing white robe, belted with a silvery cord. Unlike many others, his was still pristine. The sun peeked over the horizon making the cord sparkle and his aura shine bright.

Other creatures, some very odd looking—and she tried hard not to stare—rounded up the remaining Jinn and pressed them forward. "What's going on?" Vasya stepped into the clearing and she felt the weight of the man resting against her.

"We are rounding up the last of our prisoners."

Before Vasya could protest, Phil stepped up to them. "They won't be harmed. But they will be handed back to their leaders to be dealt with. These Jinn? They were blood bound. He'd been feeding them negative emotions from the blood the demon stole. Those emotions will need to be purged before any judgment can be passed upon them."

Christina waited anxiously; this side of Phil was one she had never seen before. It was more than a little unnerving to realize that she'd worked beside him for years and never had a clue of his real persona.

He spoke quietly to those standing around them; they bowed low and retreated and Christina wondered about those gathered around. Then he turned, arms extended and waved them back along the path they'd followed at the beginning of the night. "Come. I'll take you home and answer all you questions over a coffee."

"What about the other survivors?"

Phil looked from them to Vasya and then back to her. "They will be cared for."

Several fae emerged from the woodlands, their kindly faces and gentle gestures didn't fully reassure her. "We will ensure they are rehabilitated and sent home to their families."

Indecision warred for another minute before she nodded and watched a female minister the old man slumped to the ground beside her. The fae soothed him with soft words and he turned his head, offering Christina a smile.

Finally satisfied, Christina trailed after Phil and Vasya, the path now clear. Grit itched under her collar and smelly perspiration clung to her. Grime covered her clothes and she realized they looked like dirty runaways.

At least they'd survived the battle. She might be sore and tired but, nevertheless, they were mostly intact.

As they reached the car, Phil depressed the remote key to unlock it and it beeped in response. The mundane sound made her laugh. The others looked at her, Vasya winked and she smothered the sound, before she crawled in and relaxed.

Aches and pains made themselves known. The purr of the engine lulled her and as the vehicle swayed on the road, she fell asleep leaning against Vasya's shoulder.

Warm soft hands woke her, Vasya gently shaking her shoulder. "Come *dushka*. We are home."

Never had that sounded so good. She muttered about her need to shower.

"That would be nice. And a coffee too."

She fished the keys from her backpack as she shuffled to the door. Her legs trembled and in a moment of devil-may-care attitude, she dropped her bag to the small table flanking the doorway. It clattered and fell to the floor, but she ignored it.

They filed within the hall and Phil passed them, headed

for the kitchen. "Go clean up while I make coffee. Then we can relax and talk."

She nodded, headed to the bedroom, sure that Vasya followed. Once the door was shut she stripped quickly, feeling every twinge in her abused body. She refused to look in the mirror knowing that the ravages of the night were stamped on her face and body. Once in the shower, the water poured out with a whoosh. With stabbing fingers she washed her hair, trying to get the smell and grit out of it.

Vasya crowded in behind her, yet neither spoke and she was pleased. This wasn't the time or the place to rehash what had taken place during the night.

Satisfied with her level of cleanliness, Christina climbed out and towel dried while waiting for Vasya to finish. He turned off the water, the steam filling the small room and she handed him the towel and headed for the bedroom. She moaned as the clothes slid over her abused body.

Her hands were unsteady as she combed them through her hair and Vasya caught her eye. "You probably should have put some salve on the cuts." He caught her fingers before dragging her close and kissing her temple.

She leaned against him. "You can do it later."

He grinned and the flare of heat she saw in his eyes energized her. "Later." He laughed at her mutter, threading his fingers between hers.

The scent of coffee drew her from the bedroom to sink into the lounge with a sigh. Phil held out his hand and she accepted it. "You did an excellent job tonight. In fact, what you've done will have widespread ramifications."

She looked at him. "What do you mean?"

"It seems the demon forces in Alvonia were tied to Zuor. Many of those released tonight were citizens we were searching for."

Phil's words surprised her. "But what about the police? I mean, they weren't demons... many of them appeared during the day."

He gave a tired laugh. "The secret police are actually Jinn. News of Zuor's defeat has spread and their structure is already tumbling."

She stared. *Surely not?*

"Once you killed Zuor they had no one single head. He wasn't the strongest of the demons, but he was their best strategist. It's not over, we need the resources of the sky flyers and other clans, but the tide is swinging. Jelena has already left to head up a battalion."

He looked away but she'd caught a flash of longing on his face.

"Phil? I'm sure she'll be okay." She reached across, capturing his hand in hers.

He snorted. "Yes. She's a strong fighter. Capable. Not at all what I expected."

Christina understood. He'd claimed a deep emotion for her, yet Jelena had blown him over. She couldn't think of a way to tell him it was okay, so decided to remain quiet, hoping he'd accept her unspoken support.

"Without you four, we'd still be beating our heads against a brick wall, trying to save as many Alvonian's as we could. You've given hope to so many. And your efforts in returning the lost will never be forgotten."

She blushed red, felt the heat burn her face. "We didn't do anything, someone else wouldn't have done."

Vasya dragged her closer against his side. "We want no recognition either. What we did was for all, but the primary focus was to release Christina."

Phil inclined his head. "You saved many of those

captured. Galene is impressed, as is Dravens. They will both wish to meet with you. But not today."

"What will happen to the captured Jinn?" Christina interrupted Phil and he grimaced.

"To be honest, I don't know. They're secretive. But I've already offered my people's assistance in rehabilitation." This time he smiled and one last question remained.

"Who exactly are you?"

His laughter filled the air, the tinkle of chimes. "Are you really sure you want to know?"

She nodded.

He sighed. "My true name is Philnon Winter Wood."

He looked pained as he stared at her and she leaned in at a loss as to what that should mean to her. "And so that means?"

He sighed. "I am a son of the Winter Court. My mother is the Queen."

"Ohhh." Her breath caught. He was the son of the Queen and she'd treated him like anyone else. Upbraiding him from time to time. She bit her lip and stared at him.

He smiled but it quickly died away. "But you cannot tell anyone. I rely on anonymity to do my mother's bidding. If my true identification was known, my ability to act for my Mother, and in the best interests of my people, would be severely diminished." Phil grimaced and her stomach knotted. *His mother's bidding?*

"Huh? What? And who's bidding?"

"To help release Alvonia from the grip of the demons and to help bring harmony. The fae want to reveal themselves to humanity but first the demons must be controlled." He smiled and she was dazzled by the radiance.

The collective sounds of surprise from Gregori and

Serina filled her soul. They were both here and well. Life was perfect now. "Sounds good to me."

By unspoken agreement the four got through the day without a nap—their movements were sluggish and slow but no one really cared. As night fell, they retreated to their rooms, seeking the rest they'd denied themselves during the day.

Vasya had watched Christina all day. So far she had refused the offers he'd extended to rub salve on her scratches. Each time she responded with later and tension coiled deep within his gut.

The need to affirm their survival, in time-honored fashion ate at him, clawing like a ravening beast. By the time the dark had settled and she had joined him in the bedroom, his hunger had grown to gargantuan proportions.

Christina stood by the door, leaning back against the wood and smiled. "So?"

He nodded. "So."

Without speaking they moved, walking toward each other until they stood, facing but not quite touching. She raised her hand and he noted how it shook.

"You are fine?"

Christina smiled, heating him from the inside out. "Yeah. I'm good. In fact, I think I'm better than good."

She launched herself upwards, winding her arms around his neck and nestled in. "I don't think I've felt this good since—" She stopped.

"Since when?" He was sure he knew the answer, but he needed to hear it. He'd never considered himself needy before, and even now he winced at the connotations.

"Since our wedding."

He let the air in his lungs expel, realizing he'd been holding it since asking the question.

Now he was unable to wait. Vasya needed her against his skin, touching him.

He needed it all.

He needed it now.

Carefully he pulled away and she gifted him with a wicked smile full of delicious promise. His body throbbed with need. Christina stripped off the shirt she'd worn during the day revealing her white, cotton underwear. "One of these days, I am going to buy red underwear for you."

"Hmm promises. But this is okay for now."

"Whatever underwear you have on, or take off will be sexy, because it is next to your skin." She laughed, the sound carefree and throaty. It made his blood sizzle.

"You've got quite a way with words there." She laughed again.

He grappled with his belt, the buttons of his shirt and boots while she slipped the cotton over her hips and down long shapely legs. Bruises and scrapes revealed themselves and he promised to kiss each bit of marked skin.

Christina's eyes glittered as her gaze roamed over him. His chest expanded as her wicked tongue poked out every now and again to dampen her lips. He groaned as his erection jerked beneath the confines of his clothes.

He reached forward to cup her breasts but she batted him away. "Not yet." Her breathy whisper caught him up and shook him like a predator worrying its prey, and need surged again.

She reached behind and grasped the clasp of her bra releasing her beautiful breasts from their confines. They sagged and this time he didn't stop himself. He cupped the satiny twin globes in his hands. They felt just right. "You have the most beautiful breasts."

The ache inside grew. He had to taste the buds. Leaning in he sucked lightly on the nipple, dragging it further into his mouth. It ripened and grew beneath his touch and he groaned.

When he finally pulled away, he was breathing heavily. Naked. He needed her naked skin against his.

"I need to be inside you."

She shook against him, the quivering touch igniting fires deep within him.

Christina smelt so good. Musky arousal filled the air and his heart rhythm increased rapidly. When her fingers fluttered against his stomach, it felt like a million electrical pulses zapped him at once. He moaned, unable to restrain the sound.

He shucked his jeans, his erection springing free from the confines. Now the teasing look fled from her eyes, replaced by the hot promise of forever. He swooped in, his mouth opening over hers.

*C*hristina slid her fingers over his warm skin, feeling the slickness of sweat that came with lovemaking. He'd wanted to touch her all day. She'd known that, and deep down had wanted it too.

But hot on that knowledge came the reality that she'd probably fall asleep afterwards. So she'd fought the raging tide flowing through her veins, hoping to conceal it beneath the necessary everyday tasks. Each time she'd looked at Vasya, she'd seen the banked fire reflected in his eyes.

He'd suckled at her and now she stood, watching the

naked man run his gaze up and down her body. All she wore was the cheap panties and they were damp and irritating to her swollen flesh.

She hooked her thumbs in the bands and his nostrils flared as she slipped them over her legs, down to her ankles. Then she kicked them aside, letting him look his fill while she did the same.

But the need to touch to caress, to love him over-whelmed her and she took the final step forward, reaching out with her hand to encircled his engorged cock.

She dropped to her knees. "I love every inch of your body," she said, before slipping her mouth over him, delighting in the steely velvet of the most intimate part of his body. She laved it. Up and down, slowly at first, until the need grew more urgent.

Her movements sped up, body winding tightly with arousal as she knelt before him. His fingers tangled in her hair, holding her close. Then he stopped her motions, gulping at oxygen, his body tight, powerful muscles locked. "You have to stop." His hoarse words made her smile as she slipped off him.

"Why?"

"Because that is not what we need. Tonight I need to be buried within your body. Bringing you pleasure when I finally fill you."

She shivered at his words but rose without complaint.

When he grabbed her and held her close, the tips of her breasts brushed against his chest. Pleasure rippled over and through her. And she had to bite back the moan rising in her throat.

"Vasya," He swallowed her whisper, as he captured her mouth again. His hands roamed over her body and the sensual web he wove filled her senses.

When he picked her up, captured her in his strong arms, she wound her arms tighter around his neck, participating fully in his carnal kiss. By the time he lifted her head her senses swam.

The bed dipped and swayed below their combined weights. She barely registered it, as his mouth roamed over her body. He nipped and suckled at her throat, stopping to tease the throbbing vein before moving down to her collarbone. Every caress stole her breath.

His hands framed her face, tangled in her hair before he moved them down to her breasts, kneading them until she was wild with passion.

Christina grabbed at him, pressing her fingers deep into the sinews at his shoulders and held on tight while the roar of her body intensified. "*Vasya.*" Every breath was his, every sound yet another way to glory in his touch.

He whispered to her, telling her every way he planned to love her, touch her and bring her the ultimate fulfillment.

Finally his hands found their way down her body, resting at her stomach, stopping only briefly to whisper against her belly, "One day, I will fill you with a child."

Mindless need tore at her. She was empty and hungry for him.

"Vasya, please." Her entreaty only seemed to spur him on though. His hands gripped her thighs, pushing them apart until he could access her very core.

He pulled away and she felt the whisper of his hot breath as it moved down her body, finding the quivering mass of arousal at her core. Her legs clenched as her intimate flesh prepared itself for his invasion.

He blew on her and she stilled, panting madly. Hunting for some control of the passion that spiraled madly.

Under her fingers, she felt the molten heat of him, knew

he was as affected by their mutual passion, yet he drove her on mercilessly.

Vasya laid his tongue against her flesh and gently, tenderly using it, as he rubbed the sensitive bundle of nerves.

His touch rocketed her to the heavens and she orgasmed, dimly aware that he fastened his mouth over her and fed upon her need. His movements stopped when she came back to herself, her chest heaving with exertion. Then with the utmost tenderness, she felt him push his fingers deep within the secret recess.

Once seated, they stilled, but the heat and heaviness within her body grew again. His thumb pressed on her and she bucked once more. Arousal roared through her again and she moved under his caresses.

When he pulled away, his face looked like etched granite. Every angle taut with need: his cheeks flushed, and his eyes slumberous pools of desire.

"Vasya? Come fill me."

He gazed at her, flicked at the tiny bundle of nerves at her center with his tongue and her breath caught once more.

"Soon."

The madness descended again and she couldn't fight it. She undulated against his touch. "Vasya, please? I need you. I need to feel you inside me."

When he finally slipped his fingers from deep within her body, he painted her distended nipples with her slick moisture then suckled. Vasya moved his way up her body, before setting himself at the cradle of her thighs.

"Tonight, I hope I plant my seed within you." His soft words joined with his actions as he slid within her body. Her muscles tightened around him, taking everything he had to offer. She wound her legs around his waist, pulling him closer, hungry for the connection of their bodies, the air redolent with the musk of their heady desire.

His arms shook as he kept his weight off her body while he rocked deep and hard.

"I want that Vasya. I want your child." Every word spurred him on, and the movements grew harder and faster. She held on, clenching while her body heaved, seeking their combined release.

The trembling started deep within, molten heat scalding her senses as her inner muscles tightened and released around him. She gave herself up to the pleasure. To the liquid silver sensation coursing in her veins. Her body burned and tingled as she cried his name, arching to wring every last drop of ecstasy from the moment.

His fingers bit deep at her waist as he pummeled her, no trace of civility left. His jetting release came with a mighty roar.

They stilled. Wound around each other until finally their bodies relaxed and, as lovers do, they slept, entwined in each other's arms.

EPILOGUE

"*And in other news, the Ruling Members of Alvonia have left the government offices, where they have been under siege for the last two weeks. Sources inside the country state that the round up of secret police and the removal of many key figures has been instrumental in the overthrowing of the dictatorship.*" The woman on the television conveyed a serious look to the viewers, but excitement swelled deep within Christina.

Her heart was full to bursting as she rose and turned off the television. Sounds of shrieking echoed through the house making her smile. When Vasya, Gregori and Serina had been brought out of Alvonia, she had been little more than an empty joyless shell. Since having them back in her life there was color and optimism. Something she had been missing for far too long. Not to mention noise.

"Mama!" A little boy came running into the kitchen where she cradled her newborn daughter.

"What's up Philnon?"

The little boy bounced up and down on the spot. "Uncle Gregori says when I'm bigger I should be able to grow wings like him and fly!" The boy smiled widely and she returned it.

She laughed. "Yes that's probably true, my love."

She glanced down to the babe that suckled at her breast. Each tiny tug reminding her of just how much had changed in her life.

"Mama, will Yulia be able to do that too?" She ruffled her son's dark hair, so like Vasya's. The babe gave a tiny yawn, disengaging from her breast.

Her precious boy screwed up his face while he waited for her answer. "I don't know. She might be like your Aunt Serina and me. Only time will tell."

He gripped her hand and she laughed, adjusting her clothing before allowing her son to drag her outside, where the other adults had congregated around a long table. It groaned under the weight of the food they'd brought to celebrate.

Serina's smile caught her attention. Her sister was so excited that she'd finally passed her last exams and would soon take up her position as a teacher at the local school; a school for the children with special abilities. Philnon and his cousin Raina would be among the first enrolments.

When Yulia was old enough she would also join them. Christina looked down realizing the baby had nodded off. She hefted the sleeping child over her shoulder.

Gregori and Serina held hands, as happy together as the first day they had returned to her life. Now they lived with their daughter on the other side of the meadow, not far from Vasya, Christina and their two children. Their homes close enough but still giving them their own space.

"I have news." All eyes turned to her and she smiled. "The ruling members of Alvonia have finally given in. They left the government offices this morning."

Serina clapped her hands and Gregori gave a muted cheer.

Vasya stood. "To all those friends and family, who never got to see this day; may the victory be in their name!"

The group around the table agreed, drinking deeply.

Phil and Jelena smiled at each other, their hands entwined. They too had finally found love amongst the carnage left after the defeat of Zuor. While Jelena had initially travelled to Alvonia to lead the warriors who had remained in hiding, she'd been summoned two years ago to act as an envoy to the Winter Queen's court.

Phil meanwhile had remained in the Department working with Christina to support those they smuggled out before the total collapse of the Alvonian government. Those who now made the trek across the border needed their assistance to build new lives.

They'd survived many years of upheaval, and Christina was pleased that neither Vasya nor Gregori had been called on to participate in the battle for Alvonia. Instead their role had become that of guardians, allowing them to settle in to family life and resume their status as craftsmen.

"There will be much work to accomplish." Phil looked at her and she nodded.

"Yes. But between us, we'll do it. We've got the contacts and we'll find those who still hide."

Phil nodded. "My mother will send healers too. The reformed Jinn have already offered their support to the other blood bound in atonement."

Christina gazed around the table. Finally, she had a family, her country had a future and she had a husband who loved her.

Vasya curled his arm around her. "Peace in our time. And the winners will be us and our children."

She smiled. Her children were free of the taint of the blood demons, and together they would free others who had faced a frightening life of blood slavery.

Their work had just started but the future was indeed bright.

Konets.

BIOCYBE BY IMOGENE NIX

Levia scanned the long line of other hopefuls entering the testing chamber. The large building in the center of town was cold, and she dragged her wrap around her body, even as she craned her head, looking to the high ceiling. She'd never before had an occasion to enter the testing complex, yet she'd seen the lines of teenagers every time they passed the building.

Once she'd asked her parents why the teens were lined up and her mother's face had shuttered. Her stepfather had just shaken his head and growled. They'd stopped her questions with a carefully uttered, "You'll know soon enough, Levia." The pain in her mother's eyes had been enough to shush her questions. For endless months afterward, her parents had traveled different routes to the educational facility she attended and Levia lost interest in the puzzle of that building.

Now, as she looked around, remembering that long ago spring day, it was her opportunity to find out. But she felt a surge of concern at what lay ahead. She likely wasn't the only one, given that there were probably two to three hundred seventeen-year-olds gathered in the one place. Ahead of her, she caught sight of a couple of girls, their arms linked together and wide smiles on their faces. Scanning the crowd, she became aware that, by far, a majority of those gathered displayed both fear and trepidation.

"All female subjects will enter through doors three, six, and seven. All male subjects will enter through gates four, eight, and ten." The speaker above her was loud, and she jumped before checking the numbers etched on the black metal sign over her head.

The massive doors beside her swung open, and now an uncertain silence reigned. Many of the youngsters hung back, clearly discomforted by whatever testing regime lay ahead. This was where they'd been told their futures would be determined.

"Oh gosh, I hope they only have an aptitude and psych eval. I don't think..." Levia turned to see the white face of the girl behind her. The girl had uttered what many must silently be thinking.

Levia dragged an unsteady breath in, her hand resting flat against the plane of her belly as she looked around. No one had entered yet. It was clear many were on the verge of taking the step, but still they hung back.

She straightened her shoulders. "I'm not afraid." It was always wiser to approach things head-on, she believed. When her biological father had died, she'd been one of the few to view his capsule before it was sent into the massive gray structure built to accommodate those who'd moved onto the next life realm.

Her legs shook as she wobbled toward the entrance. Beyond the doorway, she spied sealed cubicles and her heart stuttered. Why cubicles? Usually testing—med and psych—were in eval-units, hidden only by billowing white curtains. She glanced back, noting that others had taken the first step.

"Move along, subjects." Once again, the androgynous voice of the address system blared.

Of course, given it was her seventeenth anniversary of birth, she was technically considered an adult now.

She thought longingly of baby Rald and her half-sister, Elda, waiting at home for her to return, and the celebrations to be held that night. That made her smile. She would need to make them proud of her.

She entered a row and the tall Educational Specialist, the edu-specs as her peers laughingly called them, stopped her. "Present your credentials to the scanner."

She'd done this many times since the tiny implant had been slipped below the dermal layer of her skin at birth. The small unit in her wrist heated as her details were checked.

"Enter the first cubicle, Levia Endrado, and follow the instructions to complete your assessment."

Thus dismissed, Levia moved to the first unit, laid her

palm against the scanner, and the door slid open soundlessly.

"Welcome, Levia Endrado. Take your place in the eval-unit." The soft contralto of the voice echoed after the door closed silently behind her.

"What are you evaluating?" Her voice was breathy, and she peered around.

"Your skills—physical and psychological. Your emotional and medical status. Your educational attainment levels."

It was an answer that shed little insight into the many things she was hungry to know. "Why do all seventeen year olds—" "Take a seat, Levia. Then we may begin your testing." If she'd expected an answer, she was sadly mistaken, she considered sourly. She dropped into the seat, the soft leather-like surface molding to her body. "Levia Endrado, you are required to remove all non-specified apparel." She jolted in the chair. "It's cold." "The temperature will be amended. Remove the non-specified apparel." Her misgivings grew as she dragged off the light wrap she'd brought with her, and then threw it to the floor at the side of the unit. "We will begin, Levia Endrado. At any time, should you experience any malfunctions of the unit, simply depress the red button." It glowed and she grimaced. Levia reclined against the chair and waited for the testing to begin. The first examination was based on her understanding of the political system, where she saw herself, and her knowledge of the rights and responsibilities accorded through citizenship of both her planet and the commonwealth.

The second test was mathematical and scientific proficiency. It felt like hours had passed by the time she'd finished, and she lay limp on the seat, exhausted.

"Levia Endrado, you may rise. The sanitary unit will

emerge once you trigger the yellow button at the door. Should you require refreshment, press the blue button and a restorative will be made available."

"Can I leave?" "Negative, Levia Endrado. Your needs will be catered for in this capsule." "Why?" Her voice hitched and true fear rose for the first time. Why did they keep her in the alcove? "All will be revealed at the end of the testing cycle." Levia looked at the now empty screen before hurling a curse word. It was met with silence. The urgent throb of her bladder reminded her that she needed to use the facilities, so, with

a sigh, she rose and clambered from the seat. After attending to the needs of her body, she walked around the unit, peering at the door, but it was obviously programmed remotely. She poked and prodded, but it made no difference. With a huff, she headed back to the chair.

The moment she'd settled in, the viewing screen shone bright. "Welcome back, Levia. The next sequence will evaluate your psychological reflexes, then that will be followed up with the general knowledge portion of the evaluation."

"When can I leave?" It seemed better to ask bluntly, she told herself.

"Once the examination is completed. After the next set of evaluations, you will be subjected to the physical aspect."

"Then I can go home?"

"Levia Endrado, you will now complete the psychological test. This will be undertaken by one of the center's personal evaluators."

She frowned. Personal evaluators? She bit her lip, and the sting reminded her that this wasn't something to joke about. In her seventeen years, she'd only heard of personal evaluators being brought in once before, and that was when one of the girls at her academy had been in a serious accident. Both legs were amputated and her body's ability to keep her alive had been gravely compromised. Her peers had been informed that the girl had requested the assessment before she could request her support systems be disconnected.

"Levia Endrado, are you ready to recommence processing?" The emotionless voice echoed once more and she gulped.

"Yes."

Available from Beachwalk Press

http://www.beachwalkpress.com

Direct Autographed Books

http://bit.ly/BioCybe

STARLINE BY IMOGENE NIX

Duvall McCord stepped out of line as the parade was dismissed, inwardly wincing as his new boots rubbed his feet and his new uniform scratched his neck. He looked at his

family, considering and measuring. He'd worked hard to attain the grades needed to be able to enter the academy, but it was all he'd ever wanted and dreamed of. To travel the stars and eventually captain his own ship. Now there he was on the cusp. Even as a fosterling, his room had been decorated with the ships he one day wanted to command, and at the age of twenty-three he was finally on the way.

His father, Captain Gentry, who had given up the chance of a plum command to keep his family happy, was always in the back of his mind. He now captained inter-galaxy runs for the Admiralty. He'd even given up his Star Destroyer for his wife's peace of mind. Duvall promised himself he'd never do that.

He belonged somewhere out there, among the biggest, the boldest, and the best.

His little sister, Meredith, bounced up and down, squeaking excitedly, and his parents smiled. He felt their genuine fondness for him, their foster son. They were proud of his many achievements, and if there were doubts in their minds, they were never spoken of.

Duvall was driven, almost obsessive in his desire to become the best of the best. That was why, now at the end of his time in the academy, he had been nominated as Best of his Class. The Top Graduate. The one his peers looked up to. The question had been asked and answered: was he good enough? His answer was always an unequivocal "yes." His family, peers, and instructors saw the drive and accepted it for what it was—an integral part of who he was. His mentor, Captain Gustav Elphin, had requested that

he serve aboard the Star of Ishtar, and had taken a great personal interest in this cadet.

It was acknowledged he would be on the fast-track to the stars. And, as Elphin told him again and again, emotional entanglements grounded a man; a piece of advice Duvall took seriously, so he had been careful in his social encounters. Always keeping a light touch with his lovers. Love 'em and leave 'em was his motto. He refused to let anything get in the way of his achievements and the desire to captain his own ship.

If privately his parents had any doubts about his lack of emotional ties to the women he was seen with, they kept them to themselves. No doubt they believed that one day a woman would change his mind and the attitude he had worked so hard to foster. For now, he accepted their belief that he knew what he wanted and had the drive to achieve it.

War was finally over and there was time to settle down. Long days of peace stretched out before them. The uneasy truce between the Earth Empire and the Ru'Edan, while new and tenuous, meant that there were opportunities diplomatically for the right kind of man and woman.

The rogue Admiral of the Ru'Edan Empire, Crick Sur Banden, might still be on the loose, but there was a belief that soon he would be brought to ground and that a true peace might be the outcome. Well, that was the opinion of the hopeful in the Empire anyway. The Empire held its collective breath as the newest graduates of the Earth Empire Academy marched out. They hoped to reap the benefits of those who came before.

Available from Beachwalk Press
http://www.beachwalkpress.com

Direct Autographed Copy
http://bit.ly/StarlineNix

CYBORG: REDUX - COMING SOON

21st Testing Protocol Book 1

Cyborg:Redux

Once evil reigns there is only the honest left to fear...

Clarissa was an ordinary nanny until Dr. Jeremy Colvert made her a bio cybernetic freak. On the run, it was an act of kindness that nearly brought her undone.

When Michael met Clarissa everything in his world changed—again. Now they're hiding from a world out to get them and the aim to shut down Dr. Colvert's experimentation isn't exactly going to plan.

Love might have bloomed, but there'll be no future if they can't save each other.

ALSO BY IMOGENE NIX

<u>Warriors of the Elector</u>

- Star of Ishtar
- Starline
- Starfire
- Star of the Fleet
- Starburst
- The Star of Eternity

The Star of Ishtar & Starline - Print

Starfire & Star of the Fleet - Print

Starburst & The Star of Eternity - Print

<u>Blood Secrets</u>

- The Blood Bride
- The Illuminated Witch
- The Sorcerer's Touch

<u>Reunion Trilogy</u>

- War's End
- The Assassin
- Executing Justice

The Reunion Trilogy in Paperback

<u>Sex Love & Aliens</u>

- Tangled Webs
- False Webs
- Covert Webs

<u>21st Testing Protocol</u>

- Cyborg: Redux (December 2017)
- Children Of A Greater Evil (2018)

<u>Single Titles</u>

The Chocolate Affair

A Sapphire for Karina

BioCybe

Hesparia's Tears

Tomorrow's Promise

A Bar In Paris

Blame The Wine

A Stranger's Embrace

Revenge On Cupid

Inheritance Of The Blood

The Plan

Loving Memories (2018)

Non Fiction

Self Publishing: Absolute Beginners Guide (With Suzi Love)

ABOUT THE AUTHOR

Imogene is published in a range of romance genres including Paranormal, Science Fiction and Contemporary. She is mainly published in the UK and USA due to the nature of her tales.

In 2011, Imogene Nix (the pen name not Imogene herself) was born. Imogene sat down and worked tirelessly for 3 months culminating in the books Starline, which became the first in a trilogy titled, "Warriors of the Elector."

Imogene has successfully been contracted for twenty-five titles. She has also completed several others. In 2017 Imogene decided to self publish most of her further works - a plan which is in train.

Imogene is a member of a range of professional organisations world wide, and believes in the mantra of mentoring and paying it forward.

She loves to drink coffee, wine & eat chocolate and is parenting 2 spoiled dogs and a ferocious cat along with her husband and 2 human daughters.

www.ingramcontent.com/pod-product-compliance
Lightning Source LLC
Chambersburg PA
CBHW072204130726
47910CB00011B/1860